I0708970

Mind Control
Perceivers #2

by

Jane Killick

Published by Elly Books

ISBN: 978-1-908340-21-4

ellybooks.com

Perceivers

#2

MIND CONTROL

by

Jane Killick

Elly Books

ONE

THE policeman despised Michael. The feelings of contempt and anger leaked out of Sergeant Anthony Patterson like a bad smell that tainted the air of the interrogation room. He knew Michael was a perceiver, he knew he could sense his emotions and read his thoughts, but Patterson made no attempt to hide what was going on in his head. He didn't believe Michael had any business poking his mind-reading powers into police work and he wanted Michael to know it.

Patterson was a thin, haggard man who looked ten years older than his thirty years, and wore a crumpled grey suit that looked like he'd slept in it. He sat at a wooden table in the centre of the interrogation room surrounded by its stark white walls that reflected the light back onto him. Michael sat in one corner on a hard plastic chair that made his buttocks numb, with his gaze resting on the black rubber line of a panic alarm that ran round three sides of the room. Above, at diagonally opposite corners of the ceiling, the two frog-like bulbous eyes of surveillance cameras watched and recorded everything they did.

Patterson scratched the side of his head through his wiry ginger hair and looked up from the file of notes in front of him. Across the table was the third person in the room: a terrorist suspect called Jerome Tyler. The teenager, who had been picked up in the street with a bag of explosives on his back, was the person Michael was supposed to be perceiving. Tyler was probably not much older than Michael's seventeen years and had never been in serious trouble before or done anything to get himself noticed by the anti-terrorist unit of the Metropolitan Police. Until his arrest.

Michael perceived Tyler's thoughts whispering across his consciousness. While Patterson's mind raged like a stormy sea breaking on the shore, Tyler's were like the gentle lapping of waves on the sand. Perceiving him was like listening to quiet background noise.

"Jerome Tyler," Patterson addressed him. "I have to remind you that you are under caution and you have declined your right to have a solicitor present. Do you understand?"

There was hardly a ripple on the calm sea of Tyler's mind. His only movement was to shake his overgrown brown fringe out of his eyes. His hair, dark against his pale skin, was the one mark of individuality about him. His clothes had been taken for forensic examination and he had been issued with a set of light grey sweat top and pants that almost camouflaged him against the white decor of the interrogation room.

"Where were you taking the explosives, Mr Tyler?" said Patterson.

Inside Tyler's mind, Michael sensed that he heard the words, but there was no reaction.

"You are facing very serious charges, Mr Tyler. It would help you if you answered my questions."

Tyler said nothing. He thought nothing. He continued to sit in his chair doing nothing.

"You were carrying four pounds of plastic explosive when you were arrested," said Patterson. "That's a lot of sophisticated hardware for someone your age. Do you want to tell me where you were going with it?"

Tyler's mind stirred. "Going?" The waves of his thoughts swelled and raced to the shore.

"Yes, where were you going?"

Images flashed in Tyler's head: of a bus stop sign attached to a concrete post, a graffitied Perspex bus shelter and the red flash of an approaching double decker bus with a number 10 written on the front. "I need to go," he said.

"Go where?" said Patterson.

This was not the question Patterson needed to be asking. He needed to ask if Tyler had planned to blow up the bus, like the suicide bomber who killed thirteen people on a London double decker back in 2005. But Patterson didn't know anything about the bus, he was just a norm who couldn't read minds and only knew what the suspect's words and body language told him.

Michael focussed his perception, pushing past Tyler's surface thoughts. But still, Tyler thought only of the bus. Tyler imagined himself leaning out from the bus stop, stretching his hand out into the road to hail the number 10 and seeing it pull up beside him. He imagined he would ignore the driver, touch his Oyster card to the detector and look for a quiet place to sit by the window. He didn't think about the explosives in the rucksack on his back, he didn't wish for terror or mayhem, he wasn't thinking about any allegiance to a god or a cause. He wanted only to sit quietly on the bus. And he wanted it desperately.

"I have to go *now*!" said Tyler.

"Tell me where you need to go," said Patterson. "I can help you."

Michael tried, but he couldn't see a destination in Tyler's head. Tyler's mind was stuck in a loop of getting on the bus.

Tyler jumped to his feet, scraping his chair across the floor as it was pushed out behind him.

Patterson stood too. "Sit down, Mr Tyler." He flashed a look up at one of the cameras, as if to tell the people watching that he had the situation under control. At least for the moment.

"You don't understand, I *have* to go!" said Tyler. He looked around the room, searching for a way out. He saw the door, a single brown wooden panel in an expanse of white, but also saw the policeman who stood in his way.

"Mr Tyler, you need to sit down." Patterson took a step towards him, gesturing with his hands for him to calm down.

Michael perceived the adrenaline rush through Tyler's body, giving him the power he needed to leave the claustrophobic room.

"If you sit down, we can talk about it," said Patterson in a soothing tone.

Tyler's body appeared to capitulate as he took a step back towards the chair, but Michael perceived this was a ruse. He thought about shouting out a warning to Patterson, but he was supposed to be the observer and so said nothing.

Tyler reached out as if to bring his chair back to the table, but he was really pulling his arm back to take a swing at Patterson. Patterson saw what Tyler was doing too late to stop the fist striking his stomach. The policeman cried out as Tyler ran for the door.

Michael's perception was filled with Tyler's elation as he flung open the door and ran out into the corridor. Michael slammed his hand onto the panic strip on the wall and — somewhere else in the police station — an alarm screamed.

Patterson was already out of the room and shouting after his fleeing suspect. Michael — his perception of Tyler waning as he lost his line of sight — walked to the doorway. He clutched onto the doorframe as he looked down the length of the corridor: a corridor of other closed doors that led into other interrogation rooms where other police officers questioned other suspects.

Halfway down, Tyler was running. Running hard like his life depended on it, with his arms and legs whirling in desperate circles. In his mind, the same words tumbled over and over: *I have to go, I have to go, I have to go.*

Two steps behind him, the older and taller Patterson also ran. His jacket flailed out behind him and the sound of his heavy shoes striking the floor echoed around the walls of the narrow space, as he closed in on his prey.

Tyler looked towards the end of the corridor where a final door blocked his exit. Memory flashed in his head of when he was first brought in and a uniformed police officer swiped a pass card to open the lock. It meant the door was security controlled and he had no way to get past it. In those milliseconds of realisation, his running slowed.

Just enough for Patterson to reach out for him.

Michael perceived Tyler feeling the claw of a hand grab his sweat-shirt and yank him back. *I have to go, I have to go,* Tyler's thoughts screamed.

His body tried to keep running, but he was trapped in his clothes which were trapped in Patterson's hand. His arms and legs thrashed, he slipped and fell forward. Patterson lost his grip on Tyler's sweat-shirt and he belly-flopped to the ground.

Tyler's jaw struck the floor. It split in half with a crack that echoed around the walls and thrust a spear of perceived pain through Michael's head.

Michael pulled out his perception as quick as he could, leaving the after-pain firing through his neurons.

In the corridor in front of him, Tyler was screaming and writhing on the floor as Patterson crouched on top of him with a knee in his back. He grabbed Tyler's arms and forced them behind him. Two uniformed officers flung open the security door and took over from Patterson, securing Tyler's wrists with a pair of handcuffs. They pulled him to his feet to reveal his face smeared with blood which had left a pool of red on the floor. Tyler, still struggling and screaming, was led away to the cells.

Patterson leant back against the wall and took a deep breath. He looked back towards the interrogation room where Michael still stood, gripping onto the doorframe. Michael did not like the way he looked at him. It was probably just as well that he had blocked his perception of what Patterson was thinking.

TWO

MICHAEL returned to the camp which had been his home for the past two years. The car stopped at the metal gates that secured the complex from the outside world and he remembered how he used to feel uncomfortable when he looked through the grill of the bars into the landscaped grounds of neatly trimmed grass and weedless herbaceous borders. But he now regarded it as normal. The soldier on the gate in camouflage fatigues with a rifle slung across his shoulder checked his identification, and that of his driver Hodges, and waved the car through. Michael didn't even look at the soldier's face anymore. The young man might have been a machine by the way he carried out his duties in regimented fashion. Only if Michael opened his perception would he get a glimpse into the soldier's humanity, but he had no wish to know the man behind the uniform and so he kept his mind free of thoughts that weren't his own.

Hodges drove to the Galen House, a newly constructed building designed to house young perceivers like Michael. It was a regimented house for a regimented army regime: with two rectangular concrete blocks on either side of a central porch made of toughened glass and a tiled pitched roof. To the left, the equidistant square windows on the first floor indicated where the perceivers' accommodation was, including Michael's room. Above it was a second storey with larger windows belonging to a series of offices and training rooms. To the right there was the one long window which let light into the communal area.

Hodges watched as Michael got out of the car and walked the tarmacked path to the porch. Officially, the man's job was to provide transport, but unofficially Michael knew he was there to keep an eye on him. Hodges had received training to hide his surface thoughts from perceivers, but he wasn't very good at it and Michael had easily found the information in his mind. He also inadvertently discovered Hodges suffered from post-traumatic stress from his time serving in Iraq with the Royal Anglian Regiment which, in turn, had led to a bitter divorce. It was at that point that Michael withdrew his perception and decided not to pry any further.

Michael automatically increased his filters as he walked inside Galen House. It was necessary to block out the unwanted jumble of other people's thoughts, but also to make sure his own mind wasn't open to the other perceivers who lived there.

He heard the chatter of the others before he saw them. There were nineteen perceivers assigned to Galen House, all of whom had avoided the cure by agreeing to work for the government in whatever spying capacity they decreed was in the country's interest. As part of their training, they had been put through their paces by an army sergeant who taught them everything from assembling a rifle, to conducting military manoeuvres and ironing their uniform in the prescribed manner. It was supposed to instil discipline and loyalty, they were told. Not that Michael was particularly disciplined or loyal, but he made a good show of it.

All of the others were there, sitting in twos, threes and fours around six regimentally-spaced dining tables in their regulation casual uniform of grey T-shirt and trousers. Some of them were still children — the youngest thirteen, the oldest seventeen — and all were talking across food trays of half-finished army catering. The smell of curry, vegetable lasagne and cod mornay might have been appetising if the aroma of the night's offerings weren't mixed together. The others turned to look when Michael walked in, dressed in civvies and fresh from his assignment. He was among the first few of the Perceiver Corps to be deployed in the field and, naturally, they were interested.

"How was it?" shouted Peter from the table at the far end, through a mouthful of mashed potato. The sixteen-year-old perceiver was the loudest and most bolshie of all of them. Unusually short, but physically adept, he claimed the combination made him especially attractive to girls.

Peter's question made Michael stop, halfway between the entrance and the dining tables. He didn't need to open his perception to know that the others probably had the same question. "You don't want to know," he said to the room.

"Aww, come on!" teased Peter. "Don't be such a skank."

Michael frowned at him. "You really want to know?"

Murmurs from the others confirmed that they did. He could tell many of them had already opened their perception.

"Okay," said Michael. He dropped his filters and played back the memory of Tyler crashing to the floor and feeling the crack of his jaw shooting pain through his body.

Eighteen teenagers winced and immediately shut their perception back down again.

Cries of, "Michael!" and "Whaddyado that for?" rose from the group. Michael smiled and buried the memory again. Served them right for being curious.

Michael retrieved his dinner from where it was being kept warm on the rack brought from the catering building and took it over to where his best friend, Alex, was sitting.

"That was mean," said Alex as Michael sat down beside him.

"They asked for it," said Michael.

"Even so …" said Alex.

Alex was a year younger than Michael and, unlike him, had embraced army life. He was athletic, sported a muscular frame and beat almost everyone at anything that involved running, climbing or crawling under barbed wire. He was less good at intellectual challenges, but was a fast learner and a strong perceiver. They got on because, like Michael, he didn't have much of a family to speak of. Alex came from a home with an absent father and a mother with mental health problems, so life at Galen House was the most stable he had ever had.

Michael forked over his chicken curry with the lacklustre movements of someone who wished he had ordered the fish. After the day he'd had, he wanted something bland not spicy.

Alex waited as much as thirty seconds before he said what he was desperate to ask. "Are you going to tell me what happened or not?"

Michael chewed on a piece of spicy chicken and swallowed. "I was thinking not."

Alex lowered his voice. "Seriously, Mike, was it okay?"

"They were norms," said Michael. "Norms hate perceivers."

Alex nodded as if to say he understood.

Something entered the edge of Michael's perception: an anxiety — distant at first — but getting closer.

The others sensed it too, as it got closer and became strong enough to break through their everyday filters. The chatter of the people and clatter of cutlery stopped. They all turned to face the door.

The squeak of highly polished leather from military boots and the click-click of the heels of a woman's shoes announced the arrival of two people into the building. Through the door first was a young woman. Like the perceivers, she was a teenager — maybe fifteen or sixteen years old — her naturally tall body made taller by the four inch heels on her black calf-length boots. All her clothes were black. A black baggy coat hung in folds over a black T-shirt with a half-obscured slogan and black skinny jeans which hugged her shapely legs. Even her hair was jet black, hanging straight from a middle parting down to the tops of her shoulders. It made her face look even paler than it might otherwise have been, despite the make-up she had applied to give her cheeks a red glow and her lips a strong shape of glossy maroon.

As soon as he touched her mind, Michael knew she was a perceiver.

Her anxiety intensified. *What are they looking at?* she thought.

It was a thought strong enough for them all to perceive. But still, the perceivers kept looking.

Beside her, having walked through the door almost unnoticed, was Sergeant Norman Macaulay, the officer in charge of the Perceivers Corps. He was a small man, in his forties and slightly overweight but otherwise in good shape, who had lived and breathed the army since he joined up at the age of sixteen. He always wore a dress uniform: khaki trousers and shirt ironed to within an inch of their lives, tie meticulously tied with a Windsor knot and a jacket which he kept smooth and buttoned unless he was sitting down. On his chest were a collection of medals which he wore proudly, but never talked about. He dressed like this, rather than in fatigues like many of the officers on the base, because he believed the uniform gave him authority. Michael knew this because he had perceived it from him. He had perceived everything about Sergeant Norman Macaulay over the months since he had met him, as had — he was sure — every other perceiver in the room, except the new girl.

"This is Pauline Sarkis," said Sergeant Norman Macaulay, or 'Norm the Norm', as the perceivers called him.

Some of the perceivers mumbled a 'hello', others offered a slight wave. Pauline stretched her glossy maroon lips across her teeth into a forced smile.

"Do you want some food?" Norm asked her.

"I ate on the train," she almost whispered. Her mind showed a memory of nibbling at a sandwich which had gone stale at the edges, while the English countryside sped past outside the carriage window.

"I'll show you to your quarters," said Norm. "You'll meet these reprobates properly tomorrow."

They turned towards the accommodation block, Norm's shoes still squeaking, while Pauline's heels were dampened by the carpet. Her anxiety lessened as she moved away from the group of grey-clad teenagers who stared at her. Michael blocked out her mind: there was nothing more to be gained by perceiving her any further.

Chatter rose into the room again.

Alex turned to Michael. "Why do they dump perceivers into this place without any preparation?" he said.

"Because they are norms," said Michael. "And norms hate perceivers."

LIGHTS out.

In theory, Michael had control of the lights in his own room and no one would say anything if he decided to turn them on again, but the army discipline of a regular bedtime had been instilled in him across a year of training and he couldn't shake it off. So when the lights extinguished themselves, he let them be.

Michael's room became a mosaic of shadows. Shapes sketched out in shades of black indicated the wardrobe in the corner, the chest of drawers on the far wall, his desk with a chair tucked under and his clothes piled across the back of it. The only concession to this room being his home was a two-seater sofa jammed next to the door where he would sometimes sit and read or watch the television. Only the window displayed a hint of colour from the faint glow of a lamppost on the road outside which illuminated the dark blue of the curtains.

There was a bed too, of course, but Michael couldn't see it very well because he was lying under the bedclothes.

Not as if he could sleep. Jerome Tyler's thoughts continued to persist inside of him.

Michael had perceived a lot of minds in the past and none of them had been like Tyler's. People were complicated, they thought a variety of things. If they were walking down the road, they might be thinking about all the things they had to buy at the shop, but they would also be thinking about the best place to cross the road, the disgusting state of all the litter in the street and what they planned to do at the weekend. Sometimes they would think these things one after the other, sometimes they would be thinking them all at once. They would be feeling cold from the wind, an ache in their foot from an old football injury and slightly out of breath from walking faster than usual. But not Tyler. There was one singular thought in his head: he had to go.

Even allowing for the fact that Tyler had been on his way to commit some terrorist atrocity, it didn't make sense. Surely a person like that — if they were concentrating on anything at all — they would be concentrating on the moment they were to detonate the bomb, not getting on a number 10 bus.

As the remembered perceptions turned over in his head, the noise of someone else crept into his consciousness. She — because the perception was of a woman — was lonely and scared.

He knew the emotions were from Pauline's mind. Not that he could recognise her yet — it often takes a few close perceptions to recognise the mind of an individual — but it could only be her. It was likely Norm the Norm had probably given her the room next to Michael's, which had been empty for a long time, while all the rest of the perceivers had learnt to screen their thoughts.

Michael pushed her away. He pushed Tyler away. He concentrated on his breathing and tried to relax. Sleep would come eventually.

But the more he relaxed, the more Pauline was in his head. Her anxiety at being brought to Galen House made her thoughts louder than a normal, relaxed mind. There were images of a man and a woman — her parents? — and a younger girl who looked a bit like her, possibly a sister. He perceived a sudden stab of fear as an image of a woman in a white coat flashed through Pauline's mind and the images of her family faded away.

She was broadcasting so loudly, Michael had to make an effort to block her out. Not that it was a problem, he could block signals far stronger than hers, but every time he relaxed and tried to sleep, her thoughts came back. He was often glad that his perception was stronger than anyone else in the group, but there were other times when it was a burden. This was one of those times.

Michael sat up in bed. Sleeping was useless. And Pauline's broadcast was giving him a headache.

He got up and grappled for his trousers in the semi-dark. He put them on, threw a shirt over his naked chest and padded his bare feet out into the corridor.

NIGHT lights clung to the ceiling down the length of the corridor, dimly illuminating the space below each one with faint circles. Michael padded to the next room along. Standing outside the door, he confirmed Pauline's thoughts were coming from inside it.

Michael stopped at the door. He knocked, softly and politely.

There was no reply. Images still poured from the mind inside: of people she loved, of the long lonely train ride to the base, of the perceivers laying down their cutlery to stare at her. She was on the edge of sleep, in that dreamy state where semi-conscious thoughts pass in and out.

He knocked louder.

She must have heard that because the images faded. "Who is it?" came a sleepy voice.

"My name's Michael."

He perceived uncertainty and distrust from inside the room.

He realised she had no clue who he was. "I'm one of the other perceivers," he said.

"I'm trying to sleep," said her words. *Is the door locked? Did I lock the door?* said her thoughts.

"So am I," said Michael, "but you're bleeding everywhere."

Panic from behind the door. "What?"

He realised he had used the wrong words. "You're in a building full of perceivers, you need to block your mind."

"Wait a minute," she called. There were scrambling noises from inside.

The door opened just enough for Pauline's face to peer out. She looked paler without her make-up and was dressed in a white bath-robe which appeared hastily thrown on. Her black hair lay unbrushed and untidy on her shoulders, looking more straggly because the strands were illuminated from behind by a lamp on the bedside table behind her.

"You can perceive me?" she said.

"Someone needs to show you how to block," said Michael. "Can I come in?"

She paused, keeping the door open just enough for her to look out and not enough for him to step through. She was suspicious of his motives, he could perceive it.

"I'm not going to hurt you," said Michael. "Perceive me if you like." He allowed his arms to fall to his sides and turned his palms outwards to show he was harmless. At the same time, he let his blocks fall.

She perceived him. He could feel her inside his mind. She took a good, long look.

"Okay," she said. She stood aside and let Michael in.

Her room was still regulation army issue. The wardrobe, the desk, the chair, the bed, the dark blue curtains were all the same as his. He was slightly jealous of the bedside table and lamp, which he made a mental note that he would have to ask for. She didn't have a sofa, like in his room, and in the space where it might have been were two unpacked suitcases. The only things of hers out on display were her clothes draped over the chair by the desk and a phone laid face down on the table by her bed.

Michael came in and closed the door behind him. Pauline picked up a pillow and placed it like a cushion against the headboard. She sat up against it and folded her legs up underneath her. Michael took this as a cue for him to sit at the other end of the bed. She was still wary of him, however, and he kept a respectable distance between them.

"You've not been with perceivers before, have you?" said Michael.

"What's that got to do with anything?" said Pauline.

"It's not like being around norms. You can open your mind with norms and they won't know. But with perceivers, it's different. We have to maintain blocks and filters otherwise we live in each other's heads all the time."

"Even in here?" She looked around the room with its enclosing four walls.

"Being able to see someone makes perception easier, but strong emotions and thoughts can leak through walls," he said.

Especially the thoughts and emotions of someone who had been taken from their family to live in a strange place with a group of people she didn't know. All the perceivers in the building understood that, because they had all gone through it.

"You said there are filters and blocks …?" said Pauline. "I don't understand."

She was panicking again, afraid she had made some terrible mistake. Her emotions were putting Michael on edge. He made a conscious effort to block her out. "It's a bit like going into a place where there are a lot of people," he said. "Like a school playground or a shopping centre. Do you know what I mean?"

"It's loud," said Pauline. "I mean, it's loud in my head. So many minds…"

Michael nodded, knowing that feeling. "So what do you do?"

"Make them shut up," said Pauline.

"That's a block," said Michael. "We do it all the time. We would go crazy if we didn't. If we don't want to silence them all, just stop the unwanted noise, we call that a filter."

"What's that got to do with you perceiving me?"

"It's the same method," said Michael. "Instead of blocking things coming in, you block things going out."

She looked at him as she processed this idea. "I don't get it."

"Let me show you," said Michael.

She shrugged. "Okay."

Michael shuffled up a little closer to her on the bed. He reached forward and took her hands. Warily, she allowed him, and so they sat with his fingers clasped around hers, resting on the bedclothes between them.

Her body was tense. "Relax," he said. "My father did this for me once."

"Your father?" Her body relaxed a little as she was distracted. "But adults aren't perceivers."

Michael smiled at that. "Not everything they tell you out there is true. You'll learn that in here." He remembered how his father helped him block the painful perceptions, holding him in his arms, entering his mind gently and keeping away the cacophony of other people. He could not be as intimate with Pauline. "I'm going to meld my perception with yours, okay?"

"You're going to what?" She didn't understand.

"You'll see what I mean. But if you don't like it at any time, just tell me to stop. Okay?"

"Okay," she agreed verbally, even though she really wasn't sure.

Michael had to drop all his blocks and filters to enable him to do it. For a moment, the residual babble of the thoughts, feelings and dreams of all the other perceivers, rumbled at the edge of his mind. Then he concentrated his perception on Pauline and probed deep.

She gasped. She felt it. This meant she was a strong perceiver. Probably one of the reasons she broadcast herself so loud when she arrived.

Michael allowed his perception to sit comfortably inside hers until she relaxed. Then he found her fear and locked onto it. "I imagine a wall," he said. And inside his head — inside *her* head — brick by brick he piled up a barrier to keep the fear inside. "I'm going to let go of that image in a moment, but I want you to hold onto it."

She nodded and the movement of her head rippled through her body so he felt it through his hands. In his mind, the wall wobbled a little.

"Don't move, just speak," said Michael.

"Okay," she said.

He pulled his concentration back from the wall, allowing his hold on it to dissipate. The image in their minds faded for a moment, then strengthened as Pauline latched onto it.

Pauline giggled, her attention faltered, and the wall was gone.

"Almost," said Michael. "Try again. On your own this time."

He stayed in her mind as she imagined, not a wall, but the rolling corrugated metal of an automatic garage door, gradually descending at the edge of her consciousness. Blocking not just fear, but everything in her mind, until—

The door to Pauline's room flung open and bashed against the wall behind. Michael pulled out of her mind. Pauline yelped.

"WHAT'S GOING ON HERE?" a deep, male voice bellowed.

Michael and Pauline let go of each other's hands.

Sergeant Norman Macaulay stood silhouetted in the doorway. He was, unusually, dressed in combat fatigues with the night lights of the corridor outside highlighting his balding head.

Michael jumped off the bed and stood to attention. "Sergeant!"

Pauline grasped at the bedclothes and pulled them up to her chest.

"What are you doing in here?" Norm demanded.

"We were having trouble sleeping," said Michael.

"Doesn't look to me like you were trying to sleep," said Norm.

"He was just—" Pauline's explanation was cut off.

"I don't want to know what 'he was just'," said Norm. "You, madam, are new, so I shall cut you some slack, but you young man should know better. One-hour punishment duty for you tomorrow, report to my office at oh-nine-hundred."

"I have my debrief with Agent Cooper then," said Michael.

"Oh-eight-hundred, then."

"But—"

"Are you questioning my order, Sanderson?"

"No, sir," said Michael. He hated the way Norm used his surname.

"Because, if you are, I can give you a harsher punishment than the one I have planned."

"No, sir. I'm not, sir."

"Good," said Norm. "You're dismissed, Sanderson."

Michael flashed an apologetic look to Pauline. *Sorry*, he thought.

He wasn't sure if she was perceiving him and heard his message, but he couldn't stay to make sure. He walked out of the room and into the corridor where Norm watched him until he was back in his own room with the door closed.

As he crawled back into bed, Pauline's thoughts continued to play in the background, but they were calmer and less intrusive than they were. Maybe his interrupted lesson had helped a little. He erected his own blocks to bring quiet to his mind and, despite a few moments where they weakened and allowed the images of Pauline's dreams to slip back in, he was able to drift off to sleep.

THREE

MICHAEL was furious when he came out of his debrief. Agent Cooper had listened to everything he had to say about perceiving his first suspect with the Metropolitan Police, but wasn't interested in any of his suggestions. Michael wanted to say that it would be better if he could pass information to the police interrogator while the interview was taking place, perhaps through an earpiece, so he could be of more benefit to the investigating team. But Cooper wouldn't hear any of it and said that, at this early stage, it was important for him to observe only and report back. That's how the police wanted it and that's how it was going to be until the assignment was over and an assessment was made.

Michael had already spent an hour before the meeting carrying out punishment duty picking up litter in the grounds, thanks to Norm the Norm, so it wasn't the best start to his day.

IT was mid-morning by the time Michael arrived at the police station. He found Detective Inspector Graham Jones in his office, glaring at his computer as he scrolled with a mouse on his desk. He was Patterson's boss, older than his sergeant by about ten years, displaying his seniority with the way he dressed in a smart suit of uncrinkled sober grey with a tie knotted all the way to his neck. His thinning hair, which would probably leave him virtually bald within the next five years, was clipped short and combed back. His tidiness was reflected in his desk which, apart from a stray pen by his computer keyboard, was free of clutter. The only personal touch was a framed photograph of his younger-looking self, when his hair was thick and dark, shaking the hand of a man in police uniform, probably a chief inspector of some sort.

After a few moments hovering at the open door without being noticed, Michael gave it a gentle knock. Jones raised his eyes briefly to see who it was and Michael perceived a wave of indifference. He stepped inside, reeling off his prepared apology, but stopped when he realised Jones wasn't paying any attention.

"He committed suicide," said Jones. He sat back in his chair and looked directly up at Michael.

"What?" said Michael. Not that he didn't hear, more that he didn't understand.

"Jerome Tyler," said Jones. "Came back from hospital: hung himself."

"How is that possible?"

"I don't know." Jones shook his head. "There'll be an investigation and I'll have the IPCC on my tail. Maybe I should have put him on suicide watch … Did you 'perceive' anything from him. I mean, was he suicidal?"

"No," said Michael. "He wasn't anything, really. His mind was strange, detached, almost empty. The only thing in his head was a desperate desire to get on the number 10 bus. If that's any help."

Someone knocked on the door behind him. Michael had his filters closed in the busy police station and hadn't sensed someone approach. It was Sergeant Anthony Patterson, looking even more haggard than the previous day, and now wearing a crumpled black suit instead of a crumpled grey one. Michael stepped aside to allow him in and Patterson took his place without acknowledging Michael was there. "A call's come in," Patterson told Jones. "Might be nothing, could be something. They want me to take it."

Jones was only half listening. "Michael thinks Tyler might have been planning to get on the number 10 bus."

Patterson looked across at Michael with a suspicious eye. Michael felt a moment of annoyance from him before he tightened his filters. "Was he going to blow it up?"

"No," said Michael. "He wanted to travel on the bus, but I couldn't see where."

"Look into it will you, Tony?" said Jones.

"Do you know where the number 10 goes?" said Patterson. "Through the whole centre of London!"

"You may find this difficult to believe," said Jones, "but even detective inspectors have occasion to use the bus sometimes. Of course I know where the number 10 goes."

"I mean, it's a large area to look at if we're considering a possible target and—" Patterson looked down at Michael, which he was able to do because he was a foot taller "—we don't know if the information's credible."

"It's a lead, Tony," said Jones. "Follow it where it takes you, even if it ends up being nowhere."

Jones had his doubts about using perceivers in the police force, Michael had gleaned it from him the first time they had met. But the decision was out of his hands and he was prepared to give it a go. If it was possible to see into the minds of criminals and reveal the truth that they otherwise kept to themselves, Jones knew it could be a valuable resource.

"I'll do it when I get back from this other job," said Patterson.

Jones sighed. "Fine. You can take Michael with you."

"But sir …"

"It'll give you two time to bond."

PATTERSON'S 'job' was out in Kensington, a posh part of London known by tourists for being where all the museums are. It was the sort of place where you had to have a lot of cash if you were going to live in it, with even the most modest of houses having price tags that ran into the millions. Patterson drove Michael to one such 'modest' residential street where a row of Victorian townhouses nestled next to each other in a terrace, with each one painted in a different colour to distinguish it from its neighbour. Patterson parked his grubby Vauxhall between a Mercedes and a Jaguar in the road outside and ascended half a dozen steps to a large black door set within the walls of the pastel blue painted house.

He didn't say a word to Michael and Michael kept his promise not to perceive him on the assumption that everything would become clear eventually. They spent the car journey saying nothing and with BBC Radio Five Live blasting loudly out of the car stereo. It hadn't given Michael any insight into the case Patterson was working on, but he now had a thorough understanding of Tottenham Hotspur's chances in the FA Cup.

Patterson did up his tie and smoothed down his crumpled suit before ringing the bell. A few moments later, the door was opened by a woman in a nurse's uniform. "Yes?" Her accent was not English, probably eastern European.

Patterson reached into his inside pocket and pulled out his identification, which he flashed at the woman. "I'm Sergeant Anthony Patterson and this is—" He automatically opened out his hand to indicate Michael, but he had no words prepared. He cleared his throat. "This is my associate."

"Yes, Mr Rublev is expecting you." Definitely eastern European. Or possibly Russian.

She opened the door fully and allowed them inside. This was where the relative plainness of the Victorian exterior made way for an opulent interior that oozed modern money. Dominating the entrance hall was a cloud of crystal droplets from a chandelier hanging from the ceiling, which scattered tiny rainbows of light in every direction. A cabinet made of rich, dark polished wood stood at the side and seemed only there to display a delicate vase of blue and white porcelain, an abstract glass sculpture with sticky out angles and a figurine of a slim lady in a sleek 1920s dress.

The nurse led them past the, no doubt, valuable items in the hallway and to the first door on the left. She knocked politely and walked in. "The police are here," she announced.

The front room was not as opulent as the hallway, but it had the same feeling of richness. The high ceiling made it feel spacious, even though it was not especially large by modern standards and the furniture was somewhat packed in. The centrepiece was most definitely the original Victorian fireplace, lit and flickering with a dying flame which danced over almost-spent coals.

In all that splendour, the man they had come to see appeared small and wizened. He sat in an upright black leather chair which looked like it had been wheeled in from a study. A tube was stuck up his nose, feeding him oxygen from a tank by his side.

"Victor Rublev?" Patterson asked the man.

"Who else did you think I was?" replied Rublev. His rasping, sickly voice had a similar accent to that of his nurse: almost certainly Russian.

Patterson half leant forward to shake the man's hand, but he looked so fragile, he pulled his hand away and pretended to have been lifting it to scratch the side of his nose instead. "I'm Sergeant Anthony Patterson, and this is my ... *associate*."

Rublev looked at Michael with decaying, glassy green eyes. "Policemen must be getting younger these days." He coughed, a horrible grating cough that seemed to scrape the sides of his throat. "Please sit down, I'm not royalty."

Patterson obliged and perched his bottom on the edge of an upholstered sofa opposite Rublev. Its embroidered pattern looked worn and faded, but then it was probably antique.

Michael sat next to him and opened his perception to gauge the atmosphere of the room. Patterson was somewhat overwhelmed by the wealth surrounding him and was making an effort not to think about it so he could concentrate on his police work. Rublev was anxious, and a little afraid.

Patterson pulled his phone from his pocket and, with a stylus as thin as a twig, wrote in untidy handwriting, 'Victor Rublev'. Whatever software he was using translated it into readable type. He also, Michael noticed, engaged a sound recording app.

"I want you to investigate my murder," said Rublev.

Patterson looked up from his phone, his stylus paused above the screen, writing nothing. "I'm sorry?" he said.

"It's what you policemen do, is it not? Investigate murder?"

Usually only after someone is dead, said Patterson's thoughts. "My understanding is you have evidence that you are being targeted by terrorists?" said his words.

"The evidence is here." Rublev thumped himself on the chest with his fist which set off a coughing fit that sounded like his lungs were being forced up into his throat. His nurse must have heard him because she came running in and poured him a glass of water which she held to his lips so he could sip, until the coughs subsided into wheezy breaths and he waved her away.

Afterwards, he looked even smaller, shrunken down against the black leather of the executive office chair. His skin was so pale, it was almost translucent as it stretched out over the bones of his hands and sunk in to the bumps of his skull with only a few wisps of hair left remaining. He knew he was dying and he hated it, hated it with the rage of someone helpless in the grasp of his own failing body.

Michael perceived that the man was not the victim of murder yet, but knew that he very soon would be.

"I'm sorry you are unwell," said Patterson. "Is it cancer?"

"Poison," wheezed Rublev.

"Are you certain?"

"Ask my doctors. They tell me it only takes a small piece of radiation to destroy my body a little bit at a time."

A thought flashed through Patterson's mind that Victor Rublev could be radioactive. He hid his unease by looking down at his phone and scribbling the words, 'radiation poisoning?'.

"Do you know who would want to kill you?" asked Patterson.

"Of course," said Rublev. "The Russian government."

Patterson was taken aback. "How can you be sure?"

"Who else would be planting radioactive isotopes for Russian exiles to ingest, do you think? I may not know which agent did it or how they did it, but I know it was them. The authorities in Russia and I do not see eye to eye, you might say. I made my money in the wake of glasnost and then I brought my money to the UK where I can criticise people back home with your wonderful laws of free speech. They made several attempts to kill me before, using their spineless terrorist methods, but I was careful." He smiled a wry smile to himself, which brought a little flicker of life back to his eyes. "Not careful enough, it seems."

"Do you know when you were poisoned?" said Patterson.

"Between one and two weeks ago, according to my doctor."

"We'll need a list of everywhere you went and everyone you encountered in that week."

"So many places, so many people," said Rublev. In his head flashed images of the life he had when he was well: running in the park, choosing vegetables in the supermarket, laughing in a restaurant. There were so many people: the shop assistant, another runner he often waved to in the park, the postman, a waiter, an idiot who nearly drove into the back of his car and swore at him, a man in a suit who smiled and offered his hand to shake. In the midst of all this was an image of himself as he was two weeks ago. He looked so much younger, his skin had a healthy glow and he had almost a full head of hair. He loathed the way the poison was slowly and painfully robbing him of that life.

His thoughts were interrupted by a loud burst of rock music. It was Patterson's phone. Patterson, who was in the middle of writing on the screen at the time, nearly dropped it. He frowned apologetically at Rublev. "Excuse me."

He silenced the music by answering the call, but did not speak into his phone until he got up from the sofa and walked to the corner of the room. His words were muttered and accompanied by a lot of nodding. Patterson finished the call quickly, hung up and turned to Rublev. He still wore that apologetic frown.

"I'm sorry, I have to go," said Patterson.

"But you have only just got here." Anger swelled inside Rublev. Michael perceived a string of unspoken thoughts, but they were all in Russian and he didn't understand them.

"It's an emergency." Patterson slipped the phone and stylus into his pocket like he was packing up to go. "Chances are your case will be passed to MI5 anyway."

"Your internal security services?" said Rublev. "But this is a murder inquiry. I need a British policeman. I need my killer to be arrested, I need them to face justice in a British court of law where journalists can be present."

"Then get me that list." Patterson moved towards the door. "Everywhere and everyone you encountered during the period your doctors think you might have been poisoned. I'll follow it up, I promise."

Patterson turned the door handle and Michael took this as his cue to join him.

"Don't take too long, Sergeant. I would like to know who my murderer is before I die."

Back in the hallway of opulence and tiny rainbows, Patterson headed for the front door with long, fast strides. Michael had to quicken his pace to catch up with him. "What's happened?" he asked.

"There's another kid with a bomb," said Patterson. "Except, this time, he's threatening to blow it up."

FOUR

PATTERSON'S grubby Vauxhall made a horrible banging noise as its front wheels hit the kerb and mounted the pavement, narrowly avoiding the wing mirror of the police patrol car which was blocking the road. The police car belonged to an officer in a yellow fluorescent jacket who was manning the makeshift cordon to a side street off North End Road. He had offered to move it out of the way for the sergeant, after checking his identity card, but Patterson had no patience. The officer was forced to look on and pray for the safety of his wing mirror as Patterson abused his Vauxhall and shook up the people inside of it.

He would have preferred that Michael wasn't one of those people. But he couldn't abandon him outside of Rublev's house and he didn't have time to drop him off somewhere else, so Michael had come along by default.

The car shuddered as it plonked first its front wheels, and then its back wheels, off the pavement and onto the road on the other side of the police car. The side street ran to the back of the Capital Hotel where, according to the chatter on the police radio, a teenager threatened to explode a bomb strapped to his back.

It was only possible to drive a little way up the street before it was blocked by other emergency service vehicles which had got to the scene before them. Police cars — marked and unmarked — one police van, an ambulance and two fire engines had been left higgle-dy-piggledy all over the narrow street. Patterson stopped as close as he could to them and turned off the engine.

Now that they were closer, the buzzing of busy and worried minds scratched at the edge of Michael's perception — he pushed them away.

Patterson got out of the car and went round to the boot, dis-appearing from view as he foraged for something inside. Michael got out, too, and waited for him. After the frantic drive over, with police lights flashing and siren blaring, it was nice to feel the coolness of the March air. Spring was coming, but it wasn't quite jeans and T-shirt weather yet. A strong breeze brushed at his bare arms as it was funnelled down the passageway formed by the towering office buildings around him. He wished he'd remembered to pick up his coat on the way out of the police station.

When the boot slammed shut, it revealed Patterson standing at the back of the car wearing a bulletproof vest with the word POLICE written in large white letters across his chest. He held another one exactly the same in his hand. "Put this on," he ordered, as he walked round to the front of the car and held it out to Michael.

The bulletproof vest was heavier than it looked and Michael almost dropped it as he took it from Patterson's hand. It was also not entirely obvious how a person was supposed to wear it. He turned it round several times before he decided there was no front and back, just two sides exactly the same. By the time he had slipped it over his head, Patterson was already walking further up the road and towards, Michael assumed, the hotel.

Michael caught up with him, squeezing past the higgledy-piggledy vehicles, to where the street narrowed into a one-lane road and became more of an alley. Parked across it was a white, unmarked van, like a builders' van, but with a satellite dish on top. Patterson was heading towards it. He rapped on its metal shell and announced his name before opening the back doors and clambering inside.

Michael caught the door before it slammed shut again and peered in. A single light in the roof did little to illuminate the interior which was crammed with electronic equipment. A rack of black plastic front panels twinkled with red and green indicator lights all the way down one side of the van. Three television screens, silently buzzing with static, dominated the opposite side. In front of them was a narrow desk with three workstations, manned by police officers wearing communication headsets. The one in the middle was Jones, paying no attention to Patterson who stood behind him, bent over slightly to stop his head banging on the roof. Jones had his two fingers pressed to the single headphone of his headset, listening intently to something.

No one seemed to care whether Michael was there or not, so he climbed in for a closer look.

Jones sighed and pulled the headset off so it lay around the back of his neck. Whatever he had been listening to, it had obviously finished. He looked up at Patterson. "You're here. Good."

"What have we got, sir?" said Patterson.

"IC1 male," said Jones. "Probably late teens. Claims to have explosives ready to rig in a rucksack on his back."

"Claims?" said Patterson.

"Because it's inside the rucksack, there's no way to tell for sure if it's a real bomb, but considering recent events …"

"Seems likely," said Patterson.

Jones nodded. "Looks like it's wired to a trigger in his hand. Bomb squad thinks it could be a dead man's switch."

Michael interjected. "Dead man's switch?" Then immediately wished he hadn't as the two officers glowered at him.

"If he lets go, the bomb explodes," said Jones. "We got him out the back of the hotel in the open, snipers have him in their sights, so he's not going anywhere."

"Apart from the morgue in a hundred pieces if he blows himself up," said Patterson.

"Hopefully it won't come to that," said Jones. "We've evacuated the hotel and surrounding buildings. Dogs are doing sweeps, but early indications are he's alone."

The officer sitting at the workstation nearest the door — a woman with a full head of brown hair pulled back so tightly into a bun that it stretched the skin of her face — turned to them. "We've got visual," she said and flicked at some controls on the panel in front of her.

The static flickered on the TV screens and an image appeared. The same image of a young man dressed in green, repeated on each screen like the reflection in a hall of mirrors. It was unsteady, like it was coming from a hand-held or helmet-mounted camera, but as the shakiness settled down and the autofocus locked on, it was possible to see the subject was as Jones had described: a white teenager, in his late teens, standing alone with a brick wall of the Capital Hotel building behind him. He was dressed in a pair of black jeans and a green quilted jacket, with black straps over his shoulders that presumably belonged to a rucksack on his back.

Patterson leant forward to get a better look. "Has anyone talked to him?"

"The first officer on the scene," said Jones. "The kid said he had a bomb and then, after that, no one has got a word out of him."

"Right. Okay," said Patterson, taking a deep breath, psyching himself up. "I should go."

The image on the screens zoomed close in to the teenager, blurring his features for a moment until the autofocus kicked in. The boy's face looked almost as pale as the tuft of blonde hair that blew across his forehead in the breeze of the alley. Even with the unsteady footage, he appeared to be visibly shaking.

"Get him to give himself up," said Jones. "When he does, don't do anything stupid, stand back and let the bomb squad go in. And for God's sake, don't let him let go of that trigger."

"You talk as if I haven't done this before," said Patterson.

"Suspects armed with knives and guns, yes, but not bombs," said Jones.

"It's fine, I've had the training." Patterson grabbed a spare headset from where several hung on a hook and clipped a transmitter to his belt before putting on the single headphone and adjusting the microphone so it was close to his mouth. "Excuse me," he said to Michael as he headed for the back of the van. Michael pressed himself up against the bank of twinkling lights as the smell of Patterson's nervous sweat passed by him.

"Hey, Tony!" Jones called after him.

Patterson looked back.

"Be careful. A dead sergeant is a heck of a lot of paperwork."

Patterson grinned. "Sure thing." He jumped down from the van and was gone.

Jones pulled the headset from around his neck and put it back over his head. "This is Oscar One," he said into the microphone. "Negotiator Sergeant Patterson approaching the scene. This is Oscar One, Negotiator Sergeant Patterson ..."

As he talked, Michael watched the kid on the television screens. His wide, blue eyes stared out from a terrified face. Michael opened his perception to learn more, but all the thoughts around him belonged to the police officers. He was too far away and there were too many other minds to perceive anything from the would-be bomber.

Jones and the two other officers were too busy listening to their headsets, watching the television screens or looking at their computers to even notice Michael was there. He shuffled his way to the back of the van and, with one more look to check they were still engrossed, jumped back out into the alley.

Goose pimples prickled on his bare arms. He looked around, but there was no sign of Patterson, and he assumed he had gone to the other side of the van. Michael did the same and found himself in a continuation of the alley. It was little more than a narrow tarmac strip edged with double yellow lines that led to a dead end at the back of the hotel. In front of the alley, three police cars were parked at an angle. Walking towards them, keeping close to the wall, was Patterson. The white POLICE on the back of his bulletproof vest was clear in the shade of the building next to him.

Michael took a step forward. An armed policeman stepped out from a shadow. He was clad in black armour from his helmet to his boots and carried a semi-automatic rifle. Caught by surprise, Michael instinctively perceived him and learnt that the policeman's initial assessment was that Michael posed no threat, even if he doubted that Michael had any authority to be there.

"I'm with Sergeant Patterson," said Michael.

The sergeant's name held currency with the armed policeman and he took a half step back. But the doubt remained. He looked closely at Michael's youthful face, with its minor acne breakouts, and it didn't correlate with what he was being told.

Michael strode forward with all the confidence he could muster and hoped the policeman wouldn't think about radioing back to base to check. *Patterson must know what he's doing*, the policeman thought as Michael passed him.

Patterson turned when he heard Michael approach and Michael perceived the sting of his annoyance. "What are you doing here?" said Patterson in an accusatory whisper.

"I need to perceive the bomber," said Michael.

"You need to stay out of the way," Patterson retorted.

"Don't you want to know what the bomber's thinking?"

"No," said Patterson. *Yes*, said his thoughts.

"I can help you," said Michael.

Patterson looked up ahead, they were not far from the cordon of police cars. He pushed Michael over to the wall and he felt the hard and cold bricks press at his back. He also felt Patterson's anger and perceived a wish that he could just punch Michael and get away with it.

"You're not trained, you could get us all killed," said Patterson.

"I could get information you can't get any other way," said Michael.

Patterson hesitated. Michael felt the conflict within him: he wanted the information, but he wasn't convinced Michael could get it, or that the risk was worth it.

"Jones sent me," Michael said, the lie coming out his mouth before he had time to think it through.

If Patterson had been a perceiver, there would be no way a simple lie could deceive him. But as he was a norm, with only his ordinary senses to rely on, it gave Michael an advantage. He listened in to Patterson's thoughts as the man weighed up the risks. Unlike the armed policeman back down the alley, he thought of calling in on the radio to check with Jones, but he didn't have time to have another row about the use of perceivers in the police force — a row which he had always lost. Anyway, he needed to concentrate on what he was going to say to the suicide bomber, and maybe it was better to have Michael there where he could see him, rather than wandering around the scene like a loose cannon. "Okay," he said, eventually. "But stay down, and if I say withdraw, then you get the hell out."

"Understood," said Michael.

Patterson released Michael from against the wall. He pointed to the back of the nearest police car, with its rear bumper closest to them, and indicated Michael should take up position behind it. Michael had no reason to argue.

In those last moments before he crouched down, Michael saw the position of two police marksmen, tucked into shadowy nooks between the other cars. He perceived them and realised there were four minds — which meant there were two policemen he couldn't see — focussed and disciplined, keeping control over the adrenaline running in their blood.

Beyond them, Michael perceived another mind: more intense, wild and untrained. It spewed out a fear that fluctuated between panic and terror. It was the mind of the bomber.

From his hiding place behind the car, Michael looked out and saw the teenager with his own eyes, now only metres from him. He appeared the same as the image from the television screens, but now from a different angle and infinitely more real. He *really* was shaking, trembling like a frightened stray cat, desperately alone in his small space of tarmac outside the hotel, hemmed in by the building behind him and armed police in front. The shaking made it more possible to see the blue wire which emerged from the rucksack on his back, quivering in the air before it looped round and disappeared into the neck of his coat. It reappeared at the end of his sleeve and connected to something black and plastic in his hand.

I am ready … said the teenager's thoughts … just a gentle squeeze, that's all it will take … but not yet … wait …

The teenager's thoughts changed to alarm. His head turned: he had noticed something. Michael also turned, to see what the teenager had seen.

It was Patterson. He had stepped away from the wall and stood in the middle of the alley with his arms out at his sides and his palms open. "I don't want to hurt you," he called out. "I just want to talk."

Michael returned his concentration to the bomber.

Ignore him … I have to wait … I have to wait …

"My name is Sergeant Anthony Patterson from the Metropolitan Police." He left a pause. "You can call me Tony. What's your name?"

The teenager did not reply with words, but his thoughts said: *Stephen.*

"There's nowhere to go," said Patterson. "But I can help you."

Then go away … if you go away, they will come …

"All you have to do is let my officers defuse the bomb," said Patterson. "They are experts, they can bring you to safety."

But I have to stay…

Stephen's emotions trembled like his body, scared of his own thoughts as he ran the same idea over and over in his head.

Just a gentle squeeze… it's all it will take… but wait… wait until they are here…

Michael wished Patterson was a perceiver. If the sergeant wasn't burdened by the limitations of being a norm, Michael could think loud enough to transmit his thoughts into Patterson's head so he could use that information to negotiate with Stephen. If the sergeant knew the teenager's name, at the very least, he could use that to make a connection. But, no, it was not possible. Patterson's mind could only think his own thoughts. "Why don't you talk to me, eh?" said Patterson, his voice soothing.

Can't talk… won't talk… ignore him…

"Tell me what you want and I can help you."

Michael concentrated harder. Even if Stephen would not tell Patterson, his thoughts could still betray him. But there was nothing there, an emptiness in his mind which made no sense. His only thoughts were the repeated mantra, varying around the same theme, stuck in the same place like a car spinning its wheels on liquid mud.

I'm ready… just a gentle squeeze… but not yet… wait… wait until they are here…

Frustrated, Michael shuffled in his space behind the car, his feet scraping on the grit on the road surface. He thought it only sounded loud to him because he was close to it and trying to be quiet, but Stephen must have heard because he turned his head in Michael's direction.

Realising he'd been spotted, Michael called out: "Who are you waiting for?"

Michael stood up from his hiding position behind the car so he was in full view. Patterson turned to look, his reproachful thoughts strong enough to bypass Michael's filters. Michael blocked them out to concentrate on the images whirring through Stephen's mind: white men in grey suits with white shirts, a Japanese woman in a cream skirt and jacket, a white woman in a red blouse with a bow …

… delegates …

"Michael!" Patterson spat in an urgent whisper. "Get back!"

Michael ignored him. If Patterson wasn't getting Stephen to think the right thoughts with his negotiation, then he had to.

"Are those the people you want to kill?" said Michael. "The delegates?"

Stephen's eyes widened, staring at Michael with incomprehension.

Ignore him … wait … wait until they are here …

"They're not coming back," said Michael. "Everyone's been evacuated from the hotel. It's just you, me and the police."

Stephen turned away from him and stared out ahead at nothing. His fixed, open eyes were the only part of his body that wasn't shaking.

I'm ready … just a gentle squeeze …

"It's like Sergeant Patterson said," Michael called out to him. "We can help. If you just tell us why you are doing this."

It was the question Michael wanted the answer to. Somewhere inside of Stephen's mind there had to be a reason he was prepared to blow himself up, some cause deep down that he was fighting for.

Michael concentrated. Patterson, the alley and the armed police were all banished from his mind: there was only him and Stephen. He pushed deeper than his surface thoughts, searching for his motivation. The more he found nothing, the more he pushed, getting deeper and deeper into the blankness of Stephen's mind.

He's in my head! A stab of desperate panic speared through the centre of Stephen's consciousness. So loud, it bounced Michael out of his mind.

Suddenly, Michael was aware of his surroundings.

Stephen's head whipped back in Michael's direction with angry, accusing eyes that burned into him.

"Perceiver!" Stephen shouted.

His hand reached behind — with no conscious thought — and pulled out a hand gun.

Gun! cried the thoughts from all the policemen at once.

Stephen swung the gun in Michael's direction, his finger on the trigger. *Kill the perceiver.*

A shot echoed off the walls of the alley.

Michael expected the pain of a bullet in the chest. But his lungs let out only a gasp as he saw a spurt of blood fly out of Stephen's stomach. The pain he felt was Stephen's pain: a searing hot stab through his body with a wave of shock and incomprehension that swelled in a moment and instantly cut to nothing—

An explosion — so loud it hurt — engulfed Stephen in a flash of flame. His body burst like a balloon filled with blood, throwing bits of his red-soaked flesh into the air.

The shock wave knocked Michael flying backwards. He landed on his back as bits of skin, muscle and bone fell onto him in hot red splashes.

Michael automatically blocked off all his perceptions. He lay on the ground with only his own terrified thoughts. He wiped something soft and squidgy from his eyes. It was a piece of Stephen's flesh, fused to a scrap of his green, quilted jacket.

FIVE

"**WHAT** the hell happened to you?" said Alex as Michael collected his meal of white fish hidden under a cream sauce, with chips and peas on the side, and joined him at the dining table.

The paramedics had patched him up the best they could, but he still looked a mess. Flying debris from the bomb, including (he overheard one of the bomb squad say) shards of Stephen's exploded bones, had scratched his face and arms. His back and bum ached from bruises caused by being knocked to the ground. "There was an explosion," he told his friend.

"Wow!" said Alex. "I wish my job was so exciting."

You really don't, Michael thought. Although he said nothing.

The noise in the communal room hurt his ears, which were still ringing from the sound of the bomb. Everyone was in there, and their chatter was louder than usual. On top of that, the television was on. The big screen up one end of the room was playing an early evening quiz show with all the bright lights and vivid colours of daytime TV. On the table nearest to it, a group of perceivers — led by Peter, by virtue of him being the loudest — were shouting out the answers.

"Paddington Bear!" Peter shouted.

The screen cut to a close-up of a hapless contestant who, by virtue of having been recorded several months ago in a studio two hundred miles away, paid no attention to what Peter was shouting and muttered some guess which was clearly wrong.

"No! Paddington Bear, you idiot!" cried Peter.

Peter's mates cheered when the besuited quiz show host announced Paddington Bear was, indeed, the right answer, which meant the embarrassed-looking contestant would go home with nothing and the jackpot would be rolled over to the next show.

"What's going on?" asked Michael. The communal television was usually only switched on for big events like football and it was never — and this was a strict military rule — *never* allowed on at meal times.

"The first day of the trial today, isn't it," said Alex, scooping up a fork full of peas.

Michael's body went cold. Then it went hot. The trial. He had forgotten about the trial. The smell of the fish suddenly made him feel sick. He dropped his fork to the plate and leant back in his chair. *The Perceivers Trial*, that's what the press called it. Where the man who poisoned thousands of pregnant women to create a 'master race' of people with mind powers would answer for his crimes. As far as journalists were concerned, Brian Ransom was no better than a Nazi who was finally going to receive justice before a war crimes tribunal. The United Kingdom had no death penalty, but still the population bayed for blood, and waited for the moment when he would appear in the witness box and metaphorically hang himself with his twisted ideas of how he tried to better the human race.

Michael hadn't decided whether he could bring himself to watch it. But he knew for a fact he didn't want to watch it with a group of other perceivers.

Pauline was there, the new girl, sitting on the next table. She smiled at him and he tried to smile back, but that only pulled at a half-healed scab next to his mouth. She shot him a quizzical glance as if to ask what happened, and he shook his head to say that it didn't matter. It seemed as if she wanted to ask more, but something was happening on the TV and she turned to look.

Michael looked too. The news had started. The perceivers around him hushed each other and the noise of the chattering that had been too loud, dropped to a stillness that hurt even more. A newsreader in a crisp blue blouse stared out the screen with deep brown eyes. "The Old Bailey hears how Brian Ransom conned thousands of British women into taking vitamin pills laced with the genetically-engineered perceiver virus."

Michael couldn't listen to it. Not in public. He got up from the table as quietly as possible. Alex asked if he was okay, but Michael waved away his concern. No one else noticed, they were too engrossed by the news on the TV.

He had planned to go to his room, but when he reached the corridor, he realised he didn't want to stay in a building full of other perceivers, where part of his brain would be concentrating on shutting out the rest of the world. He turned, instead, to the door and found himself in the grounds of the camp. The sun had gone down now and there was only a haze of the daylight still in the sky. The street lights had taken over and cast their orangey glow across the road and across the grass. The sun had taken what little warmth it had given the day and brought the night chill to the air. Michael shivered and realised, for the second time that day, he shouldn't have left his coat in the police station.

He could have gone back in for a jumper or something, but the cool breeze on his face was actually refreshing. He started walking, with no particular plan of where he was going, and ended up in the car park.

HODGES was still there, giving his car one last check over for the night, and wiping the back windscreen with a chamois leather. He stopped, mid-wipe, as he heard Michael's approaching footsteps. He had taken off his tie and undone the top button of his shirt, which somehow made him look more human. He always wore a suit and tie to drive Michael around, like it was some kind of uniform, a barrier between him and the rest of the world that meant he did not have to show everyone his real self.

"Shouldn't you be inside?" said Hodges.

"Yes," said Michael.

"Had a row with someone?"

"They're watching the trial."

"Ah," said Hodges, as if he understood. Maybe he did, maybe he didn't. Michael could have looked inside his mind to check, but it was nicer to believe the man knew him enough so he didn't have to explain himself.

Hodges gave up wiping the back window of the black Audi A4, folded up his chamois leather and popped it in a pocket on the inside of the passenger door. He pushed the door closed again, pulled a set of keys from his pocket and pressed a button on the fob. The car responded with a bleep and a yellow flash of all four indicators. Michael's body shuddered at the suddenness of it.

Hodges smiled a sympathetic smile at him. "I had a friend who witnessed a bomb explode once," said Hodges. "For a week afterwards, he couldn't stand any kind of loud noise. There was one time, someone accidently dropped a glass and smashed it — we found him several minutes later hiding under the table."

"It's not the explosion," said Michael. "It's the—"

"The trial, yes you said." Hodges pressed the button on the car keys in his hand again, and the car responded like before, with four simultaneous clicks as the locks of each door released. Michael shuddered again. His heart was racing.

Hodges opened the nearest rear door. "Sit down," he said.

"I'm fine," said Michael.

"Sit."

There was something in Hodges's tone that suggested it was not open to debate. Michael sat with his bum on the edge of the back seat and his legs dangling out of the doorway. "Was that in Iraq?"

"Yes," said Hodges.

"Must have been awful."

"Some of it was," he admitted. "But I was a soldier, I wanted to see action."

Michael thought about it for a moment. It seemed wrong, to him, that someone's job should be going to war. "Did you ever see a suicide bomber?"

Hodges folded his arms and leant back against the body of the car. The dim glow radiating from the street lights highlighted the lines of his face, etched by experience. "I saw the aftermath once," he said. "A young man had gone into a marketplace with explosives strapped to his body and set them off. He killed more than a dozen people who had simply gone out that morning to buy vegetables. Mindless."

"Why do they do it?" asked Michael.

"Isn't that more your territory?" said Hodges. "Figuring out what's going on in people's minds?"

"I'd still be interested in hearing what you think."

Hodges took a deep breath and let it out in a long sigh. "They think their life has no meaning, they can't see themselves having any sort of future, they can't see themselves getting ahead in life through education or work or bringing up a family. Then someone comes along who tells them that their life can have meaning in death. So they choose death, and they don't care who they take with them."

"Is that what they think when they pull the trigger?" Michael was remembering Stephen, and the thoughts that didn't explain why he did it.

"Who knows," said Hodges. "I suppose they're thinking of whatever mixed up cause someone has drummed into their head. The young man in the market in Baghdad shouted 'God is great' in Arabic before he blew himself up. As far as I am concerned, no god who endorses killing wives and mothers as they buy vegetables to feed their family can be considered 'great.'"

A wave of disgust and grief poured from Hodges, seeping through Michael's perception filters. It lasted only a moment before the former soldier pulled back his emotions and locked them away inside himself.

"Was the explosion you witnessed a suicide bomber?" said Hodges.

"Yes," said Michael. The memory of it was still fresh, unprocessed, painful like the bruises on his back.

"Did you see inside his head?" said Hodges.

"I did," said Michael, "but I couldn't see why he was doing it. I tried, but there was nothing there. He kept saying to himself that he was ready to set off the bomb, but he didn't seem to have a reason. There was no desire to die, there wasn't any sort of cause in his head. And I probed deep into his mind — deeper than I should."

The memory of Stephen pulling the gun on him was suddenly there. Accusing him of being a perceiver before the sniper shot him and it was all over. *How could Stephen have known? How could a norm possibly have known?*

"So perceivers don't know everything," said Hodges.

"I wouldn't go that far," said Michael. He said it as a half joke to try to lighten things up, but even through a smile, his words sounded melancholy.

Hodges shivered in the night air that had suddenly got colder now that the sun had completely set.

Michael realised the man was supposed to be off shift. "I'm sorry, you should be going home."

"That's true," said Hodges.

But Michael didn't want to leave the safety of the car where he could be alone with his thoughts and no one else's. "You have your own car, don't you?" Michael asked. "I mean, you leave this one here and drive your own car home?"

"What are you getting at, Michael?"

"Can I stay here tonight?"

"In the car?" said Hodges.

"It's inside the base," said Michael. "It'll be safe."

The man frowned and pulled the keys from his pocket. He pressed a button and the boot popped. He went round to the back of the car and rummaged around while Michael wondered what the hell he was doing.

Hodges returned carrying a blanket which he threw at Michael. "The AA says always carry a blanket in your boot in case you break down in bad weather," he explained.

Michael clutched the soft wool of the material to his lap. "Thank you."

"Mm," said Hodges, doubtfully.

Michael pulled his mobile phone from his pocket.

"What are you doing?" said Hodges.

"Texting Alex," said Michael. "Getting him to cover for me."

Alex replied almost immediately: 'Sure thing, geezer,' said the text, followed by a yellow face icon that winked at him.

Michael giggled.

"What?" said Hodges.

"He thinks I'm off with some girl," said Michael.

"That wouldn't be such a bad idea at some point," said Hodges. "But not in my car. Semen stains are hell to get out of the upholstery."

Michael smiled, even though it pulled at that scab by his mouth, and unfolded the blanket to spread it out over his legs. Hodges made to leave.

"Hodges?" Michael stopped him.

The man turned back. "Yes?"

"You won't report this, will you?"

"Michael…" His voice was doubtful, almost apologetic.

Michael realised it might have been a request too far. "Sorry, I don't want you to risk your job…"

Hodges put his hand on the roof of the car and leant forward so he could look Michael in the eye. "I wouldn't do anything to hurt you, Michael. You perceive that, right?"

It had been a long time since Michael had looked into Hodges's mind to find out his motives, but when he had, he had found no malice there. He decided to trust him. "Good night, Hodges."

"Good night, Michael."

Hodges walked off to wherever he had parked his own car. Michael watched him go, reflecting on how tough it must be for him to serve two masters.

SIX

THE first rays of the sun woke Michael, prodding him from sleep like an alarm clock that had been set too early. He felt the grogginess of semi-consciousness for one blissful moment before he decided to move and the bruises on his back complained with a spasm of pain that ran down his spine, into his pelvis, and up into his skull.

He groaned.

Sleeping in the back seat of a car was not the best medicine for someone caught in a bomb blast. But it had the advantage of being gloriously quiet. He opened his mind further and perceived the silence. He was cocooned in an emptiness where no one was lying awake worrying, or missing their family, or having inappropriate sexual thoughts about an actress from the television. He was alone with his own thoughts and it was beautiful.

He also needed a pee. Michael struggled to sit up in the car, his back complaining with each muscle movement. The blanket was caught up round his feet and required several kicks to get the damn thing off him. "Ow, ow, ow!" he said to himself.

Finally, he was able to shuffle along the seat, open the door and step out into the fresh air to taste clean oxygen. His breath turned to vapour as he exhaled into the open air. It had been a clear night, causing the temperatures to drop and bring a frost, which the early morning sun was already burning away. In the brightness of daylight, the car park seemed like a tarmac field, stretching out to the hedge boundary, big enough for a game of football. Hodges's car sat like a molehill in its space, metres distant from the twenty-or-so other military molehills which had been parked there for the night. In the shade of several towering trees, a row of khaki jeeps reminded him of the many bumpy trips he'd taken in them to reach ghastly military exercises on Salisbury Plain.

Michael walked away from them to the nearest hedge where he unzipped his trousers and released his bladder with that glorious sensation of physical relief. A stream of yellow urine arched into the undergrowth, discharging its warmth in vapour that rose into the air with a musty human smell. As he squeezed the last urine from inside of him, the presence of another mind crept into the edge of his perception. He hadn't been paying attention and the mind was suddenly close. Along with the smell of coffee.

He turned.

Pauline stood there, all in black like he had first seen her, with a steaming mug in her hand. Her gaze automatically dropped to his groin.

"Shit!" said Michael, caught by surprise, grabbing his willy and shoving it back in his trousers. Heat coloured his cheeks.

Pauline was grinning. "Morning," she said.

"Don't you knock?" said Michael.

She looked around the half empty car park, closed a fist and rapped on thin air. "Like this?"

"Ha bloody ha." His face still felt as red as an over-ripe tomato and he knew she had probably perceived his embarrassment. He should never have let his guard down, even when he was alone.

"I brought you some coffee," she said, holding out the mug. A twist of steam rose gently into the cold of the morning and it smelt like civilisation.

Michael took it and sipped. His whole body warmed at the prospect of coffee stimulation as he swallowed and tasted its welcome bitter earthiness. "How did you know I was out here?" he asked.

"Alex," said Pauline.

"Alex?"

"He winked at me in a suggestive way this morning," she said. "I thought he was hitting on me. Turns out he thought I was out with you all night."

"Oh." Michael laughed.

She didn't find it funny. "What have you been saying?"

"I asked him to cover for me," said Michael. "You know, make it look like I'm asleep in my room so Norm the Norm doesn't know. When we do that, it's usually because the other person wants to be with a girl."

She rolled her eyes. "Boys!"

Michael drank from the mug. It was more lukewarm than hot, having been carried all the way from Galen House, but it was still more than he expected. "Thanks for the coffee."

"I tried to find you last night to talk to you, but Alex said you left when the news about the trial came on."

"Yes," said Michael.

"Don't you want to see that bastard pay for what he's done?"

"Not really."

"If it wasn't for him, my mother wouldn't have taken that stupid pill," she said.

"I'm not saying he didn't do anything wrong," said Michael. "I'm just not sure I want to watch it laid out in front of me on television."

"Don't you want to see him face his crime?" said Pauline, getting angry. "That pill changed my DNA before I was even born. If it wasn't for him, they wouldn't have taken me away from my family, I wouldn't be…" Her voice cracked. She stopped talking before it became too obvious. But her emotions gave her away; the pain of separation was easy to perceive.

"You didn't have to leave home," said Michael. "Not after the Perceivers' Law. We have a right not to be discriminated against." He remembered how hard perceivers had fought to make that law a reality. He remembered the elation as he sat in the Houses of Parliament and heard the Prime Minister, John Pankhurst, promise that perceivers would be allowed to live freely in Britain without fear of persecution.

"How long have you been in here?" asked Pauline.

He thought back to when he had first come to Galen House. It was a long time. "Two years," he said. "Give or take."

"You don't know what it's like out there." She pointed into the distance, indicating the world outside the camp. "They find out you're a perceiver and you're a second class citizen. The law says you can live with it like a normal person, but people don't let you. Like that boy last year who jumped off Beachy Head because he was bullied for being a perceiver. No, in the real world, they find out what you are in school screening and they strongly 'suggest' you take the cure. Pankhurst said some nice things, but no one listens to him anymore. My mum says he's a fool who'll be humiliated at the next election. My mum says…"

Talking about her mother, Michael perceived, brought back the memory of the home that she missed and she stopped herself from saying more.

"There was always the cure," said Michael.

She shook her head, the pain of the decision was still raw. "Perception was already part of me," she said. "I didn't know how I would cope if it was taken away. Besides, it was too late for me, my family would never trust me again, they saw me as an alien in their house. They were happy when we got the knock on the door and I was invited to join this place. I'd screwed up school anyway, so when they offered me a job as a perceiver, I took it. Maybe the cure is right for those whose perception is weak, but I couldn't do it."

"I'm sorry," said Michael. He felt her anger and frustration, and understood it. It reminded him of making that horrible choice himself, except he didn't have a family to leave behind. Not really.

"Ransom did that to me, he did that to all of us," said Pauline. "I want to see it all laid out in front of him in court, then I want to see him take the stand and squirm as he explains why he did it. They say the creation of perceivers has changed the world, that's not something one man should be allowed to get away with."

She had every right to be angry. Michael had been angry once. But there was nothing he could do about it, so he decided not to waste his energy. The perceivers genie was out of the bottle and now they had to deal with it. Ransom had claimed that, given enough time, evolution would have turned the whole world into perceivers. All he had done was hurry evolution along a bit, in his twisted, utopian belief that a generation of people who could perceive each other would promote understanding.

"There would always have been the natural borns," said Michael.

Her eyes narrowed. She didn't understand. "The what?"

"The natural borns," said Michael. "The perceivers who would have existed anyway. I'm a natural born, my mother didn't take a pill."

She shook her head. "Perceivers are teenagers, we were all born in those years when women thought they were getting free vitamin pills that would make their babies healthy. No one knew about it until we reached puberty and we started perceiving."

"They didn't know about it because the natural borns kept it quiet," said Michael. "How do you think Ransom knew what DNA to splice into those vitamin pills? DNA that already existed in the few people like him who'd been born with it."

Michael suddenly stopped. In his rush to explain, he had let slip that Ransom was a perceiver. Something a lot of people had taken a lot of trouble to keep quiet.

"You're wrong," said Pauline. "Why would you think that?"

"I know it because—" He stopped himself. He wanted to tell her, even though he knew he shouldn't. He felt her probing into his mind, trying to find the information in there and increased his blocks. "Get out of my head!"

She frowned at him, embarrassed she'd been detected and frustrated that he was hiding something from her. "You know because of what?"

"Can I tell you something, Pauline?" said Michael. "Something that I haven't told anyone else in here?"

"Sure," she said. Her tone had changed and maybe she perceived it was something personal.

"I know because Ransom is my father."

He perceived her as she stood there, processing his words. They confused her. Part of her was still angry, but mostly she was unsure if she believed him. "But your surname is Sanderson, not Ransom."

"I took my mother's maiden name. I didn't want people to know."

"But you're telling me," she pointed out.

"Yes," said Michael. He still wasn't entirely sure why.

"And you live here with the rest of us. Spying on us?"

"No," said Michael. He stepped forward, he wanted to put a hand on her arm to reassure her, but she stepped back from him. "Let's say that me and my father are … 'estranged'. He didn't give my mother one of his pills, he created me in a lab with his sperm and the egg of a natural born woman perceiver. He wanted me to inherit perception from both parents, to be stronger than anyone else."

"So you're not the same as me," said Pauline, maintaining her distance.

"I guess not," said Michael. There was water in his eyes, blurring his vision. He fought to stop it turning to tears.

"I should be getting back," she said. "I have to get ready for training."

Michael perceived her mentally distancing herself from him. It made him ache inside. "Do you see why I'm uncomfortable watching the trial? I believe Ransom deserves to be punished, but I'm afraid the court will expose things which should remain secret."

"Sure, I understand," said Pauline. "But I'm going to be late."

She turned away and started walking. "Thanks again for the coffee!" he called after her.

"Your flies are still undone," she called back without turning round.

Michael's hand shot down to his trousers and felt the gap where he had forgotten to do the zip up. He fumbled with the zip as he watched the black-clad figure of Pauline, small in the distance, walking out of the car park and back towards Galen House. He worried that he had exposed himself more than he should.

SEVEN

MICHAEL saw Patterson limping down the corridor. Part of the bomb had lodged in his leg when it exploded and severed a muscle. He'd been standing closer to the blast than Michael and caught more of the force of it. His bulletproof vest had protected his vital organs, but a gash on his arm had required stiches and the bandage the hospital had put on could be seen poking out of the end of his shirt cuff. He also had a severe cut across his right cheek, the sharp red line of the scab looking like it might turn into a scar worthy of a movie villain.

Patterson stopped a few steps from Michael, his anger so loud that Michael had to increase his filters to shut it out. Around them, other policemen and women walked past, some in uniform, others in business suits. Several of them disappeared through the door into the briefing room.

"You lied to me," said Patterson.

"I'm sorry," said Michael. Sorry for his injuries, not so sorry for the lying.

"You told me Jones said you could be there, but it was all bollocks. You disobeyed me and spoke to the suspect and nearly got us killed."

"But I saw into his head," said Michael.

"So did I," said Patterson. "As bits of it splattered all over my body."

Michael's attention was caught by Jones walking down the corridor carrying a bunch of cardboard files. He was wearing the same suit as yesterday, he had loosened his tie and undone the top button of his shirt to reveal where the grime of sweat had worn into the material. It didn't look as if he had slept much, if at all.

Patterson noticed Michael was looking at something behind his shoulder and turned to see who it was. "What's he doing here?" Patterson asked Jones as he approached, referring to Michael.

"Orders," said Jones. Michael got the sense that Jones didn't like it either, but with his filters on high to block out Patterson's strong emotions, he wasn't sure.

"If it wasn't for him, we could be questioning the suspect right now," said Patterson. "Instead of scraping him off the pavement."

"If you have a problem, Tony, you could rest at home like the doctor told you to," said Jones.

"I can't rest," said Patterson. "Daytime TV does my head in."

"Then shut up and get into the briefing room."

Patterson gave Michael one last glare and stepped sideways with an exaggerated limp to get past him.

"And you," said Jones, pointing his finger at Michael. "Make yourself scarce."

MICHAEL hid himself away in the observation room; a broom cupboard of a space with little more than a desk, a couple of chairs and a monitor which displayed a feed from, usually, one of the interrogation rooms. On this occasion, the display had been flipped to a feed from a single camera in the briefing room. At some point in the past, a senior officer had decided to film the briefings for whatever reason and had had the camera installed. Whoever that officer was, he or she had either moved on to another job or retired because no one could remember who it was. But the camera had stayed, allowing Michael to take advantage.

He wasn't allowed into the briefing room. As far as the other officers on the team were concerned, he was hanging around the department because he was some sort of trainee or police cadet. They didn't know he was a perceiver and, apart from Jones and Patterson, they weren't allowed to know. So Michael was banished to the broom cupboard where he could sit back with his feet on the desk, open a can of Coke and slurp it as loud as he liked, while the police business unfolded on the screen in front of him.

The camera was set on the ceiling, giving him a bird's-eye view of a long table with, he counted, twelve police officers sitting around it, their faces indistinct because of the distance and wide angle of the lens.

Jones, at the head of the table, brought everyone to order. "We've got a busy day, so let's crack on. Baker's been looking into the kid's background — Tania?"

A woman with long blonde hair spoke, rattling through her information like she was on a timer. "The bomber was Stephen Bailecki, seventeen years old, no criminal record, no red flags on the terror watch list. Average kid, as far as we can tell. But the interesting thing is, he lived on the same estate in Kennington as Jerome Tyler, the other kid with explosives we arrested."

Murmurs of interest from some of the others.

"We went down there yesterday, spoke to a few people. Nothing popped. We've confiscated his computer, tablet, yadda: forensics are looking at it now."

"What about his target?" said Jones.

"I've been looking into that," said one of the other men around the table. Michael recognised him as the chubby man with a big nose he'd seen around, but couldn't remember his name. "There was a trade conference at the Capital Hotel, so we're working on the assumption that he wanted to disrupt the conference, but … it's a weird one. The attendees were from various countries and were there to discuss oil and gas exports — hardly the sort of thing terrorists usually go after. I'm looking into the background of the delegates to see if they might have been targeted for another reason, but I'm drawing a blank so far."

"Hasn't someone accepted responsibility for the attack?" said another voice. Michael didn't see who it was because he was in the middle of taking a swig from his Coke can. It was frustrating watching people on a screen when he couldn't perceive them. Like watching a movie with empty shells of characters walking and talking, and supposedly having emotions, which he couldn't feel.

"The Army Against Fossil Fuels," said the chubby man in response to the question. "Unfortunately, the media have picked up on that one so the press are all talking about it, but there's no record of these people ever existing before. I think it's a lone nutjob wanting some publicity on the back of the bombing."

"Probably," said Jones. "But check it out anyway."

"On it," said Chubby.

A delicate knocking sound stopped their discussion as the police officers in the briefing room all looked in the direction of the door.

"This will be the PCSO," said Tania Baker.

Michael could tell the person who walked in was a woman by the way she moved. She wore a blue hat which, because of the angle of the camera, obscured her face.

Baker asked her to sit down. "This is PCSO Gillian Barnes who's based at Kennington Police Station. She's fairly sure Tyler and Bailecki hung around in the same gang that she deals with as part of her beat."

Patterson shuffled up his seat so Barnes could take the spare chair next to his. As she sat down, she removed her hat to reveal her short cropped black hair. She wore a PCSO uniform of white shirt and blue tie, which distinguished her from regular police officers.

"Thank you for coming, Officer Barnes," said Jones. "Anything you can tell us would be of benefit."

"I didn't know anything about them being terrorists," she told the assembled officers. "I swear, if I had known, I would have reported it."

"No one is blaming you, Officer Barnes," said Jones. "We just want to know what you know about them. It could be really useful to us."

"They hung out on street corners, much like any kids of that age," said Barnes. "Talking and playing with their phones. I moved them on a few times and told them to keep the noise down late at night, but nothing out of the ordinary. A couple of them were given cautions for minor crime, shoplifting and stuff, but nothing major. They're not involved in drugs, not dealing anyway. The big dealer on the estate got arrested a while back and the users that are left go elsewhere to score. I suspected Tyler was involved with criminal damage on some parked cars about six months ago, but I was never able to prove it."

"Did they, perhaps, have contact with strangers from outside the estate?" said Jones. "Anything recently?"

"Not that I saw. But, then, if anything happened outside of my patch, I wouldn't have known." She paused, fiddling with the rim of her hat on the table in front of her. "Perhaps they were … what do they call it …? Bedroom terrorists? I don't patrol their bedrooms."

There was a little snigger from some of the officers. Michael wasn't sure if she was making a joke or if the officers found her funny. It was so hard trying to judge people without perception.

Barnes was asked a few more questions, which invoked very little more information, she was thanked for her time and allowed to leave.

Jones concluded the briefing by dishing out assignments to his assembled team and dismissed them.

Michael tossed his empty Coke can in the recycling and left the broom cupboard.

THE PCSO was standing outside the briefing room, holding her hat and fiddling with the brim, when Michael saw her again. He was trying to find Jones and was walking back down the corridor, having visited his empty office. As he passed, he perceived a bewildered feeling from her. It was strange how he felt her turn from an image on the screen to a real person in that moment.

Michael peered through a glass porthole in the door to the briefing room and saw only the table surrounded by empty chairs. He could have gone inside to double-check, but his perception told him it was empty. Jones had probably gone to the canteen for a coffee. Either that, or he was avoiding giving Michael an assignment, which was entirely possible.

"Excuse me," said the PCSO. "I don't suppose you could direct me to the ladies?"

"Um … sure," said Michael.

The women's toilets was not a place he tended to hang out, but it just so happened it was next to the gents, so he knew where it was. He was about to explain to her where it was when he caught something else from her mind. As she relaxed, and the feeling of being lost dissipated, it revealed that she was worried about what she had said to the police officers.

Intrigued, he decided that simply giving her directions would be a missed opportunity. "It's probably easier if I show you," he said.

"I don't want to put you to any trouble," she said.

"No trouble," said Michael.

He walked down the corridor, focussing his perception and making sure she followed him close. She was thinking about Tyler and Bailecki, the image of their faces mixed up with a group of other teenage faces in her memory. She remembered them gathered by a shop somewhere under a street light, and it made her feel uneasy. There was something about them that unsettled her, something that she couldn't articulate. She would have felt stupid to have told a room full of a dozen detectives about her intuition. *But maybe I should have,* she thought. *If only they had been drug dealers, then the money they had would make sense.* Many of them were from one-parent families and she used to think all the gadgets and clothes and jewellery they had were from absent fathers trying to buy their love. But, after the bombing, she wasn't sure that was true anymore.

Michael was so concerned with perceiving her thoughts, that he almost walked straight past the women's toilets. He covered himself by making a play that he was heading for the gents. "Oops, sorry," he said, feigning a laugh like norms do when they are trying to convey they have been a bit stupid. "This one's yours." He pointed at the door marked with the silhouette of a figure in a dress.

"Thank you," she said, and went inside. Michael just caught her relief at being moments away from emptying her bladder before he pulled his perception out.

He leant back against the wall for a moment and thought about what he had perceived. If even a norm had an uncomfortable feeling about the teenagers in the gang, there had to be more to them than just hanging around on street corners.

MICHAEL did not expect to find Patterson in Jones's office. But there he was, slumped in a chair by the door, broadcasting negative emotions like a rotten apple sends out the smell of decay.

"Inspector Jones not here?" said Michael.

Patterson looked across the desk at Jones's empty chair. "I may not be a perceiver, but I have a feeling in my water that he is, in fact, somewhere else."

Michael glanced behind him at the rest of the office who, in theory, could hear them through the open door. The officers in the open plan area were either on the phone or absorbed by their computer displays and apparently didn't notice.. "Do you know where he is?" said Michael.

"Reporting our lack of progress to the boss," said Patterson. "What did you want Jones for anyway? Because there's a queue and I was here first."

"It doesn't matter," said Michael.

"Clearly it does, or you wouldn't be here."

"You wouldn't want to know, it was something I …" Aware of the other officers in the main part of the office, he stepped inside so he could close the door. "It was something I perceived."

"Try me," said Patterson. "It'll kill time before Jones gets back."

Michael realised he was now firmly inside the office with Patterson. Making an excuse to leave would be an admission of defeat. It was easier to explain. "The PCSO wasn't telling you everything," he said.

"She barely told us *anything*," said Patterson.

"I think she was too embarrassed to say. The teenagers in the gang have more money than they should for regular kids in that neighbourhood. That's assuming they're not living off the proceeds of crime, which she thinks they're not. She also thinks they're a bit weird."

Patterson chuckled. "Being a bit weird is not a crime. If it was, we'd have half of London locked up."

"There's something going on with that gang," said Michael. "Something not involving drugs, or even religious extremism. You didn't look into their heads, Sergeant Patterson, their minds weren't like the minds of ordinary people."

"Then we shall discover whatever it is they were hiding with diligent police work. They will have a digital trail on their phones or computers, they will have told someone or been seen by someone and that person will tell us. I don't need a perceiver telling me that they have weird minds. In my experience, anyone planning to kill themselves is always a bit screwed up in the head."

"Okay, so you don't believe in the power of perception, I understand that. But look at me."

Patterson allowed his gaze to drift up and down the length of Michael's body as he stood in front of him. Michael half caught his thoughts as Patterson regarded the cuts on his face and reflected on why Michael was the one to have escaped with just a few scrapes in the explosion, while he was injured by flying shrapnel. "Not a pretty sight," said Patterson.

"I'm seventeen years old," said Michael. "I'm their age. I can talk to them like adults can't talk to them, and I can see inside their heads while I do it."

"But you're not trained," said Patterson. "You're going to screw it up like you screwed up Bailecki."

The jibe hurt, even as Michael tried to ignore it. "Then brief me. I can go in there like one of them, talk to them like one of them. Maybe find out where the explosives came from, why they did it, who they're going to target next."

He perceived that Patterson, despite himself, was warming to the idea.

"We're not sure the gang has anything to do with the bombing," said Patterson. "The two of them might just have met on the estate and the rest of the gang has nothing to do with it."

"I can find out for sure," said Michael. "And if it helps to persuade you, if I go onto the estate undercover, it will mean I'll be out of this police station and out of your hair."

The door opened and the inside handle bashed into Michael's bruised back. He winced.

Jones was standing there with one hand on the outside door handle and the other balancing a croissant on top of a cardboard takeaway mug of coffee. A combination of sweetness and bitterness floated into the room. "What are you two doing in here?" he said.

"Michael has an idea," said Patterson.

Michael felt Jones's surprise as he raised his eyebrows at his sergeant. "This is an idea you like?"

"Actually," said Patterson, "I think I do."

EIGHT

THE flat smelt stale. Opening the door and walking inside disturbed the air for the first time in many months and caused the dust to circulate again. Michael and Patterson gagged on it as they stepped inside.

"I don't believe I'm doing this," said Patterson as he closed the door behind them.

They had walked directly into the living area, dimly lit by daylight that filtered through the thin curtains patterned with large roses that must have once been red and were now kind of pinkish. The place came 'furnished', in that it included an old fake leather sofa and a coffee table stained with the rings of many hot mugs. The wooden veneer on the coffee table, just like the paint on the walls, was starting to chip off.

Patterson walked across to the window and threw open the curtains, disturbing another layer of dust which made him cough and then sneeze. "Bloody hell, they could have cleaned it first," he complained.

"It's fine," said Michael. It made a change from Galen House. In the dirty flat, there was no one to give him orders, no automated system to put his lights out and no perceivers to guard his thoughts from. It was almost like a holiday.

With the curtains open, it was easier to see the room. It really was rather dingy. Michael sat on the sofa and a cloud of dust rose into the air. He didn't think to hold his breath until it was too late and he let out several sneezes.

Laughing at him, Patterson wandered over to the space on the other side of the front door to where there was a kitchenette area, furnished with cheap cream laminate units. He opened a few drawers and a few cupboards and neither the handles nor the doors fell off, which was a good sign. He next tried the doors of the oven, the microwave and the fridge.

"Oh my God!" said Patterson.

"What?" said Michael from his position on the sofa where he couldn't see easily into the kitchenette.

"Mouse droppings."

"Charming," said Michael.

"No wonder the kids on this estate spend most of their time hanging around outside," said Patterson. He pulled a handkerchief from his pocket and wiped his hands. "I'm going to drive to the supermarket to get some cleaning products. Are you going to be all right here on your own?"

"I think so," said Michael. "Unless they're giant alien killer mice."

Patterson looked at the base of the fridge where he had seen the droppings. "No, I think they're just the regular kind."

"That's all right then."

"I'll see you later," said Patterson, heading back to the door.

"Bye, *Dad*," said Michael, grinning.

Patterson gave him an irritated stare and left. The door slamming shut in the frame echoed around the bare walls. Michael savoured a moment of being alone.

Their cover story was that Michael and Patterson were father and son and had just moved to the area because Patterson had a job at a nearby warehouse. Michael could tell everyone that his 'dad' was on the night shift, which allowed Patterson to go home to his own bed at night and be scarce in the day when he was supposedly sleeping.

Over the course of the week it took to get approval for the operation, the media interest in the bomber had faded to almost nothing and the police inquiry had come up against several dead ends. Tests showed the explosives being carried by both teenagers were from the same batch of PETN, a common substance used by the military and civilians (for jobs such as quarrying) and could have been smuggled in from almost anywhere. As Tyler and Bailecki appeared not to have gone outside of Kennington in recent weeks, it was almost certain someone else had done the smuggling. Analysis of their phone records, emails and internet use revealed no contact with any potential smugglers and a sniffer dog sweep of their homes found no traces of PETN. Either they were very clever at hiding their tracks, or someone else was very clever on their behalf.

The officers who had interviewed the other teenagers on the estate came to the conclusion that they knew nothing about Tyler and Bailecki's terrorist plot. For a while it looked like Michael's idea of going undercover and infiltrating the gang was going to be kicked into the long grass. But Michael managed to write a persuasive report stating his case and, with pressure from Patterson, the operation was finally approved.

A 'ding' from Michael's pocket broke into his thoughts. He pulled out his phone: it was a text from Alex.

'How's the new place?' it said.

'Like Buckingham Palace!' Michael texted back.

He turned the phone round and took a picture of the sofa sitting alone against blank walls, and sent it to Alex.

'The Queen's really let the place go,' Alex replied.

Michael found an animated chuckling face to text back to him.

'You should invite me round — if it's all right with Her Maj,' smiley face.

Typical Alex, thought Michael. He put the phone back in his pocket.

Silence returned.

Michael opened one of the windows, letting in a bit of fresh air, some London pollution and the sound of nearby traffic. He toured the place a bit more, checked out the bathroom (basic) and the bedroom (at least it had a bed) and came back to where he started.

Although the quiet was lovely, it soon got boring. Michael decided he might as well go outside and see if he could find the teenage gang he was supposed to spy on.

MICHAEL negotiated three flights of stairs of the seven storey building down to ground level. Emerging outside, he found he had come out the back way which led into a communal garden area, surrounded by other rectangular blocks of flats. He imagined, in the sunlight, the grass and the shrubs and the children's play area would look pleasant, even inviting. But as the dusk sucked the last of the light out of the day, the foliage and climbing frames became little more than dark blobs in a darkening landscape.

Perceiving there was no one close, he passed through an alleyway to the front of the building. The road was not especially wide and was made narrower by the cars parked down one side of it. Two boys, aged ten at the most, were taking it in turns to ride a skateboard down the dotted white line in the middle, in a dangerous game which risked them being run over by some maniac motorist who preferred speed over safety. In the moment that he perceived them, he understood that the danger was part of the attraction.

The only other person on the street was a woman walking her dog, a little brown shaggy thing with legs going like the clappers to keep up with her long strides. As she passed, Michael perceived she was counting the days to see how soon she could take a pregnancy test. He let her frantic thoughts disappear into the distance before he followed her. Not because he wanted to follow her as such, but because she was walking in the direction of the local shops which, if he had remembered the maps he had studied correctly, was where the gang liked to hang out.

The shops sat on a wide paved area with a sculpture of twisted metal in the centre which someone had presumably decreed was 'art'. Down the middle was a single row of street lights, sending their orange glow out to where the passageway was bordered by rows of two storey buildings. Each row had five retail units with accommodation or storage above. Three of the shops were boarded up and the rest looked run-down, even in the half-light of the early evening. The only one that was open was a convenience store at the far end with a front plate glass window through which a white light blazed out onto the street.

Unusually for him, Michael saw the teenagers before he perceived them. Five figures were silhouetted by the light from the shop window: three tall and skinny, probably male; one short and dumpy with a chest that definitely marked her out as female; and a fifth sort of middling in that he was neither particularly tall or short nor thin or fat. Michael ran through the descriptions he had memorised of Tyler and Bailecki's friends and was fairly sure he knew who they all were by the time he got close enough to see enough detail. He was only wrong with regard to one of the tall lanky people, who turned out to be female with long dark hair tucked up into her baseball cap, and not one of the ones he'd read about in the police files.

He kept his eyes fixed ahead as he walked towards the shop, but his perception was entirely focussed on them. He expected them to have minds like the other two, empty of anything apart from the one thing that they were doing or planned to do. But what he actually perceived were the minds of normal teenagers, filled with the music they liked, the other teenagers they fancied, the memory of a row with their father and the thought of buying alcohol. All jumbled up together in a group. The only thought he singled out was from the tall girl with her hair tucked away, who checked him out as he passed.

Embarrassed, Michael walked into the shop. It was one of those places that was packed floor to ceiling with pre-packaged everything, all marked up ten per cent more than the supermarkets. It had all the sort of things people were likely to run out of and couldn't be bothered to walk further to get, like toilet paper and toothpaste.It would look odd for Michael to walk out of the shop empty handed and so he bought a chocolate bar and a can of Coke.

When he stepped back outside, the teenagers were standing in exactly the same place as when he went in, as static as the twisted metal art installation up the other end of the block.

"Hiya!" he said, needing to make some kind of connection.

The fat girl, whose name he knew was Laura, was the only one who looked up from contemplating her shoes, a pair of the latest Nike trainers in blue with silver trim, not yet grubbied by the experience of being worn. He filtered out the others to perceive her and got a litany of her first impressions of him. Michael, she thought, was weasely and annoying and not in the least worth shagging. She also had an aching back from standing up so long and was hoping one of the other two would soon move so she could take a turn leaning against the lamppost.

"I just moved in," said Michael, adopting a smile which he hoped norms would find friendly. "Is there much to do around here?"

"Ain't nothing," said the skinny woman, stepping out from the shadow. She was older than the others, maybe nineteen and stood with her hands plunged deep into her jacket pockets, making her pointy elbows stick out like a chicken. Her mind spewed boredom. She was looking for some action, of either the violent or the sexual kind. But not, she decided, with Michael.

"Depends what you're looking for," said one of the skinny guys, a black boy, sixteen years old with an acne problem. He was Chad, according to the Metropolitan Police files, a college student with a dubious attendance record. His mind danced along with the music that still played in his ears, flipping between thinking about the breasts of a woman who lived across the hall from him and wondering if could get the skinny girl (who was called Cheryl, according to his thoughts) to buy him a beer from the shop.

"There's a boxing club meets on a Thursday," said the other skinny guy, pulling out his phone — the latest model which Michael would have bought if only he had the money — and putting his music on pause. He was a white sixteen-year-old called Eric, known to the others as E-boy. He had spikey ginger hair and freckles that speckled his nose. Michael perceived his mind flash to a memory of standing at the sidelines of a boxing class while, at the same time, clutching the inhaler in his pocket and hoping he wouldn't have an asthma attack in front of the others.

"Boxing? You?" Chad laughed. "You couldn't knock down a feather."

"I was just saying," said E-boy, "there are a few clubs he could join."

"Yeah, like the Wednesday knitting club," Chad sniggered, as if it were the cleverest joke in the world.

The others joined in with mocking laughter, especially the average-sized kid, a fifteen-year-old called Dave. Michael took a moment to focus on him and immediately sensed that he was more intelligent than the others, laughing the loudest because of a desperate need to be accepted by them. His thoughts revealed that he believed standing out in the cold was better than being at home with his bonkers mother and skank of a sister, even though part of him wanted to be at home studying for the physics test he had in the morning. Not that he would tell the others because he was clever enough to know that they had no time for a school swat.

Cheryl hid her smile behind the collar of her jacket which she had pulled up to protect her neck against the wind. "This is *boring*," she announced. "Let's go to the chippy." She turned on the heel of her very high heeled boots — also new and expensive-looking — and walked off in the other direction.

The others turned and followed her. Not because she was their leader, but because they had nothing better to do.

Michael stood and watched, realising they were not ready to accept him, and continued to perceive them until they were too far away. Their thoughts were full of little else other than fish and chips, and it made him hungry.

It was all very disappointingly normal. Perhaps the officers who had interviewed the gang were right: the other teenagers had nothing to do with Tyler and Bailecki's terrorist activities. Tyler and Bailecki might have acted alone and being part of the gang was just a coincidence. Perhaps the whole operation to infiltrate them would lead to nothing more than uncovering a dodgy source for expensive trainers and state-of-the-art phones. As he walked back to the flat, he realised he would have to write all this up in his report. He wondered how the hell he was going to make it look good.

NINE

MICHAEL received a subtle waft of lemon as he opened the fridge to take out two cans of Coke. It was a better smell than the one which had greeted him when he first looked inside, which could only be described as putrid. Michael had attacked the smell with one of the cleaning products Patterson had bought from the supermarket, and now the fridge epitomised the meaning of clean.

He closed the fridge door to the accompaniment of a massive, "Yeeees!" from the sofa where Alex was sitting playing a game he had rigged up by connecting his mobile phone to the television. The second hand beat-up TV set had arrived soon after they moved in because Patterson was one of those typical oldies who couldn't seem to live without one. Patterson was a bit miffed, therefore, that almost as soon as it had arrived, it had been commandeered by one of Michael's friends, relegating Patterson to the kitchen.

"I hope you're not going to turn this place into a party flat," said the policeman, looking up from the work he had spread all over the kitchen counter. He was sitting on a kitchen stool and supposedly working on his laptop computer, despite the bits of paper laying scattered next to it. Because oldies, it seemed, couldn't seem to live without paper either.

"He's only here for a few hours," said Michael. "I've got to go out tonight to see if I can catch up with the gang again."

"Well, good," said Patterson. "I don't want this place full of teen-agers with loud music and drugs and girls."

"Yes, *Dad*," said Michael, as he breezed past him with two Coke cans in his hands.

Patterson frowned. "Don't call me that."

Michael chuckled and returned to the sofa with the drinks while Patterson returned to concentrating on his work.

Alex had somehow managed to take up almost the entirety of the three-person sofa by sprawling across it. So Michael stood there until Alex realised and shuffled up a bit to make room. He plonked himself down, handed over a Coke and Alex paused the game. On the screen, the animated figure of a soldier in full army fatigues stopped progressing down a dark alley with his M16A3 rifle.

"You should ask the new girl to come over," said Alex with a sug-gestive smile.

"Pauline?" said Michael. "I don't think so."

"Come on, she's into you!"

"I really don't think so," reiterated Michael. "She needed someone to be friendly when she first got there and it happened to me. I have a feeling she doesn't want to be friendly anymore."

"That, Mike, is why you have such a bad track record with girls." Alex lifted the ring pull of his Coke and it let out a brief fizz. "Anyway, how's this case thing going that you're working on?"

"Oh good," said Michael, allowing Alex to pick up on his lie.

Alex gave him a quizzical glance. Perceivers usually avoid lying to each other because they know the other person is be able to tell.

Michael acknowledged the glance, giving the cue for Alex to open his perception further.

I think I've done the wrong thing, Michael thought in his head, knowing that Alex could read those thoughts. *I think the gang is just an ordinary group of teenagers, not a terrorist cell. When they find out all this has been for nothing, all those people that said putting perceivers in the police force wouldn't work will be proved right.*

They won't do that, said Alex's thoughts. *They need us.*

Their secret conversation was interrupted by the sound of Patterson's shoes hitting the hard kitchen floor as he hopped off the stool. He noisily gathered up all his papers and shuffled them into a pile. "Right!" he said. "I'm off for my night shift."

"I'll see you tomorrow, then," said Michael from the sofa.

"Yes." Patterson closed his laptop and thrust everything into a black holdall which looked nothing like it was designed to contain office paperwork, which was sort of the point. "Don't spend too long playing on my television and forget what you're supposed to be doing tonight."

"Yes, *Dad*," said Michael.

"And don't call me that!"

Michael laughed. They said goodbye to each other and Patterson left the flat.

"Seriously," said Alex after the door had closed. "They need us. This early stuff we're doing like you messing around in the police and me in the court, it's just gearing up for putting perceivers everywhere."

"The public won't accept it," said Michael.

"Maybe not yet," said Alex. "But eventually they will have to. I mean, at the moment, I know what I'm doing in court isn't making any difference. I can stand there and perceive the witnesses as they give evidence and I can report back whether they're lying to my handler and she can inform the barristers, but at the end of the day it's not making any difference. If the jury decide to convict an innocent man or free a guilty one, I have no control over it."

"Then what's the point?"

"The point is," said Alex. "It won't always be like that. Soon, I'll be reporting directly to the barristers myself. Then I might be called as an expert witness who can see into the mind of the accused, just like they call a psychiatrist sometimes. Eventually, they'll do away with the jury and the barristers altogether, they'll just appoint a perceiver to say whether someone is guilty or innocent."

"The public doesn't trust us enough," said Michael.

"At one time, they didn't trust CCTV cameras. But the need for the authorities to spy on people was greater than the public's need for privacy and now they're everywhere. Just like we will be eventually. They want us to spy on people, Mike, and they're going to find a way to make it happen no matter what everyone else thinks."

A buzzing sound emerged from the kitchen. At first, Michael thought it was the sound of one of the humane mousetraps Patterson had bought, indicating it had caught a rodent, but the buzzing was swiftly followed by a blast of rock music.

"What's that?" said Alex.

"Patterson's phone," said Michael, recognising the tune. He got off the sofa and went over to the kitchen where he found it vibrating on the side near where Patterson had been working. For a moment he thought about chasing after him, but decided it wasn't worth it and answered it. "Hello?"

"Ah, Sergeant Patterson, good," said the person on the other end of the phone, a woman whose voice Michael sort of recognised but couldn't immediately place.

"It's—" Michael started to say, but the person on the other end sounded like she was in a hurry and just kept talking.

"This man keeps on ringing, and I keep telling him you'll be back in tomorrow, but he won't have any of it. His name's Victor Roo … um … Victor Rublev, he says he has that list for you. I said he could email it in, but he's not having any of that either. He says he wants to give it to you in person."

"Well—" Michael began.

"I tried to say you were busy and I could send a police constable," the woman motored on, "but guess what? He was having none of that either. So, anyway, I just gave in and took all the details and decided to let you deal with it. Have you got a pen?"

Giving in, Michael decided, was clearly the best strategy when it came to the woman whose voice he now recognised as Detective Constable Tania Baker. "Yes," he said, pulling out his phone and opening the note app.

"His name is Victor Rublev and he's at University College Hospital in Euston Road. He said could you come tomorrow because he hasn't got long, whatever that means. I told him you were a very busy man, but—"

"He wasn't having any of it," Michael finished for her.

"Exactly. So I've passed on the message and now I can finally go home. See you in the office tomorrow. Bye."

"Bye," said Michael, but she had hung up before he even finished the word.

Alex was watching him from the sofa. "What was all that about?" he said.

"Another case Patterson was working on."

"Important?"

"Not sure," said Michael.

"So, are we going to have another game or what?" said Alex.

Michael looked at his phone, it was approaching eight o'clock. "For another half an hour or so, then I really need to go out, and you need to get back to camp before you get in trouble with Norm the Norm."

"Who cares about him?" said Alex.

"Just remember you said that when he puts you on toilet cleaning duty."

"It'll be worth it." Alex grinned. Michael came back over, hooked up his mobile phone to the game and started to play.

THE gang hung around the play area like it was their domain, and not somewhere for little children. It was the same five teenagers that Michael had met outside the shop. Laura had squeezed her large bottom onto one of a pair of swings and was kicking up the dirt underneath with her new Nike trainers as she slowly pushed herself backwards and forwards. Chad and E-boy were leaning against the climbing frame as if it were a lamppost, both concentrating on the displays of their identical swish phones. Dave was atop the slide, enjoying being higher up than everyone else for once. And Cheryl stood at the gate, her pointy elbow resting on the top of the railing as she played with her long, lime green painted fingernails.

"Hello again," said Michael as he descended from the block of flats and out into the open, as if it was a pure coincidence that he was there.

The ones at the climbing frame did not so much as look up from their phones. Dave followed their example and pretended not to notice. Laura looked up from her shoes. *It's that weasel again*, she thought.

Cheryl glared at him. "Whaddoyou want?" she said.

"I did what you suggested," said Michael. "I looked at some of the clubs down at the Community Centre, but I don't think boxing and knitting are for me."

"Are you for real?" said Cheryl. She was annoyed that he'd interrupted her contemplating her nails. Michael perceived that she'd just paid to have the manicure done and wasn't sure if lime green was her colour. "Hey, Chaddyboy!" she called over. "This one thinks he's a right comedian!"

Chad and E-boy dragged their attention away from their phones and, almost in unison, pulled at the cords of the earphones so they plopped out and hung down by their knees. They sauntered over towards Cheryl with a swagger that was supposed to make them look tough to those who weren't perceivers. Michael, of course, could sense that it was all for show. Dave pushed himself down the slide, but because his bum was bigger than a five-year-old's, he had to push himself almost all the way down to the bottom. Laura watched from her swing.

"It's just," said Michael, as he perceived the group of teenagers so he could judge the best way to ingratiate himself without being too obvious. "Where I used to live there were a bunch of us used to hang out. Otis and Jennifer and Jack, and it was such a laugh. We did *crazy* stuff all the time. I just wondered if, maybe, I could hang around with you."

Chad laughed. Big, deep guffaws like someone with twice his lung capacity. The others joined in, except for Cheryl, who maintained the pout of a skinny fashion model. It was all fake. Like the swagger, they did it for show. "You wanna hang around with the cool kids, is that it?" said Chad.

"Something like that," said Michael.

He perceived them all and they were all wary of him. They saw him as too much of an outsider, too keen, too polite. But, still, they didn't outright reject him and that in itself seemed odd.

"What about it, Chad?" said Dave. "James said we need more people."

The name sent a quiver of discomfort around them. It was a name, Michael perceived, Dave should not have used.

"You said we were going to find more girls," protested Laura, kicking up the dirt from under her swing.

E-boy turned to her. "We need to replace Stephen and Jazz after they—" *died*, said his thoughts "—left. *They* weren't girls."

"There's always been too many boys in this gang," Laura moaned.

Chad took a few more steps to join Cheryl where she stood at the gate. He bent forward and leant both his forearms on top of the railings so he could look up at Michael. He maintained his air of superiority while, inside his mind, there was an anticipation of cruel excitement. "Do you think you're worthy?" he said.

Michael paused. He didn't want to sound too eager, but on the other hand he didn't want to be rejected. "I suppose so."

"Then prove it," said Chad.
 The excitement mounted within the others.
"How?" said Michael.
 Chad grinned.

TEN

PATTERSON had brought the television into the flat and the television had brought the news. Michael had turned it on because there was sod all else to do inside on his own during the day. The news had pictures of his father dressed in a suit, walking towards the Old Bailey flanked by people Michael didn't know, who he assumed to be his legal team. Running around him were photographers and a camera crew. Ransom didn't acknowledge their presence, nor did he try to dodge them as he entered the stone edifice of the legal building.

"Today the court heard from a witness who claims her daughter was 'poisoned' by the pills Brian Ransom gave to pregnant mothers through his company, Ransom Incorporated," said the voice of a male correspondent as pictures of outside the court continued to play on the screen. "Marianne Croucher told the court: 'I thought I was taking a vitamin pill, something that would make sure my baby was born healthy, but it turned out I was taking a poison that would scar my daughter for life.' Mrs Croucher went on to say that her daughter showed the first signs of being a perceiver at the age of twelve and was cured at the age of thirteen. But, visibly emotional, she told the court that by that time, the damage had already been done and her daughter has not been the same since."

The television report cut to the image of the reporter, a greying man in sober brown suit and tie, standing on the road outside the Old Bailey. "Mr Ransom sat listening passively in the dock throughout this morning's testimony. He denies twenty counts of Administering a Noxious Substance with Intent to Cause Bodily Harm and the trial—"

Michael switched it off. He couldn't bear to hear any more.

He thought of Alex, who had been assigned to work in the court system, and took his phone out of his pocket. He checked the display, but he had no messages from anyone.

He sent Alex a text: 'How ya doin'?'

The text went through, but no reply came back. The display dimmed with inactivity and eventually went to black.

Michael awakened it again and saw the notes he had jotted down the night before. It reminded him, he was going to tell Patterson that he had left his phone in the flat. He called the office.

"I'm sorry, Sergeant Patterson isn't here at the moment," said a male voice he recognised as the chubby detective he could never remember the name of. "I could take a message, or you could try him on his mobile."

"No," said Michael. "Can you tell him he left his mobile in the flat."

"Ah," said the detective. "What flat?"

"He'll know what I mean."

"Okay."

Michael thanked him and finished the call.

He read the note on his phone again. He hadn't written much down apart from Rublev's name and the name of the hospital, but he remembered Detective Baker's words. She had said Rublev hadn't got long which, seeing how ill the Russian looked at their last meeting, probably meant not long to live. He also remembered the promise Patterson had made to him. If Patterson wasn't around, Michael decided, then he would have to honour that promise.

He turned off the TV and consulted his phone for the best way to get to Euston Road.

MICHAEL breathed in the smell of cleaning fluid, its perfume so artificial it added a cloying taste to the air. His body absorbed its germ-killing properties with each mouthful, but he wondered if the clinical air also contained tasteless radioactive particles that would burrow into his lungs and wreak damage inside of him. There were no radiation warning signs or people wearing hazard suits around Victor Rublev's hospital bed, but Michael suspected there was a reason he was being kept in his own private room, and it wasn't only because he had the money to pay for it.

Rublev lay shrivelled in his bed, a shell of a man who seemed to have shrunk inside his own skin. Despite the tubes that fed liquid and drugs into a vein in his arm, his body looked desiccated, with translucent loose skin that gathered in wrinkles around his sunken eyes, on his withered neck and over the atrophied muscles of his arms. Light from the bright but cloudy day filtered into his window by the bed, reflecting off the pristine painted white walls and highlighting the array of medical equipment that sat in homage around his bed. It did nothing to lift the darkness where Rublev lay in a hospital gown, draped around his fading body like a shroud.

Michael perceived Rublev's ghostly presence drifting from one half-thought to another, but Rublev did not sense Michael until he reached the side of his bed.

The man's thoughts coalesced into recognising the world around him. "Sergeant Patterson's friend," he croaked in a whisper just loud enough to be heard over the air conditioning.

"Sorry we couldn't come sooner," said Michael. "Sergeant Patterson is investigating the terrorist bombing at the Capital Hotel."

"I heard," said Rublev, struggling with each syllable. "Why do young people want to throw their lives away when there are so many others desperate to hang onto life?"

Rublev gasped for air, his throat rasping as it forced life-giving oxygen into his lungs. Rublev knew, in his mind, that talking strained his body and he accepted the coughing fit that followed, shaking the bed as the spasming momentarily blocked his ability to breathe.

Michael perceived the pain in the man's chest, and his desperation as he fought against it. "I'll get a nurse," said Michael.

"No!" Rublev gasped. He grabbed at Michael's hand where it rested on the side of the bed and gripped it tight. As tight as if he were a fit and healthy man.

"They can do … nothing …" he gasped.

Michael did not pull away and Rublev lessened his grip. It took several long minutes, but his breathing returned to a staccato kind of normal. Through it all, his mind was lurching between lucid understanding of where he was and dream-like memories of his past. Michael saw bits of London that he recognised — from the distinctive sign for Tottenham Court Road tube station, to the tower that held Big Ben. There were images of unfamiliar places in which Rublev remembered himself as a younger man of tall, slim build. They might have been glimpses of his home in Russia, but Michael associated Russia with cold and snow, and these images were all sunny. One face kept returning in those memories: a young woman smiling, in a white summer dress decorated with yellow flowers that swished as she walked.

"In the top drawer," said Rublev with one large and difficult breath.

Michael used his free hand to open the drawer of the bedside cabinet which was empty other than for a few scattered medical leaflets and a sealed envelope with 'Sergeant Patterson' written on it in calligraphic script. He pulled out the envelope and showed it to

Rublev. The man squinted. Michael held the envelope closer until the Russian was satisfied at what he saw and relaxed back into the pillow.

"All. In. There," he managed.

"I'll give it to Sergeant Patterson," said Michael. "He may have some follow-up questions, if that's okay."

"No questions," gasped Rublev. "All. In. There."

Michael put the envelope in his pocket and felt the man's hand weaken its hold around his own. "Stay … with … me …" he whispered.

Rublev panted a hard-fought breath. *I'm going*, said his thoughts, and then the words turned to Russian, tumbling through his mind in sentences that Michael did not understand. *Skazhi Andrei Orlov … pozhalsta … skazhi Andrei Orlov chto on bil prav.*

Rublev panted another breath. Memories spiralled in images of distorted faces and places washed in red or brown or blue colours. An older man with grey swept-back hair and layers of clothing — shirt, tie, cardigan, jacket, overcoat — smiled at him then faded away. The face of the woman in the summer dress appeared in one moment of clarity before she was eclipsed by the grotesque grins of men in suits and the twisted facade of a grey concrete building.

Rublev willed another laboured breath into his body and pain shot through his chest.

Fear gripped him. He was drowning in a room of plentiful air, reaching out for oxygen. Michael perceived Rublev gasping for life, but his body was not responding, not breathing.

Darkness grew inside Rublev's mind. He felt each painful beat of his heart like a hammer blow to his chest, but still not strong enough to force his blood to pump very far. The bleak reality of nothingness encroached as he struggled to cling on to each hard-fought moment. Tumbling Russian words became meaningless syllables as memories were extinguished. It hurt so much that he detached himself from his body. Memories became blobs of flashing red, brown and blue lights that winked into the darkness and turned into dim and infrequent blurs as they drifted away. Night drew in, with no moon or stars, a blanket of black. It encased him in its cocoon of nothingness, sucking the last spark of light until his mind became a vacuum and his body stopped.

Michael's mind was alone. He realised he was holding the hand of a dead man.

He pulled his hand clear, stumbled backwards and banged into a piece of medical equipment.

"Help," he meant to shout, but his voice barely obeyed him.

He ran into the corridor. "Help! Help!" Medical staff bundled past him. "He's dead, he's dead!" he shouted at them.

But they did not listen. They called for equipment and they called for drugs and they pumped at the poor man's body, but Michael perceived that the life that was in it had already gone. It was gone forever.

ELEVEN

THEY passed through the alleyway to the front of the block of flats, Michael and the gang: Chad, E-boy, Laura, Cheryl and Dave. It was properly dark now — perfect for clandestine law breaking — with most people safely inside their homes for the evening. The only movement was the two boys on their skateboard, whooping and giggling as they took it in turns to speed down the road, weaving in and out of the white lines like a slalom.

'Do something illegal, but don't get caught' was the gang initiation mantra. 'If you get caught, you're on your own.'

Flashes of memory from the others revealed they had all done it. Mostly petty theft from shops and some criminal damage, but it was Chad's initiation that was legendary. He had swiped the hat right off the head of a policeman and ran off so fast that only an Olympic sprinter could have caught him. When he finally met up with the rest of the gang at Kennington Park, they had all tried on the hat and took pictures of themselves — to much hilarity — before finally leaving it atop the war memorial. Every now and then they would laugh at the memory and Chad would fail to mention how the policeman had recognised him and called at his flat the following day, causing him to have a massive row with his mum.

"What are you going to do?" Chad asked Michael.

Michael was thinking. An idea was percolating. A smile was forming. "You'll see."

He walked down the road, trying to be cool and natural, adding a little swagger to his step like he had seen Chad do. The others followed at a discreet distance. He checked for traffic and crossed the road, heading for the kerb opposite.

At the last moment, he turned and stepped towards one of the boys who had just got on his skateboard. With a quick push, the boy was unbalanced and landed on his bum. "Hey!"

Michael didn't care. He put one foot on the skateboard, pushed off with the other, and was suddenly flying down the road. The wind blew his hair back from his face as he sped away from the boys until their protesting cries faded away behind him. With the toe of one foot, he revved against the tarmac to increase his speed, maintaining his balance like a professional, remembering the time at the camp when he'd practised on Peter's skateboard before Norm the Norm had confiscated it.

He swerved closer to the parked cars, reached out his fist and slammed it against a wing mirror, bending it backwards. It hurt, but the adrenaline dulled the pain as he wobbled further down the road, regaining his balance and reaching out his fist again for a second hit.

So absorbed was he by the thrill, so free were his perceptions of any minds around him, that he didn't hear the roar of a car engine as it came up the road in the other direction. By the time he saw it, it was metres away, with the black bonnet with its Peugeot insignia eyeing him like a charging bull.

Michael swerved, but the skateboard did not turn easily. He heard rubber skidding on tarmac as the car braked and veered off in the other direction.

He felt the breeze of the car's headlight brush past his leg with next to no room to spare. In that moment of relief as he missed being struck — and the driver shouted abuse from his window — Michael realised he was heading for one of the parked cars.

His legs struck the grill of one of them, catapulting him over the bonnet as the skateboard continued with momentum down the road without its passenger.

Michael's body thumped onto the metal and slid, uncontrollably, into the windscreen.

The thrill evaporated and was replaced by pain that encompassed his whole body. Adrenaline was still firing, but it was not enough to dull the million aches in his arms, legs, chest and head.

He was lying, he realised, curled in a foetal position on the car bonnet, facing a shattered windscreen. Something warm and wet ran down his nose and dripped on the green painted surface of the car: his blood.

Michael's perceptions became full of other people. It was the gang. A mix of concern and glee and amusement, circling around him as they got close.

Out of the corner of his eye, he saw the boy retrieve his skateboard from the gutter and run back up the road to where he had left his brother.

Michael heard himself groan.

"We need to go." It was Chad's voice. "Can you get up?"

Michael turned his neck to look at Chad. It made his head spin, but at least he was able to do it without breaking his spine. "I think so."

Michael did not so much stand up from the car as shift his body, sliding down the bonnet until he was caught by the hands of several teenagers who allowed his feet to gently find the road surface. He leant on a shoulder, which turned out to belong to Dave, and tested his legs to see if they would bear his weight. He groaned again. Several times.

"Am I part of the gang now?" asked Michael.

"We need to vote on that," said Chad.

But as he was hurried away in pain, Michael's perceptions told him that they all would be voting in his favour.

HOT tweezers stabbed at the skin under Michael's cheekbone as they were wielded by the unsteady hand of Sergeant Patterson. Michael winced and felt moisture gather in his eyes. He blinked away the pain, gripping the edge of the kitchen work surface so he didn't fall off the stool, as Patterson locked onto the pebble of windscreen glass and pulled it from his flesh.

A fevered wave of relief ran through him as he heard the tweezers and their target plop into the bowl of boiling water and disinfectant on the kitchen work surface. A ribbon of his blood snaked up from where the glass had dropped to the bottom. Patterson dipped a ball of cotton wool into the bowl and pressed it against where the glass had been. Michael flinched instinctively at the sting, then held himself still as the heat from the liquid cleansed his wound.

"Not only am I pretending to be your dad," said Patterson, "I'm now pretending to be your mum as well." He dropped the bloody ball of cotton wool into the bin which he'd pulled up beside him and reached for another from the packet he'd bought from the shop. He dipped it in the bowl and dabbed it against several other cuts Michael had sustained to his face.

"Thank you," said Michael. Having to speak stopped him from wincing again.

Patterson might not have found Michael that morning, sprawled out on the sofa with a bloody piece of toilet paper stuck to his cheek, if he hadn't popped by to pick up his mobile phone. Patterson tried to pretend he was angry, but his emotions revealed he was actually shocked by the state Michael was in.

"What on earth were you thinking?" said Patterson.

"I wanted to impress the gang," said Michael.

"You made an impression all right — on the windscreen of a dark green Renault Clio."

"That bit wasn't planned," said Michael.

"Uh-huh," said Patterson. He dropped the second bloodied cotton wool ball into the bin. "I think you're done, but I still think you should get a doctor to check out some of those bruises. You could have broken something."

Michael hopped off the stool and immediately regretted not doing it more gracefully, as the judder aggravated all his bruises at once. It hurt, but not bad enough to suggest he'd broken any bones.

"How did you know what car it was?" said Michael.

"I had a look at the police log," said Patterson, picking up the bowl and taking it to the sink where he poured away the bloody disinfectant.

"Will I be arrested?"

"I can make sure that doesn't happen. Not that I condone breaking the law." *Oh God, now I'm beginning to* sound *like his father.* "So the gang are prepared to accept you now that you've nearly killed yourself, are they?"

"Yes," said Michael, moving slowly — hunched over like an old man — across to the sofa. "They've arranged a meet up tonight. They pretended like it's nothing special, but I perceived they want me to meet their leader."

"The leader?" said Patterson. "Doesn't he hang around with the others?"

"I don't think so. I tried to perceive more, but it's difficult when you've bashed your head on a car windscreen."

"Serves you right."

Michael sat on the sofa and felt the soft cushion of its seat embrace his bottom. It was more comfortable than the kitchen stool. It also allowed him to rest there, and resting stopped him aching.

As he shifted position, he heard a crinkle in his pocket. It was Victor's letter. He had forgotten.

He pulled it out. The envelope was scrunched up a little, but still stuck down. "I went to see Victor Rublev yesterday," he called over to Patterson who was clearing up in the kitchen.

"Who?" he said.

"Do you remember the Russian we went to see? The one who said he was poisoned."

"Bollocks!" said Patterson. "I forgot all about him. Being nearly blown up can do that to you."

"He wanted me to give you this."

Michael held out the envelope. Patterson came over from the kitchen and took it. Puzzled, he slid his finger under the flap and tore an opening at the top. He pulled out a folded piece of paper, hand-written on both sides in the same script which had adorned the envelope. He scanned it, trying to figure out what he was reading.

"It's the list of everywhere he went and everyone he saw during that week he thinks he was poisoned," Michael explained.

Patterson raised his eyebrows. "That's a long list. Perhaps he can narrow it down a bit in identifying potential suspects."

"He can't," said Michael. "He's dead."

"Oh," said Patterson. He paused. "I'll get someone to look over the list."

"Can't you look over it?"

"I'm up to my eyes in other cases," said Patterson. "Not to mention playing nursemaid to over-enthusiastic undercover operatives."

"I was in his head when he died," said Michael, turning cold at the memory. "I think his body only kept him alive that long so he could pass on that envelope. I don't think it would be right to give it to someone else."

Patterson sighed and looked at the list again. The very long list. "We don't even know for sure he was poisoned."

"He died in hospital, the doctors there must know," said Michael. "Why don't we ask them?"

THE hospital was full of death. As soon as Michael walked in, he felt the perceptions of desperate relatives afraid that it would be the last time they would see their loved ones, of people lying in beds wondering if they would ever see their home again, of staff who lived with death every day, but still became sad every time they lost a patient. The perceptions triggered the memory of being inside Rublev's mind and the terror as death ate away at the last moments of his life. It was a glimpse into hell and it scared him because, even at seventeen, he knew that he would one day be in that situation with nothing to save him. So he blocked his perception, closing down every stray thought and feeling from outside himself to be alone inside his own mind where he could suppress the memory of Rublev.

Patterson leant back against the nurses' station with his arms folded. He was impatient and somewhat irritated that he'd been per-suaded to make the trip to the hospital — Michael didn't need to be a perceiver to know this because Patterson moaned about it on the drive over. At least, when he wasn't moaning about the appalling state of London traffic.

Michael waited next to him, breathing through his mouth so as not to take in the hospital smell, as the nurses fluttered around them like they were part of the furniture. They did not make eye contact or acknowledge them in any way, apparently too busy to care.

A woman in a doctor's white coat, glasses and short-cropped hair approached them with the grimace of someone who had been rudely dragged away from whatever else she was doing. "The famous Sergeant Patterson, I presume?" she said.

"Famous?" said Patterson, pushing his bum away from the nurses' station so he stood up straight. He held out his hand for her to shake.

She obliged with subdued enthusiasm. "Mr Rublev talked about you. He said you were the British policeman who was going to solve his murder."

"It *was* murder, then?" said Patterson.

"Unless he accidentally came across a banned toxic substance and decided to drink it," said the doctor, dryly. "That would be my guess."

"Sorry, I didn't catch your name …?" said Patterson.

"Mrs Reynolds, consultant oncologist," she said. "Original tests showed the cells in Mr Rublev's bone marrow had died and cancer was suspected, but it was clear it was no cancer that I had ever seen before. His body was eaten from the inside by something more powerful."

Michael chipped in. "He said it was radiation poisoning, is that true?"

Mrs Reynolds noticed him for the first time.

"This is my associate," said Patterson. "Michael Sanderson."

"What happened to you?" she said, looking him up and down.

Michael realised the cuts on his face from landing on the car were still visible. He hurriedly tried to think of an excuse. "Car accident," he said.

She nodded. "Yes, radiation, that's what we believe. I'd never seen anything like it before, but one of our nurses worked on a similar case in Germany and he suggested we get in a Geiger counter. It was pretty alarming, I can tell you. We took the advised precautions, but a number of staff refused to go anywhere near him, and I don't blame them."

It was Patterson's turn to nod. "We'll need access to his medical records and, obviously, there will have to be a post mortem."

Mrs Reynolds looked puzzled. "The body has already been taken away by the coroner. My staff informed the correct authorities, Sergeant. Don't you people talk to each other?"

Patterson managed an embarrassed smile. "We've had a lot on," he said.

She frowned. "I will get my secretary to send you any files that you need. It's just a shame, Sergeant Patterson, you weren't able to visit Mr Rublev at the hospital while he was still alive."

Having had the last word, she turned on her heel and walked off, leaving Patterson looking somewhat bemused as nurses, busy on other tasks, continued to flutter round them.

TWELVE

MICHAEL took a series of buses back to the flat from the hospital, while Patterson headed for the office to catch up on the Rublev investigation. Michael had perceived guilt in Patterson's mind that he hadn't taken Rublev seriously on their initial meeting and, even though he had a legitimate reason for being distracted by other things, he felt he'd failed to do his duty.

Patterson had suggested calling Hodges to drive Michael back to Kennington, but turning up at the estate in a chauffeur driven car would not have created the correct impression. Besides, while Michael was on assignment, Hodges was probably allocated another job. So he rode London Transport, like he had done the day Rublev died, meaning it was late by the time he got back. He made himself some something to eat from the bits and pieces Patterson had left in the fridge, and waited until it got dark.

MICHAEL went to the play area, but the gang wasn't there. He went to the shop, but they weren't there either.

With nowhere else to look, he decided to stand and wait for a bit, leaning against the lamppost like he had seen Chad and E-boy doing the other night. After five minutes, he thought a figure in a hoodie emerging by the empty shops at the other end of the pedestrianized walkway could be one of them. But he was mistaken, it was a different teenage girl.

After what had to be about half an hour feeling the cold steel of the lamppost at his back and half-heartedly playing a game on his phone, he decided the gang wasn't coming and he needed to look elsewhere. He thought, as he dawdled past the boarded-up shops, that none of the gang had said what place, time or day they would meet him again. They had just said that they would. If they weren't at one of their usual hangouts, then perhaps there was some event on television they had all stayed in for, like a big football match. Michael wasn't into football. He sort of liked it, but he had no memory of growing up supporting a team or playing with friends in the park or at school, so he didn't keep track. He checked the TV schedules on his phone as he walked back towards the block of flats.

The road where the two young boys had once ridden their skateboard felt eerily quiet. Only one car passed him the whole time, with the rumble of its tyres sounding an empty echo as the noise bounced off the buildings, and faded to nothing. He turned into the communal garden where dim outlines of the play equipment were visible in the light coming from the windows of the surrounding occupied flats. It was still devoid of teenagers, as if the Pied Piper of Hamlyn had taken them all away.

He turned towards the back entrance and almost bumped straight into a figure standing in the dark.

It was Dave. Almost indistinguishable in the alley, hands buried in the pockets of his moss-green parka, he stood resting against the wall with his face shaded by the hood of his coat pulled up over his head.

Michael hadn't perceived anybody there. He didn't have his blocks erected, only his everyday filters, so he should have picked up on Dave's presence. It scared him that he hadn't.

He made the effort to perceive him now. A ghost of a mind whispered inside of Dave's head. The intelligence that Michael had perceived when they first met was replaced with the dull machinations of a consciousness that was barely thinking. His eyes stared at Michael from out of the hood of his coat while his thoughts only said, *collect him.*

"Dave," said Michael, aware as he spoke that the breathiness of his voice gave away his anxiety. "I didn't see you there."

"Come with me," said Dave. He turned and walked in the other direction.

"Where are we going?" said Michael, following.

"To where you can become one of us," said Dave.

The name *James* formed in Dave's mind.

"I thought I became one of you last night," said Michael, keeping the conversation going in the hope that Dave's mind would reveal more.

"That was just the initiation," said Dave.

He would not say any more, even though Michael asked him a couple more questions. In the end, he gave up talking and concentrated on perceiving.

Dave's mind reminded him of the emptiness he had perceived in Jerome Tyler and Stephen Bailecki. The only thing Dave thought about was where he was going, with a list of directions playing over and over in his head. *To the main road, take a left. Walk past two streets then turn into Ebbern's Road. At the industrial estate, enter the second block of buildings on the left and go to the second unit with the blue door.*

It was like one of those children's songs that build up line-by-line, but backwards. As Dave carried out each instruction, that part of his mantra fell off the list. Eventually, only one instruction was left:

Go to the second unit with the blue door ... Go to the second unit with the blue door ... Go to the second unit with the blue door.

At last, they were there, and the mantra stopped.

The blue door was made of painted wood and not dissimilar to the front door of the flat he was living in. It was set into the side of an industrial unit, a utilitarian brick building with a metal shuttered front and a sign, *A.F.G. Limited* — painted in red letters above the shutter — which had got smudged and gone streaky where rain had got in.

Dave knocked on the door.

After a moment, it was opened by Cheryl. She stepped back and let them inside.

If Michael had been paying more attention to his perception, he might have noticed that her mind, too, was devoid of much thought. But he only perceived her presence as he walked into a square hallway lit by a dusty bulb hanging from the ceiling. The purpose of the hallway seemed only to act as a conduit to a steep set of stairs. Like the bulb, it was undressed, with no carpet or covering on the wood.

Cheryl took them up to the first floor landing which was laid with a worn sticky carpet that must have had something spilt on it in the past because Michael's shoes ripped themselves free with each step, as if it had been laced with a trail of syrup. The trail ended at a door which Cheryl opened without knocking.

It had the chill and mustiness of a room which hadn't been heated for a long time. It must once have been an office because two desks were shoved up one end of the room, one of them still with a landline telephone on it. The phone, like everything in the building, looked like it hadn't been touched for a long time: it was covered in dust and had a cable that ended in a tattered pair of brown and blue wires where it had been pulled out of the wall. There were two chairs, one a coffee-stained office chair with grubby purple upholstery, and the second a sturdy varnished wooden chair with arms which looked like it had been stolen from behind a teacher's desk.

The final three members of the gang were there: Chad, E-boy and Laura, each standing round the edge, having claimed a wall each to lean on. They were not talking, they were not looking at their mobile phones, they were merely leaning, their thoughts only revealing that they understood Michael had arrived. Like Dave, their personalities were dulled. It was like perceiving them through tracing paper: he could see the outline of them, but he couldn't perceive the detail.

"Dave, you found him," said Chad.

"It was easy," said Dave, closing the door behind him.

Michael turned to look as he heard the click of the latch. It sounded ominous. Perhaps it was the creepiness of being shut in a room with five people who felt like half-people.

"What's going on?" said Michael. He looked at all of them in turn, perceiving the answer in their heads.

You're here to meet James… You're here to meet James… You're here to meet James…

Chad took the wooden chair from where it was tucked under one of the desks and pulled it to the centre of the room, turning it to face the far wall. "Sit down," he said.

"Why?" said Michael.

"You must sit down," said Chad. *Sitting down is next*, said his thoughts.

Michael nervously sat in the chair and stared at the grubby white wall ahead of him. He perceived the others carefully and continued to feel no threat from them. But he also perceived that they had no notion of what was going on any more than he had.

Michael thought back to the basic undercover training the Metropolitan Police had given him. There were two golden rules: not to draw attention to himself and always have an escape route. He realised he had just broken both of them. He gripped the arms of the chair nervously and sat up straight against its high back, waiting for the gang's next move.

He was suddenly aware of the smell of coffee. Not stale like the spillage on the office chair, but freshly made. The door clicked again. Someone new had entered. Michael's perception immediately honed in and he sensed a mind younger than the others: male and curious. He sensed him for only a moment before the mind clammed shut and Michael's perception was kicked out. Michael tried to get back in, but he was blocked.

The mind belonged to a perceiver.

Michael rushed to put up his own barriers as the young male walked round to the other side of the chair and faced him.

He was a boy, with curious hazel eyes that stared out of a face that was still soft without the hint of stubble. He was barely a teenager, maybe thirteen years old, and yet he stood with the assuredness of an adult, dressed in a smart, clean, ironed light blue shirt and black trousers, holding a steaming mug of coffee in his hand.

"You're a perceiver," said the boy, who had to be James.

"Yes," said Michael. He couldn't deny it, it would have been obvious as soon as James's perception touched his mind.

Michael reached out to the others. Their minds were still open to him, but they were blank and told him nothing. They merely watched and waited.

"Don't worry about them," said James.

Michael felt a chill as he realised James was aware of what he was doing. Even though the boy was immature, his ability was advanced. Michael did as he was told and withdrew his perception, deciding he needed to concentrate only on the boy.

"Unusual to find a perceiver of your age who hasn't been cured," said James.

"Is it?" said Michael. He felt the boy's perception trying to worm its way into his head and maintained his blocks.

"They don't like people like us wandering around. I hear some people try to resist, but once they know what you are, they keep hounding you until their paperwork says you've been turned into a norm."

"I hid my ability," said Michael. "In the early days of the cure programme, they weren't as organised as they are now."

"Liar!" screamed James, throwing his mug of coffee aside, sending an arc of brown liquid flying through the air and falling to the carpet — hot drips landing on Michael's face — until the mug smashed against the wall. Ceramic pieces crashed to the floor.

Michael wiped the splashes from his cheek.

"Why have you been trying to get into my gang?" demanded James.

"I just moved into the area and I wanted new friends," said Michael, still trying to wrap his lies in truth. "And your gang's the one with new phones and trainers and stuff."

James's face sneered in anger. Michael could only guess that's what he was feeling because he couldn't perceive through the boy's blocks. James slapped his hand across Michael's face, leaving a stinging impression on his cheek. "Don't lie to me! Why?"

James leant in close, the remnants of coffee still hanging on his breath, and stared with wide hazel eyes. Michael felt him pushing at his blocks, harder and harder until he had to concentrate to keep them steady. James let out a cry of effort as he kept up the pressure. He grabbed Michael's face with both hands and clasped his fingers around Michael's jaw.

Michael's blocks wobbled, he let out a little bit of himself, as he shook his head to try to physically break free, but James held him tight. His perception started to pulse, like a battering ram pulling back for hit after hit, jabbing again and again at Michael's barriers. But Michael was strong and experienced and he kept the young perceiver out.

"Argh!" cried James in one last exasperation of frustration as he tossed back Michael's head. Michael's skull hit the back of the chair, giving James his only piece of frustrated pleasure.

James stepped back, breathing heavily as he paced in front of Michael, working off his anger.

Michael thought about running. Chances are, if he timed it right, he could get through the door and down the steps before they realised what was happening. But there was more to understand. The gang was run by a perceiver, that was clear. Why he was out on the streets leading a gang of older teenagers, and why they were happy to let him, Michael didn't understand. If he ran, he might never find out. So he elected to continue to sit.

James walked across to Chad and stared directly into his face. The older teenager did not move, did not flinch. Like a guard outside Buckingham Palace, he stared straight ahead as if he wasn't even aware James was in front of him. James walked on, stopped in front of Dave and did the same thing. He repeated it with Laura and Cheryl and E-boy. Michael thought about trying to perceive what was going on between them, but he feared James would detect him and so Michael relied on only what his eyes showed him.

James returned to stand in front of Michael. "You won't take over from me, you know," he said. "They know me, they don't know you."

"I don't want to take over," said Michael. "I want to join."

"You can never join," said James.

In that moment, Michael decided to take his chance. With one concerted effort he concentrated his perception on James, blasting the boy's blocks with all of his power.

James, taken by surprise, stumbled backwards.

He lost control for a second — Michael perceived a whiff of the boy's superiority, his assuredness of power, the pride in his own ability — before James closed the doorway to his mind.

James's eyes grew angry and he pointed a long, accusatory finger at him. "Perceiver!"

Like a war cry it echoed around the room. The troops began their advance.

The five norms left the walls they were leaning against and marched, in parallel, to the centre of the room. Screaming: "*Perceiver! Perceiver! Perceiver!*"

They clustered around him. Chad grabbed the hoodie he was wearing, lifted him from the chair and threw him to the ground. Michael's body slammed to the floor. He felt the carpet under him — still damp with coffee — as his head banged down hard, sparkles flickering across his vision.

He screamed, kicking and lashing out with his fists as Chad ripped at his hoodie, pulling his arms from the sleeves. Chad tossed it across the room as Dave descended and grabbed his T-shirt. Michael looked directly into his face and perceived his mind: blank except for one instruction, *strip him naked.*

"No!" Michael cried, struggling as his T-shirt was pulled over his head, blocking out his view of Dave and disrupting the focus of his perception. With his T-shirt off and his torso naked, he worked to perceive the teenagers again. They had become one, the five minds all engaged in stripping him without a single thought of their own.

Michael kicked as his trainers were pulled off and his heel struck bone. He perceived the stab of pain in Laura's jaw, but she didn't yell or back away. Instead, she tossed the trainers behind her and came further up his body where she put her hands on his groin. He recoiled –as much as it was possible while being pinned to the ground — but she felt no taboo, no qualms, no sexual awareness as she undid his fly and yanked at his waistband, forcing his jeans down his legs. Four pairs of hands held his naked arms, shoulders and torso to the damp carpet as he fought to maintain his modesty. But as the cold of the room touched his genitals, he realised he had lost.

Someone — he wasn't sure who — pulled the socks from his feet and so there he lay, arms and legs splayed out on the floor, stripped naked and held down by the five gang members. Michael could struggle, he could move his limbs by as much as a few centimetres, but he couldn't break free.

He felt fear for the first time: his own fear. He was vastly outnumbered, no one knew where he was, no one would hear his cries for help on the desolate industrial estate. He could not reach his phone which had been tossed away with his clothes and his perception couldn't help him.

James observed while he stood with folded arms as the other members of the gang did his dirty work for him. Michael still perceived nothing from James, but there was a smile on the boy's lips which suggested satisfaction.

"Put him on the chair," said James.

Michael's perceptions of the others changed with the new instruction. Their hands pulled at his arms and shoulders, lifting him from the floor and placing him on the chair. His buttocks landed hard on the rigid cold wood of the seat as his spine slammed against its upright back.

Tie him up … tie him up … tie him up … the perceived whisper went around the five minds.

"No don't!" cried Michael. "I can sit here, you don't need to do that."

But Chad already had the wire from the ripped out telephone in his hand. E-Boy held Michael's wrists down to the arm of the chair as Chad wrapped the wire around it, cutting into his flesh, tight enough to restrict blood flow to his hands. All the while, the others held him down. Michael tried to resist at first, but realising it was a waste of energy, he stopped and let them do it.

They knotted the wire to secure his wrists and then they found an old computer cable to bind his ankles to the legs of the chair. Another was wrapped around his chest so he was forced to sit upright.

"What are you doing?" said Michael. But there was no use appealing to the five. The only other person thinking for himself in the room was James, who had taken up position perched on the edge of one of the desks.

The gang stepped away, leaving him shivering and helpless, naked on the chair with goose pimples of cold and fear rising on his skin.

Michael focussed his perception again, trying hard to get into James's thoughts, but he was still unable to get past his blocks.

"You're not getting into my head, *perceiver*," said James, using the word like it was an insult.

Michael let his perception go. If the boy was that strong, then there was no way he was getting past those blocks without distracting him in a significant way. Something he couldn't do while tied to a chair.

James stood from the desk and walked towards him. He leant forward so he was face to face with Michael. "You're not taking over my gang, *perceiver*."

"I didn't want to take over, I just wanted to be a part of it," Michael repeated.

He felt James's perception probing to get into his mind again, but Michael kept him out.

"You're not going to be part of anything," said James. "Not now that you've found out about me."

He stepped back from Michael, giving E-boy and Dave a passing glance as he took a wide, circular route back to his vantage point on the desk. Immediately, E-boy turned away from the others and left. Dave went round the room gathering up Michael's clothes and brought them into a pile a short distance from his feet. He stood next to it: waiting.

E-boy returned holding a syringe. Michael thought he was going to be drugged until he perceived the instruction in E-boy's mind: *take his blood.*

Michael looked at James. "What are you doing?"

But James merely smiled in answer, keeping the secret of his plan locked up behind his mental barrier.

The sound of ripping paper caused Michael to turn to see that E-boy had ripped open a sachet containing a sterile wipe. E-boy rubbed it across the inside of Michael's elbow where a vein was close to the surface.

"Why do you want my blood?" said Michael.

James did not answer. The minds of the others didn't seem to know.

Michael shuddered as the needle came towards him. He thought of resisting. He couldn't break free of his bonds, but he could move enough to make it difficult for E-boy to pierce his vein. But that risked the needle plunging anywhere into his arm, piercing a muscle or even breaking off inside his body if he struggled too much. So he let E-boy do it, breathing in sharply as he felt the prick on his skin. Michael watched E-boy's freckly face as the blood flowed into the syringe. It betrayed no emotion.

E-boy withdrew the needle, sponged over Michael's skin with the same wipe, even though it was no longer sterile, pressed it down hard for a moment and dropped it to the floor. The pressure had not been long enough to clot where the needle had pierced the vein and a spot of blood oozed out onto his skin.

E-boy walked towards the desk, discarding the needle as he went and passed the vial of Michael's blood to James.

"That's all I need," said James, secreting the vial in his pocket.

All you need for what? Michael was about to ask, but before he could say anything, something triggered Dave to move. He pulled a cigarette lighter from his pocket and flicked the catch so a flame was born. It danced in the unseen breeze.

Michael perceived the only thought in Dave's head: *fire*.

"What are you doing?" Michael asked James.

James looked on, not seeming to care, as Dave lowered the flame to the clothes.

"Dave, don't!" Michael pleaded. "You don't know what you're doing!"

The cigarette lighter made friends with the cotton of Michael's T-shirt and spawned a larger flame that reached up into the air in a new, more vigorous dance.

He realised, in that instant, they intended to burn him. To burn him to death.

Panic gripped him. He contracted the muscles of his arms and legs to break free from the chair, but the bonds held him tight. The more he struggled, the more the wires bit into his flesh.

Walk away, the five were thinking. *Walk far away… and forget…*

The gang retreated into the dark where he could no longer see them.

"No, don't leave me!" He struggled to break free from the chair, but he was as much part of it as the varnish that made the wood shine. "You can't leave me here!"

In front of him, James left the desk. Michael looked at him. Directly at him, into his eyes, trying to find humanity in him. "Please," he heard himself beg. "I'm a perceiver like you."

James returned his stare and said nothing. The fire grew larger.

"This is *murder!*"

James turned away and followed the other gang members out of the door.

"For God's sake!" Michael shouted after him. "At least call the fire brigade!"

At the last moment, as he disappeared from view, James allowed one thought to slip from his mind. A thought he knew Michael would hear: *Goodbye, perceiver. Forever.*

THIRTEEN

FIRE burned the bundle of clothes a metre from Michael's bound and helpless naked body. Myriad orange and yellow cones leapt from the pile, snatching oxygen from the air to bring back to the base of each flame where they continued to consume the material.

Michael felt the fire's deadly heat getting stronger. It wasn't yet burning him, but the hairs on his shins were close to scorching and it was only a matter of time.

He had hoped the fire would burn itself out when it reached the damp nylon carpet. But, within the black smoke rising into the air, was the smell of melting artificial fibres and he feared the fire would soon gain hold of the dry wooden floorboards underneath.

He pulled at the telephone and computer wire wrapped round his wrists and ankles, but all it did was make the knots tighter. With every effort, he wriggled his right wrist, jostling his hand to try to slip it underneath the restraint, but his hand was too large and the gap was too small. They had bound him to the chair well.

Water was in his eyes, from the increasing smoke and the fear of being burnt to death. Except, he realised, he wouldn't burn to death. The smoke would kill him first. Taken into his lungs instead of oxygen, he would be so desperate to breathe, that he would gasp down more and more of the poisonous air until he passed out. While unconscious, the fire would spread to his naked body and eat the flesh off his bones until the only thing anyone would find in the debris would be his charred skeleton.

Michael coughed. The smoke was thicker. He looked above him and saw how it gathered at the ceiling.

The fire had almost exhausted the fuel in the clothes and was spreading. It bit into the floorboards as it crept in all directions to look for new food.

Michael coughed again. In reflex, he drew in another contaminated breath of heat and carbon. His body spasmed in repeated, desperate coughs.

He didn't have long. If he was going to get out of this, he had to do something now.

It was then he saw the corner of his phone, sticking out from what once must have been the pocket of his jeans. The plastic casing was melted and the screen blackened and warped. Even if he could somehow tip over the chair and reach it with his fingers, it would be useless.

"Help!" he cried out, even though there was no one there to hear him. "Help!" He kept calling until the coughing made him stop.

His only hope was to get free of the bonds.

He looked at the tight knots in the wire that bound him, as smoke choked up his eyes and filled his mouth with its toxicity. If he could reach them with his teeth he might be able to undo them.

He yanked his shoulders forward and felt the wire across his chest cut into him, forcing him back against the chair.

He looked at the knots, so easy to undo if only he could reach them. As his mind clouded, he imagined untying them. He wished they would untie, with all his will.

A knot appeared to loosen.

He was hallucinating. He had to be hallucinating.

But he wanted it to be true. He wanted it so much to be true.

He focussed his will to loosen it even more.

Before his eyes, the intertwined ends of the wire slackened. They slithered back the way they had come, untying the knot like a snake under the power of a snake charmer.

Through shallow, smoke-filled, choking breaths, he watched the impossible. The two ends of the wire untangled from the knot and fell free from his wrist.

Michael lifted his unbound hand to his face, shaking as he wiggled his fingers to see if it was true.

No time to think. Not able to breathe. Heat blistering his legs. He used his fingers to pick at the knots holding his other wrist. In seconds, that was free too and he was untying the knots that held his ankles. He grabbed the wire around his chest with both hands and forced it over his head.

He stood up.

Stumbling, oxygen deprived, not able to see, he ran to where he remembered the door to be as his bare feet burned on hot ashes on the floor.

Out onto the landing where the air was slightly cleaner, he felt along the wall to the staircase.

He took one step, then misjudged his footing and went tumbling down the uncarpeted stairs in a jumble of bumps that didn't hurt him at all. Nothing could hurt him now that he was high on freedom.

He ended up in a ball at the bottom.

His hands slapped out in front of him and hit a wall. He kept slapping until he hit wood: the door.

Pulling himself to his feet, Michael found the handle and turned.

He stumbled out into the fresh, un-burning air, gasping at it.
Coughing and wheezing and stumbling. But free.
Free and alive.

FOURTEEN

MICHAEL concentrated on the tied laces of his training shoe, as it sat at the end of his bed. He willed them to untie. In his mind, the laces weaved around each other, unravelling the knot until they broke free of each other and each one lay separately on the duvet. In the real world, the laces didn't move and remained steadfastly tied in a bow.

Michael propped himself up straighter against the pillow at his headboard and took a deep breath. He stared at the trainer again with all his strength: directing his brain power and commanding the laces to move.

The trainer sat there. The bow did nothing.

Michael let his breath go and his throat spasmed. He coughed and gasped as his lungs protested at having their regular oxygen intake disrupted. He reached for the box of tissues next to him on the bed and spat into it. His sputum was no longer black from the soot of the fire, but his lungs were still producing mucus as they tried to heal from their ordeal.

"My God, are you all right?" came a female voice from the doorway.

He had been concentrating so hard on trying to undo shoe laces that he hadn't perceived her coming. It was Pauline. She wore the regulation grey T-shirt and trousers they all wore in the camp, but it didn't suit her and the clothes sat on her body like they had been put on a manikin by a shop assistant. She still kept her individuality with the precise black lines of her eye make-up and her jet black hair, which she wore hanging loose, against regulations.

Michael nodded in answer to her question. Speaking would require air from his lungs and they were too busy trying to recover from holding his breath.

"Are you sure they should have let you out of hospital?" said Pauline.

"Doctor said—" he took a croaky breath "—it's fine as long as I don't exert myself."

Pauline stepped inside and looked over to the chest of drawers where a jug of water sat next to an empty glass among a collection of half a dozen 'get well' cards. She poured him a glass and brought it over. Michael accepted it gratefully, took a sip like the nurse at the hospital had told him, and felt the lukewarm water soothe his throat.

"I see you got my card," she said.

Michael looked over, and among the pictures of cute animals and pastel coloured flowers was a card with a picture of a killer whale on the front and the message, 'get whale soon'. He smiled. "Yes."

He reached down and put the glass on the floor by the bed. He still hadn't got around to asking for a bedside table like Pauline had in her room. "I didn't expect to see you," he said. Not after their encounter last time.

"If I said I was just passing, would you perceive I was lying?" she said.

"I would," said Michael.

"The truth is, Alex sent me."

"Ah, Alex," said Michael, nodding. He would have to have a word with his friend.

Pauline sat on the other end of the bed and yelped as her bum landed on top of the trainer. She reached underneath herself and pulled it out. "What's that doing there?"

"Nothing," said Michael. "Put it on the floor."

She dropped the trainer to the ground where it tumbled until it hit the chest of drawers and came to a stop.

"How's life in the army?" Michael asked her.

She rolled her eyes. "I thought I was here to use my mind, but they keep making me march up and down. What's the point in that? And who cares that my step is one millisecond later than everyone else's? I'm still getting there, aren't I?"

Michael laughed. Then regretted it because it made him cough again.

"Do you want some more water?"

He waved her concern away and sat taking slow and steady breaths until the coughing subsided.

"It's about discipline," said Michael. "They want all their soldiers to be the same, to keep in step, so they follow orders."

"I won't be ordered about by anybody," said Pauline.

"You're wearing the uniform," he noted.

She frowned and pulled at the neck of her T-shirt as if it were some distasteful scrap. She let go of it and allowed the T-shirt to drop back against her chest. "Grey marl! *Not* my colour. I only wear it to keep them off my back. It's like school uniform, isn't it? You hate it but you wear it on the outside because you know, on the inside, you are the same person."

"At least the army pays you."

She scoffed at that. "Not much."

"It adds up over a few months," he said. "Or you can do what Peter did, get credit on your salary and run up a massive debt."

"Not sure it makes up for all the marching."

"You get lessons on perception too, right?" said Michael.

"Yeah, mostly about focussing and stuff."

"Not anything new?" he asked.

"What do you mean? You say it like there's something new to teach."

"I've been thinking," said Michael. "Maybe there's more to perception than sensing people's thoughts and feelings."

"Wouldn't we know about it?" said Pauline.

"Not necessarily. I mean, you didn't know there were adult perceivers or natural borns until I told you. It makes me wonder what other secrets they might be keeping from us."

"If we were being told lies, then we would perceive it."

"Not if the only people they allow close to us don't know the truth."

Pauline laughed like it was ridiculous. "What are you talking about?"

Michael returned the laugh, releasing his tension, but being careful not to engage his whole lungs. "I don't know," he said. "The smoke must have addled my brain."

"Alex said…" She paused. "Alex said the fire was deliberate, that someone tried to kill you."

"Alex should stop spreading gossip," said Michael. He really would have to have a word with his friend when he next saw him.

"Is it true?" said Pauline.

"Yes and no." James had meant for him to die, he was certain of that, but he didn't think the other gang members had meant to hurt him. They were James's puppets, following his orders without question, like soldiers running into battle to face death, just because someone more powerful than them told them to do so.

"You're younger than me," said Michael all of a sudden.

"I suppose," she said, surprised.

"You would have gone through the perception screening programme. What happens, exactly?"

She blew out a mouthful of air as she remembered a tense time in her life only a few months ago, the strain still showing in her voice and the traces of emotion that escaped through her filters. "Someone comes to your school and takes over the head teacher's office and they call you in, one by one, to speak to them. I remember thinking it was really stupid because all they do is ask you a bunch of questions and anyone trying to hide would just lie. But now I think the man who screened me was an adult perceiver and he must have known what I was the minute I walked into the room, so it didn't matter what answers I gave him."

"Wouldn't you have sensed he was a perceiver at the time?" said Michael.

"Not if I wasn't expecting it and not if he had his blocks up," she said. "That's something I've learnt in here. To be honest, I was so nervous that day, I daren't perceive anything from the moment I got to school to the moment I got home."

"They test everyone, right? No one could slip through the net?"

"Everyone," said Pauline. "At our school, they came three years running, testing all the age groups where children were going through puberty. Anyone who didn't come to school that day was sent an appointment to go to a special clinic, and if they didn't turn up, they got a home visit. There was one boy in our class they had to physically drag out of his bedroom for the test while he was screaming about his human rights. It was stupid because it turned out he was a norm."

"The reason I'm asking," said Michael, thinking about James. "Is that I met this perceiver kid who said something odd. He said: 'once they know what you are, they keep hounding you until their paperwork says you've been turned into a norm.'"

"What does that mean?" said Pauline.

"I think he meant the authorities believe he's had the cure."

"And he hasn't?"

"No."

"You're talking about the perceiver kid who tried to kill you in the fire, aren't you?" she said.

Michael smiled. "Alex talks too much."

"Alex said he was really strong. Someone like that's going to attract attention, get invited to join the Perceivers Corps or be pressured into taking the cure."

"You think so?" said Michael.

"It's what happened to me," said Pauline. "I know you think the Perceivers' Law protects people like us who opt to live on the outside, but I didn't get the impression that was a choice I had. For perceivers with weak or average power, maybe, but for strong ones like us — and the kid who tried to kill you — no chance. When Agent Cooper knocked on my door after the screening, I got the impression that if I tried to live an ordinary life on the outside, they would always be watching me, afraid of what I might do with my power. I wasn't told that in so many words, of course, but I perceived it in Agent Cooper's thoughts — I'm sure he thought those things on purpose."

Michael leant over the side of the bed and picked up his glass of water, using it as an excuse to look away from her. Maybe he had been naive to think society would turn their backs on prejudice against perceivers just because of a law.

"So you think," said Pauline, "this perceiver kid somehow forged the records to show he'd been cured when he hadn't, to keep the authorities off his back?"

"After what you've told me," said Michael. "I think that's exactly what he did."

"Then there has be a record of it somewhere."

"That's what I was thinking."

"So, where do we look?" said Pauline.

It was the question he'd been asking himself ever since he'd had time to think about what James had said in the derelict office. The only problem was, he didn't like the answer. "I know someone who works in the cure programme, but I haven't seen her for a couple of years, it might be a bit awkward…"

"Awkward?" she said. "Do you want to find out who tried to kill you or not?"

"Perhaps you could come with me."

"I'd like that," said Pauline. "Except, I'm not allowed out of the camp, I have some more stupid marching to do."

"I can get you a pass," said Michael. "We can say I need someone to look after me because of my—" he coughed a couple of times "—medical condition."

"Like I'm some kind of nurse?" said Pauline, offended. "Bit of a gender stereotype!"

"Norm the Norm loves stereotypes, they fit nicely into his regimented view of the world. He'll give you a pass for that, I bet you."

DOCTOR Rachel Page wasn't used to being around perceivers and her irritation at being disturbed in her office was obvious behind her smile as soon as Michael knocked and walked in. When she saw who it was, her surprise turned to delight and she stood from her desk to welcome him, taking off her reading glasses as she did so, laying them beside her computer as she stepped out to greet him.

"Michael," she said, her smile becoming genuine. She walked towards him and they met in the middle of what was a small, but tidy and private office with a chill breeze that blew in from the window which was open a crack beside her desk. Michael perceived she wanted to hug him, but self-restraint and thinking better of it held her back. It was then she remembered Michael's power and her standard blocks went up, dulling the emotions he was getting from her.

"Hello, Doctor Page," said Michael.

"You're virtually a man now," she said.

Michael looked down at himself. He felt just the same as he had two years ago when they last saw each other. "Am I?"

Page, too, had changed. She was dressed for work in a smart navy trouser suit and her hair, once long, had been cut into a brown bob. It made her look a little younger.

Pauline entered through the open door, following Michael slowly and apprehensively.

"And who's this?" said Page.

"I'm Pauline."

Page turned back to Michael. "Girlfriend?"

"A friend," said Michael. "Who is also a girl."

Pauline looked at the woman they had come to see. "You're a perceiver," she said.

Page's standard blocks weren't enough to mask her discomfort at the word. "Come in, my dear, and close the door," she said.

Pauline did as she was asked, still wary, but comforted by the fact that Michael was so at ease.

"Most people here don't know that about me," said Page. "I need to keep it that way. This building is full of people whose job it is to cure perceivers, after all."

Her office was one of many in a small 1980s office block in the Docklands area of London, surrounded by banking and financial firms. There was no company name on the front of the building, just a plaque with the street name and number. It was probably by design that the administrative hub of the cure programme was secreted a distance from the centre of London where it would attract little attention.

"Doctor Page," said Michael. "We've come to see if a perceiver — a *child* perceiver — could be recorded as having had the cure when they actually haven't."

"I see," said Page. "Straight to business, is it?"

"Is it possible?" pressed Michael.

"Nothing is impossible, although it's highly unlikely. But if you've come to ask me to fudge the records for a friend of yours, then the answer is no. With my history, it's not a risk I can take."

"No," said Michael. "But I think someone might have already done it."

Page became interested. "Who?"

"I don't know who might have done the fudging, but the perceiver's name is James. Is it possible to look him up?"

"It should be."

Page went back round to her side of the desk and sat down. She closed the active window on her screen — a list of numbers in an impenetrable spreadsheet — and initiated some software which opened with a blue logo with CCL written in the centre.

Cure Clinic List? thought Michael, although it probably stood for something more sophisticated.

Michael and Pauline stood behind Page and peered at the screen.

"His name is James …?" said Page.

"I don't have a surname," said Michael, suddenly realising with embarrassment that he might have come on a wild goose chase. "But he's about thirteen years old."

Page sat back in her chair and gave him a despairing look. "Do you know how many thirteen-year-olds there are in Britain called James?"

Michael didn't answer, but he was willing to bet quite a few.

"Except," said Pauline, "we know he lives in Kennington, or around there. There's got to be only a handful schools he could have gone to. And Michael knows what he looks like, right?"

Michael nodded. "Oh yeah, that face is etched into my brain."

"So …" Pauline pulled out her phone and her fingers danced across the screen. "There's only six high schools in that area where he could have been a pupil. If you've got access to school photos, you can pull up pictures of everyone called James of the right age group in those schools and we should find him."

"Brilliant!" said Michael. "I knew there was a reason I brought you." He took the phone from her and showed it to Page.

Page squinted at it. "God, I'm getting old," she said to herself and put on her reading glasses. She took the phone and laid it beside her computer keyboard. "If I search for boys named James in years eight, nine and ten in those schools over the past three years, we should find him. Assuming he went to one of those schools and you've got his name and age correct."

She made several attempts at the search, muttering about it not being the sort of thing the database was designed to do, before coming up with a result. There were twenty-two matches.

"Can you pull up their photos?" said Pauline.

"Um … yep," said Page. With a few clicks of her mouse, she displayed the details of the first James, which included a photo in the top right hand corner. He was a black boy and definitely not the one.

"Not him," said Michael. "Can you pull up the next?"

She nodded and pulled up another record of a boy called James. This one was chubby with ginger hair and also rejected. They went through six more photos like that before they found the one. James stared out of the screen with those same hazel eyes he'd used to stare into Michael's face. He looked even younger in the photo in his school uniform, but it was definitely him.

"That's James," said Michael.

Page clicked again and pulled up a different record. "His name is James Hetherington, he's just had a birthday, so he fourteen years old," she said. "It says here he was screened last year. The result was positive and he was cured."

"That's the fudge," said Michael. "The kid I met definitely wasn't cured, he was strong, he could control other people with his mind."

Page turned to him. "Control people?"

"I don't know what you'd call it, brain washing or programming, but he was able to make the norms in his gang do what he wanted, as if they had no free will. I think he also did the same to that kid who blew himself up outside the Capital Hotel."

"That's not a power perceivers have," said Page.

"As far as you know," said Michael.

"Your father and I did a lot of testing in the early days, Michael. We never found anything like that."

"Maybe not in natural borns, but what about the ones who were created by the vitamin pills? Maybe your tests didn't cover everything."

Pauline interrupted. "Is there a way to find out how the fudging happened?"

"Possibly," said Page. She brought up another form on her computer. "It was signed off by Doctor S.O. Lucas. That must be Saul Lucas. I remember him, an uptight little man. He was a norm, used to oversee the injections at the cure clinics, he left the project a while back." She peered closer at the screen. "I don't recognise that clinic code, though."

Next to James Hetherington's name was a four digit code, AP93. Page double clicked to copy and paste it back into the original software. It brought up the name Harrow Bridge Clinic, Greater London. Michael perceived her concern before she said anything. A glance over to Pauline revealed she perceived it too.

"Wasn't that the place that was firebombed in the early days of the perceiver riots?" said Michael.

"Yes," said Page. "We had to close it down and move somewhere else. There hasn't been a perceiver cured in that building for more than two years."

"So somebody lied on the form?" said Pauline.

"It would seem so," said Page. "I would have put it down to human error, someone putting down the wrong code when they were tired, but if you say he *wasn't* cured ..."

"It has to have been deliberate," said Michael. "Maybe he controlled the mind of this Doctor Lucas person to falsify the records."

"I need to inform Cooper," said Page. She reached for the telephone on her desk, but Michael's hand got there first and stopped her picking it up.

"No," he said. "I'm working with the police, they can look into Doctor Lucas. If anything comes of it, I'm sure it'll get reported back to Agent Cooper. There's no point in telling him until we know what we're dealing with."

Michael took his hand away and perceived Page's regret at not feeling his touch any longer. She allowed her own hand to slide from the telephone and come to rest in her lap. She looked at Michael and allowed a thought to slip from her mind: *Are you doing okay?*

Pauline must have perceived it too because she stepped away from them. Embarrassed, Michael perceived, at intruding in a relationship she didn't understand. "Thank you for your help, Doctor Page," she said. "Come on, Michael, my pass says I have to be back before dinner." She was at the door already, holding the handle ready to open it.

"Could you wait for Michael outside for a minute?" said Doctor Page. "I just need to ask him something."

Pauline took a moment to get Michael's reaction. He nodded at her. *It's okay*, he said in his thoughts. She perceived him and closed the door behind her with the gentle click of the latch.

Page swivelled round on her chair so she could look at him directly. "She's a nice girl," she said.

"You didn't want to talk to me alone about Pauline," said Michael.

"No." She felt uncomfortable, then she realised Michael could perceive her discomfort and she blushed a little. "I would like, if you don't mind, to *really* know how you are doing."

Her perception brushed at his mind, as if gently knocking to come in. But the memory of nearly dying in the fire was too fresh and if he let her in, he didn't think he could hide it from her. Instead, he strengthened his blocks and sensed her disappointment.

"You have to believe me when I say I'm fine," he said.

"I'll believe you if you want me to." She withdrew her perception.

"Look, I need to go," said Michael. "Me and Pauline have a train to catch."

"Then promise me before you go, Michael, that you will visit your father."

He had perceived there was something festering in her head that she wanted to say to him, but he hadn't probed, so the mention of his father caught him by surprise. "No."

"He could be sent to prison."

"That's got nothing to do with me."

"You could show him your support," said Page.

"I don't support what he did, you know that."

"But still," said Page. "He's your *father*. He misses you."

"It's his fault I don't remember being brought up by him."

"In a way, it's my fault as well," she admitted.

"Pauline's waiting."

"Of course," said Page. She didn't hide her disappointment, but let it flow out of her so she could be sure he perceived it.

Michael shut it out, but it had already got in and he couldn't forget it. He headed for the door. "Thanks for looking up that stuff on the database," he said and stepped into the corridor.

Pauline was waiting. "Who was that woman?" she said as they walked off together towards the lift.

"My biological mother," said Michael.

Her surprise filled his perception. "Your family are weird."

Michael laughed. "Yeah."

She giggled too and they laughed together all the way to the ground floor.

FIFTEEN

THE journalist looked pale, his white skin tinged with a green that allowed his neck to blend into the olive colour of his jacket. He had thrown it over the faded black T-shirt he was wearing when the police came because he thought it made him appear more respectable. Instead, he looked like a washed out drug addict as he desperately clutched a paper cup of machine-dispensed coffee like he was in withdrawal.

Michael knew this because he sat with him in the interrogation room, perceiving him. The journalist, whose name was Oscar Elkins, thought it was disgusting that a teenager was allowed to observe what was going on. *What is it with the Metropolitan Police these days?* said his thoughts. *Have they embraced 'bring your son to work day', or something?* It made Michael laugh inside. It was odd, sometimes, seeing what other people thought of him.

Elkins didn't think much better of Patterson, who sat across the interrogation table from him, using the fake smile that was supposed to make him appear friendly. Elkins wasn't fooled. He was a strong believer in freedom of the press and free speech and he wasn't impressed by being dragged out of his flat and down to the police station just because he had interviewed Victor Rublev for *The Daily News.*

Patterson smoothed his already-smooth tie against his belly and shuffled in his seat. "Thanks for coming in, Mr Elkins," he said.

"I didn't think I had a choice," said Elkins.

"I need to remind you that you are not under arrest, but this conversation is being recorded."

"How long is this going to take?" said Elkins. He felt like he had a hangover even though he hadn't been drinking. He'd forced down breakfast that morning, but wished he hadn't because the wholemeal toast and jam sat in his stomach like a stone, refusing to be digested. It made him want to give up on the idea of eating healthily and go back to processed white bread.

"It shouldn't take long, Mr Elkins," said Patterson, trying a little too hard with his smile. "I want to ask you about the murder of Victor Rublev."

Shocked, Elkins sat up straight, spilling his coffee over the edge of its cardboard cup so it ran down his fingers. "Murder?"

"Yes," said Patterson.

"I heard he died, but I thought he had a heart attack or something. Murder? Are you sure?"

"Yes."

Memory flashed in Elkins's mind of his interview with Rublev. Strangely, not of them sitting in the Filigree Restaurant chatting over afternoon tea — which police investigations had confirmed they did — but of sitting in his flat listening back to the recording of the conversation. He remembered trying to make out Rublev's Russian accented words over the noise of chinking china cups and background piano music. "You don't think that I . . . ? I'm a journalist, I attack people with words, I don't shoot or stab them."

"We believe Mr Rublev was poisoned within a two week window," said Patterson. "Your meeting with him was right in the middle of those two weeks."

"We had tea and cake," said Elkins. "Not arsenic and cyanide." He rubbed his hand around the collar of his jacket where the wool blend scratched at his neck. He felt suddenly sweaty. Moisture gathered under his arms and on his chest. It made him look guilty to Patterson, but the only emotion Michael perceived from Elkins was confusion.

"The doctors believe he ingested a radioactive substance," said Patterson. "You were sharing food with him, perhaps you slipped in something when he wasn't looking."

"No!" Elkins's indignation was genuine, as was a nagging fear he was about to be fitted up for a crime. The journalist had interviewed many political activists, of which Rublev was the most recent, and he'd heard many horror stories about the authorities abroad arresting and imprisoning people who didn't agree with their point of view. But he never thought he would experience that in Britain. "What reason would I have to kill Rublev? He was a valuable source for my articles, he's no good to me dead."

"Then take me through it," said Patterson. "Everything you did on the day that you met Rublev."

Elkins sighed. He took his jacket by the lapels and flapped them against his chest, fanning in some cooling air. He remembered, that morning, packing his bag with his notes and his recording equipment, and realising the batteries were dead. "I had to get off the bus early to buy some batteries," he said. "But I'd left plenty of time, so it wasn't a problem. I often buy a newspaper from the little shop near the canal, and it's a nice walk if it's not raining, so I don't mind. I met Rublev at the restaurant, did the interview and came home."

Elkins had skipped over the vital bit of the story, even in his head. Perceiving his memory was like watching a film on normal speed, only to have it fast forward during the good bit. Elkins, however, didn't seem aware that he'd missed anything out.

"Perhaps you could go into a little bit more detail about what happened at the restaurant," pressed Patterson.

"Oh," said Elkins, surprised. "Well I … I must have handed in my coat when I got there. Did I hand in my coat? It must have been a jacket, because I left the flat wearing a jacket. Yes, yes that's right, because it wasn't cold enough for a coat."

Elkins's memories were mixed up with other times he'd been to the Filigree Restaurant. Evidently, it was his favourite place to meet foreign political activists when he was working on a story. He remembered handing a long coat to a man in a white shirt and black waistcoat and black tie, but he also remembered putting on his brown padded jacket that morning. His mind made allowances, mixed up the memories, and suddenly it was the *brown jacket*, and *not* the winter coat, that he recalled handing to the man at the cloakroom.

"I sat at the table by the window … actually, Rublev didn't want to be public, so we sat in a corner out of the way … or maybe that was when I met Naoki Yang last year … does it really matter where we sat?"

His mind was trying to remember, but every time he honed in on something particular, it became fuzzy. Like a bar of soap in the bath, he could see glimpses of it beneath the bubbles, but every time he tried to grab it, it slipped away. The concentration made him feel ill and a layer of sweat formed on his face, giving it a glassy sheen.

"The details are important, Mr Elkins," said Patterson. "It would help to tell me everything that happened, everything that you saw. Maybe it wasn't you who poisoned him, maybe you are a witness to who did."

"Yes, right," said Elkins, taking a few deep breaths, relieved that the police didn't necessarily think he was a murderer, even though he still felt nauseous. "So I …"

The soap slipped away again. He couldn't remember. He tried to take a run at the events by going back to the flat and the memory of packing his bag, realising he needed batteries, putting on his jacket because it wasn't cold enough for a coat, getting off the bus and heading for the shop. And coming home again … listening to the recording of his discussion with Rublev, remembering the lingering taste of tea and cake in his mouth, even though he had no memory of actually eating it.

As he mentally took himself back to the restaurant, his mind swam with images of a waiter standing with a notebook ready to take his order, of a three-tiered stand of sandwiches arriving on a table, of trying not to spill tea down his tie. But, in his mind, every time he looked across the table at his companion, he saw a Chinese man, or an elderly German man, or a woman. He didn't see Rublev. The harder he tried to remember, the more his mind looked into darkness.

The nausea mushroomed inside of Elkins so suddenly that Michael tasted the sick in his own mouth. Revolted, he pulled out his perception.

"Oh no," said Elkins, his face now almost entirely green and shiny with sweat. He stood up so quickly that his chair fell over. He rushed to the door, but he didn't even have time to reach for the handle before he was controlled by a vomiting spasm. He reached out his palm for the wall and rested his weight there as he retched. The contents of his stomach came flying out in an arc of lumpy, orangey gloop that splattered to the floor and on his shoes, splashing back against his trousers and the wall. He stood panting, looking down at the puddle of vomit he had created. The smell of bile and semi-digested food rose into the room.

Patterson stood. Michael perceived the policeman was about to hit the panic alarm when they were interrupted by a gentle double tap on the door.

Without waiting for an answer, the person opened the door to reveal herself to be Tania Baker. She lifted a foot to step inside, saw the vomit she was about to tread in, and thought better of it. Her nose wrinkled.

"Get the doctor, Tania," said Patterson.

"We've got the results back," she said, somehow feeling the need to finish what she came in to do. "They're positive."

"*Tania.*" Patterson glared at her. "*Doctor!*"

"Right," said Baker, and disappeared into the corridor.

INSPECTOR Jones closed down his computer and looked across his desk to where Michael and Patterson were sitting. He was tired, Michael perceived. His head was full of recent conversations with detectives, the details of several cases merging together with his life outside the police station. His wife was annoyed he forgot to put the rubbish outside for the bin men that morning, he'd had to scale back surveillance on a terrorist suspect he personally felt was still a risk, and his doctor had told him off for forgetting to take his statins. The usually neat man had loosened his tie a little and undone the top button of his shirt, allowing a couple of grey chest hairs to peek out.

"I don't understand why you don't arrest Oscar Elkins," said Jones.

"Because he didn't do it," said Patterson, sitting forward in his chair, excited by all the thoughts going round in his head.

"I thought Tania's report said they found traces of radiation at both the restaurant and his flat. That puts him square in the frame, doesn't it?"

"Yes," said Patterson. "And no."

Jones put his fingers to his temple and rested the weight of his head on them as he closed his eyes for a moment to hold onto sanity. "It's been a long week, Tony. I haven't got the energy to listen to you unravel some Agatha Christie plot."

"Oscar Elkins almost certainly poisoned Victor Rublev," said Patterson. "As you say, we found traces of radiation at both his flat and the restaurant, so he definitely came into contact with the offending isotope."

"More so than if he'd been an innocent bystander, according to Tania's report," said Jones.

"Right," said Patterson. "Which kind of knocks any theory on the head that someone might have bribed a waiter to do it. We're checking into all the restaurant staff, of course, just in case. However, it's fairly certain Elkins was the conduit, especially as he was one of the names on Rublev's list."

"Then charge him."

"I would, except…"

"Except what?"

"Have you read the article Elkins wrote based on his interview with Rublev?"

Jones put his other hand to his other temple and rested his weight on both arms. "Tony, I'm starting to get a headache. Can we just assume that I'm not as well read as I appear?"

"The article isn't exactly what I would call neutral journalism," said Patterson. "He practically worships the guy for standing up against the Russian government. So wanting to murder him seems unlikely and, even if he was the killer, I would've expected a journalist with the intelligence of Elkins not to have poisoned himself at the same time."

"He's definitely suffering from radiation poisoning, then?" said Jones.

"A mild form, the doctor thinks. We're just waiting on the result of tests to confirm."

"We've still got enough to charge him," said Jones. "It'll put him under pressure to talk, if nothing else. I've read the transcript of your interview with him and he didn't tell you anything about his meeting with Rublev. That suggests to me that he's hiding something."

"Michael has a theory about that," said Patterson.

Jones turned to Michael, as if only noticing him there for the first time, then back to Patterson. "Are you two friends now?"

Patterson smiled at that. "I haven't invited him to my birthday party yet, but let's say I think he has skills which could be useful."

"So," Jones asked Michael. "What's your theory?"

"I perceived him," said Michael, "and I don't think he was hiding anything. He genuinely doesn't remember anything about his meeting with Rublev."

"Perhaps he's getting old," said Jones with a chuckle. "I forgot my car keys this morning — had to go back into the house to get them!" He looked to Patterson to share in his little joke, but all he got back from his sergeant was a serious expression and the chuckle died on his lips.

"This isn't ordinary forgetfulness," said Michael. "When he tried to access that part of his memory, he came up against nothing. A blankness. Not like he has forgotten, but like he hadn't laid down the memories in the first place."

"Similar to people not remembering the trauma of a car crash?" said Jones.

"Possibly," said Michael. "It's the same sort of blankness that I perceived in Tyler and Bailecki. Do you remember I said there was nothing in Tyler's head except the need to get a bus? And Bailecki's mind was stuck in a loop waiting for the delegates so he could detonate the bomb? It was like the minds of the gang who left me to die in the fire. I think someone got into their heads and pushed them into doing it. Elkins doesn't remember poisoning Rublev because the person who programmed him didn't want him to remember."

Michael's words stopped and quiet came into the room. Only the fan in Jones's computer rumbled softly as it worked to keep the electronics cool.

He perceived the reaction of the policemen. Patterson had already accepted the crazy theory and was hoping his boss would do the same. Jones was confused, as he tried to process the implications all at once.

A loud knock made all of them jump. Michael turned to see the chubby policeman open the door and lean in.

"Sorry to interrupt," he said. "But there's some CCTV footage you need to see."

THEY crowded around Chubby's desk which seemed to exist as an anti-monument to the neatness of Jones's office. A plastic supermarket sandwich container lay empty beside his computer mouse, half a mug of cold coffee sat on top of a stack of paper files, and there were at least four pens strewn around, none of which was inside the dusty pen holder. No one, however, was looking at the mess. Michael, Patterson, Jones and the remaining three members of the team were all focussed on the screen of Chubby's computer. It showed a paused video image of a canal towpath from the vantage point of a camera mounted on a narrowboat.

Chubby — sitting in his swivel chair at the controls — clicked the mouse. The image unfroze and the grass at the edge of the towpath rocked gently in the breeze of a dry, overcast day. A woman in a knee-length navy coat, walking a small black dog, came into frame. Her face was away from the camera as she strode past in sturdy walking boots, her dog jerking on its lead as she tried to keep up with it.

"This is footage from a canal boat owner on the Grand Union," said Chubby. "He had his barge broken into a couple of times by a bunch of yobbos, so he installed CCTV a couple of months back, lucky for us."

The woman and her dog soon walked out of shot and the assembled police officers, along with Michael, witnessed several seconds of nothing other than willowing grass. Then a man entered the frame: first his arm, then his back and finally the back of his head. Michael recognised the brown padded jacket he wore as the same one Elkins put on before heading to his meeting with Rublev.

"That's Elkins," said Patterson.

"Yes," said Chubby, not realising that his pride at having found the piece of evidence was being picked up by the perceiver at his shoulder. "He got off the bus early, as he said, to go to the shop before his meeting. From there, it seems he took the scenic route to the restaurant — typical arty-farty journalist type — and this is where we pick him up."

The video continued to play and nothing significant happened. Elkins walked down the towpath until he disappeared into a shadow and out of shot.

"Fascinating, Detective," scoffed Patterson. "That's going to blow their socks off in court."

"Wait," said Chubby, not knowing that Michael was perceiving how he loved to turn on the suspense, so his colleagues would appreciate his detective work all the more. "You can just about see the bridge he's walked under at the end of the towpath."

Michael strained to see the bridge Chubby was talking about, but that part of the picture was out of focus and it still looked like a shadow to him.

"This is the bridge from the other side," said Chubby, and with another couple of clicks, brought up a second video image, this time looking down on the towpath from above. It had a good view of a brick Victorian road bridge that arched across the canal, as well as the steps leading up the bank to street level. The woman and her dog appeared from out of the shadow of the bridge and continued to walk along the towpath. "It's the CCTV from the pub on the bank on the other side of the bridge. The landlord reckoned dealers were selling drugs there, so he installed the camera — gotta love the Big Brother society, right?"

"Get on with it," said Jones.

Chubby did nothing, just let the footage play. Michael perceived the anticipation of the police officers around him as they leant forward, waiting for something to happen. For a moment, nothing did. If it hadn't been for a bird flying past, the video would have looked like a still image.

What the others didn't know, and what Michael perceived, was Chubby's silent amusement as he sat back in his chair and waited for someone to figure it out. The longer they watched, the more amused he became.

"Hold on," said Patterson. "Where's Elkins?"

Chubby turned around with a grin. "Exactly. He walks under the bridge and that's where he stays for …" He turned back to the controls and fast forwarded the footage. "… about ten minutes."

At high speed, it was possible to see the flow of the water in the canal, but that was all that moved, until a flash of brown appeared from under the bridge. Chubby returned playback to normal speed to show Elkins come into view. Elkins turned from the path to climb the stone steps cut into the bank and, for one moment, his face looked almost directly at the camera. It was definitely Elkins. Apart from his cheeks being a little red from being out in the fresh air, he looked perfectly normal as he walked out of shot.

"From there, he went straight to the restaurant," said Chubby. "We don't have the whole lot on CCTV, but I timed it and I don't think he stopped anywhere else."

"What was he doing under the bridge?" said Patterson.

"Having a cigarette out of the wind, probably," said Jones. "Or checking his email on his phone."

"I don't think so," said Chubby. "Because you haven't seen the best bit."

Everyone waited. Chubby soaked up the dramatic tension like a comedian waiting to deliver his punchline. He watched the screen with the others.

Another figure emerged from under the bridge. Smaller and thinner than both Elkins and the woman with the dog, he wore a black hoodie rather than a coat or jacket. It was a teenage boy. The boy took three steps down the towpath before he turned to climb the steps and Michael saw his face. Recognising him immediately, he felt suddenly hot.

"That's James Hetherington," said Baker, vocalising what Michael already knew.

"Who's that?" said Jones.

"The kid Tony thinks was in the same gang as the bomber," she added. "Tony asked me to track him down, but he seems to have gone AWOL. His mother says he hasn't been home for a week."

Michael put out his hand to rest on the back of Chubby's chair as his mind put two and two together.

"What's the Hetherington kid from my bomber inquiry doing in CCTV footage from my radiation poisoning inquiry?" said Patterson.

"I don't know," said Chubby. "What I do know is they spent ten minutes under that bridge together, out of the view of any cameras."

"Are you sure?" said Patterson.

"CCTV shows Hetherington going down to the canal from the pub side and walking under the bridge about half an hour before Elkins shows up. He stays there until just after Elkins leaves. Suggests to me they had a meeting, don't you think?"

Patterson shook his head. "At this moment, I don't know what to think."

But Michael knew. And it scared him.

SIXTEEN

SIX o'clock in the morning and Michael was the only one in the dining area. It was blissfully quiet, not only in sound, but in perceptions. The others were still in bed, either asleep or dozing, waiting for their six-thirty alarm call.

Breakfast had been left at the far end of the room on two wheeled trolleys with metal racks onto which twenty trays were dressed exactly the same. A bowl of cereal in the nearside right hand corner, a spoon opposite it on the right, a portion of milk in an insulated cup behind the spoon, and a piece of fruit in the final corner. Michael chose a tray with muesli and a banana on it, more out of habit than anything else, placed it on the nearest table and sat down.

James Hetherington filled his mind, as he had done in every waking moment since he had seen the boy's hazel eyes stare out of that CCTV footage. Which was almost every moment of the sleepless night he had just had.

Hetherington had turned the journalist into a killer, he was sure of it. The cameras hadn't seen what had gone on under the bridge by the canal, but Michael didn't need to see a video to know what happened. The boy had used his perception on Oscar Elkins. Perhaps he caught his attention first, by asking something crass, like if he had the time. Then, when the journalist stopped, the boy slipped into his mind and took control. He found a way into his subconscious and planted a series of instructions. They would have been simple: *Slip the poison into Rublev's tea when he is not looking and make sure he drinks it.*

Perhaps Elkins resisted, knowing somewhere deep down that what he was being asked to do was wrong, but Hetherington would have perceived it. He would have reassured the journalist, maybe told him that the radioactive isotope was really a lump of sugar that would sweeten the tea the way the Russian liked it. And, because Elkins hadn't expected to be invaded by a perceiver on the day he walked along by the canal, he would have accepted the explanation. Because no one stops a stranger and asks them to poison someone, it's unthinkable.

The instructions would have sat in a dark corner of Elkins's mind, like a subroutine in a computer, waiting to be triggered. To anyone looking in from the outside, they would see nothing had changed. They would see a journalist on his way to interview a Russian dissident, like he had interviewed so many other political refugees in London over the years. Until Elkins sat opposite Rublev and a waiter brought them tea, activating the subroutine. The touchpaper was lit and the fuse burned, wiping out all memory as a fire swept through Elkins's consciousness. It left no trace, other than a memory gap that Elkins couldn't explain and only another perceiver could see.

Hetherington had pushed him into committing murder, a slow painful murder that ate a man from the inside until he was sent gasping to his death.

Like he had pushed the members of his gang to strip Michael naked, tie him to a chair and leave him to burn.

Hetherington was the power behind Tyler and Bailecki. He had made Bailecki carry explosives to a hotel and kill himself for a cause he didn't even know. A job, perhaps, that Tyler was originally supposed to do before he was arrested.

Michael looked up from his tray of muesli to see other perceivers had started to come in for breakfast. One of them was Alex. Michael perceived his far-too-awake-for-that-time-of-the-morning cheerfulness before he saw his shape among the other grey-clad teenagers.

"Morning!" said Alex as he passed Michael's table. "Didn't your mother tell you not to play with your food?"

Michael looked down at his muesli. There were tracks in the cereal where he'd twirled his spoon around in the bowl subconsciously while thinking about Hetherington.

Alex collected his own tray and brought it over to the table. "Am I early or are the people with the coffee late?"

Michael looked around. Normally, a delegation from the catering corps brought over urns of tea and coffee for the morning meal, as part of an arrangement to keep perceivers out of the mess hall and out of the way of regular soldiers. The corps were uncharacteristically late. Not that Michael cared.

"Can we talk?" he asked Alex.

"Sure!" Alex poured milk over his bowl full of cornflakes.

"Not here." Michael kept his voice low.

"After breakfast," said Alex. "Should have five minutes before roll call."

Michael didn't respond. He sat impatiently, allowing his emotion to bypass his filters.

Alex perceived him. "You mean *now*?" he said. "Right *now*? Before breakfast *now*?"

"Outside," said Michael. "Away from the other minds." He stood.

Alex frowned and allowed his spoon to fall back into his cornflakes. "You're definitely going to owe me a favour," he said. He grabbed the orange from his tray and got up from his chair. He paused for a moment, swiped the banana off Michael's tray, and joined him as he headed for the door.

As Michael and Alex were leaving the dining area, Pauline was arriving for breakfast. She looked different with her hair pulled tight away from her face and tied in a scrunched up ball at the back of her head. If it hadn't been for the familiar perception of her personality, Michael might not have recognised her in the grey uniform that they all wore.

But Pauline was perceiving them too and she could tell something was going on. "Where are you off to?"

"For a walk," said Michael.

"Can I come?" she said.

"No," said Michael.

"If you like," said Alex.

Michael shot Alex a reproachful glance.

"Great!" said Pauline.

Michael would have thought of some appropriate words for Alex to perceive if he didn't think that Pauline would perceive them too. It wasn't that he didn't like her — in fact, he liked Pauline a lot — but he wanted to share his theory with an experienced perceiver.

It was too late, however, and Pauline tagged along as they left Galen House into the haze of the spring morning. Only a month ago, it would have been dark at that time, but now the few street lights that glowed were superfluous in the early daylight, which would have been bright if it wasn't for the fog which had descended over the camp. It made Michael shiver, and he realised that coming out in a T-shirt hadn't been the best plan.

The complex was already busy with soldiers going from one building to another on whatever business they were on. The threesome were almost run over by the catering van as it careered round the corner, bringing freshly made coffee and tea to Galen House. Alex let the mournful thought *coffee* slip from his mind as they walked past it. Michael and Pauline chuckled.

After only a minute, they had left the activity behind to enter the quiet of the car park. The army vehicles — jeeps and personnel carriers — sat like khaki standing stones: cold, still and damp in the morning fog. Michael led the way past them to where Hodges always parked his vehicle, pulling out the keys from his pocket as they got near.

"Are we having the meeting in your office?" asked Alex.

"Something like that," said Michael. He pressed the button on the remote and the car unlocked itself.

"Bagsie sitting in the front!" declared Alex, like an excited five-year-old. He was at the passenger door and opening it before anyone could object. "You two can sit in the back."

"Oh we can, can we?" said Michael.

Alex grinned. He didn't let out any thoughts from behind his perception barriers, but he didn't have to. He was an incorrigible matchmaker.

Pauline shivered as she reached for the door handle. Not because she was uncomfortable about the idea, but because she was cold. She was thinner than the other two and goose pimples had appeared on her bare arms.

"Hodges keeps a blanket in the boot," said Michael.

He opened the boot and found Hodges kept a lot of stuff in there, including a bottle of spare screen wash, jump leads, a tyre iron and a spare set of clothes. It wasn't so much a car boot as a cupboard. Michael retrieved the blanket and passed it to Pauline who was now sitting in the back of the car. She wrapped it around her shoulders and draped the ends over her knees, as he got into the seat beside her. He wanted to shuffle up to sit closer and to feel her body warmth next to his, but self-control stopped him.

"As snug as a bug in a rug," said Alex who was kneeling up in the front passenger seat, facing backwards so he could see their faces. He still held the orange and banana in each hand.

"Who you calling a bug?" said Pauline.

"Michael, obviously," said Alex, with another one of his grins.

He looked at the two pieces of fruit, turned round for a second to put the banana on the dashboard, then turned back again and dug a thumbnail into the orange peel. A tiny spray of juice spat out to the side and the smell of citrus filled the car. "So," said Alex. "What's on that very perceptive mind of yours?"

Now that they were all sitting in the car and the other two were looking at him, Michael wasn't sure what to say. Alex kept peeling his orange, making Michael feel hungry.

"Did you find out any more about that perceiver who fudged his paperwork at the cure programme?" said Pauline.

"Who's this?" said Alex, opening the passenger door window just a crack and posting his orange peel through it so it fell to the ground.

"James Hetherington," said Michael. "Yeah, I did."

"Well?" said Pauline.

Michael took a moment. He wasn't quite sure how it say it. Saying it, rather than thinking it, made it somehow more real. "I think he used his perception to kill people."

He perceived their shock and their scepticism. He would have thought the same if he hadn't been inside the heads of those Hetherington had manipulated.

"Perception doesn't kill people," said Alex.

"Like guns don't kill people," said Michael. "It's what you do with them that makes the difference."

"Is that what you were talking about before?" said Pauline. "That there's more to perception than they're telling us."

Michael nodded. "I think this kid goes into people's heads and programs them to commit murder or kill themselves."

"Why would he do that?" said Pauline.

"He likes the power it gives him," said Michael. "From what little I was able to perceive I got the impression he loves controlling his little gang. It makes him feel superior."

"It's not possible, Mike," said Alex, separating a segment of orange from the rest of the fruit. "Our power is, like, passive. We sense minds, we don't control them." He popped the piece of orange into his mouth and chewed.

"You've never heard of anyone using their perception for anything else?" said Michael.

"No," said Alex. "Have you?"

"Yes, for the cure," said Michael.

Alex stopped chewing. Pauline continued to watch. Both were intrigued.

"You don't know how they cure perceivers, do you?" said Michael.

"Of course we do," said Pauline from under her blanket. "It's an injection."

"That's what they tell people." Michael looked at both of them, realising neither of them knew the truth. "The injection is a sedative. It helps to stop people resisting the real treatment. Once the person is docile, two other perceivers go inside their mind and cut off that part of the brain which allows perception to happen."

"No," said Alex. "Mike, you're wrong. The cure's been around for, like, more than two years. If that was the case, we'd know by now."

"Do you think so?" said Michael. "With everything you know about the army and the intelligence services, do you think they would let out that sort of information? Parents are willing to let their children have an injection if it will make them 'normal', but letting someone inside their brain …?"

"Is that what your mother told you?" said Pauline.

She did, but Michael didn't want to say in front of Alex.

"Okay," said Alex. "So say that's true, what's that got to do with killing people?"

"It means there's more to perception than they're telling us," said Michael. "If you can close off perception by going into someone's mind, maybe you can do other things too. Things that no one has tried yet, or things that only strong perceivers can do. Most perceivers either get cured before they master their power or they get sent here like us and get trained so they never find out."

"I still think it's far-fetched," said Alex.

Michael sighed. He couldn't disagree with Alex, it did sound far-fetched. But that's why he wanted to talk it through with him. "The Hetherington kid was strong. As strong as me. Maybe that's why he can do things that we never thought of. Maybe he would have been a natural born if his mother hadn't taken the pill, and maybe the combination of the two allowed his power to be even greater. I don't know…"

"We should try it out," said Pauline. "On a norm. See if we can get inside their head and make them do stuff."

"Kill people?" said Alex in alarm.

"No!" said Pauline. "Something safe. Like, I don't know, flashing their naked bottom at Sergeant Macaulay."

"Norm the Norm?" Alex laughed. "I'd love to see his face."

Michael felt a familiar presence at the edge of his perception. "Hodges," he said.

"Brilliant idea," said Alex. "We could get him to do it."

"Not what I meant," said Michael.

There was a knock on the passenger car window and Alex jumped so much he dropped his orange over the back of the chair. It hit Michael on the toe and bounced off under the driver's seat.

Hodges was outside the car, looking inside with disapproval. "I hope you're going to clear up all this orange peel on the ground before you leave," he said.

Alex wound open the window fully and looked down at the mess he had created. "I was trying not to drop litter in the car."

"Hmm," said Hodges. He leant through the window and saw Michael sitting in the back seat. "I didn't give you a set of keys so you could have a picnic in here with your friends."

"Sorry," said Michael. "We wanted somewhere private to have a meeting."

"A meeting about what?" said Hodges.

"Something you could help us with," said Alex.

"No," said Michael. There was a reason he had a personal vow to stay out of Hodges's head and he wasn't about to break it.

"Yes," said Alex. "You want to help us, don't you, Mr Hodges?"

"If I can," he said.

"No, it's all right," Michael told him. "We'll find someone else."

"To do what?" said Hodges. "You know, if you're up to something and I don't report it, it could get me into trouble. So you might as well tell me what it is."

"Okay," said Michael. "But you don't have to do it if you don't want to."

"Try me," said Hodges.

SEVENTEEN

HODGES stood in the car park as the sun burnt off the last of the early morning fog and highlighted the imperfections in the tarmac. Alex leant on the bonnet of the car about two metres away, brushing the grit and dirt from what was left of the orange he had dropped in the footwell. Pauline sat on the back seat with the door open and her legs swinging outside. She had let the blanket drop from her shoulders so it lay on her lap where she could keep her hands and forearms warm.

Michael stood centimetres from Hodges, his eye line level with the knot of the tie of his chauffeur. "Are you sure about this?" he said.

"Better that I do it than someone else," replied Hodges.

"I promise not to do anything else when I'm in there."

"I trust you, Michael."

Michael wasn't sure Hodges was right to trust him. He had only ever used his perception to look inside other people's minds and never to alter them. It was an untried procedure on a norm who didn't have the mental capacity to resist a perceiver's power. If something went wrong, it was Hodges's mind that was at risk.

"Alex, can you monitor me?" Michael asked.

"Sure," said Alex. He stood up from his position resting against the car and handed the orange to Pauline, freeing himself of all distractions.

"Okay," said Michael to Hodges. "You shouldn't feel anything. But if you do, or if you're worried at any stage, just say and I'll stop. Alex will watch what I'm doing as a safeguard."

"It's fine, Michael. I'm ready." The man took a deep breath and Michael perceived his nervousness. So, he wasn't as confident as he pretended. And yet he was willing to put himself — to put his mind — in the care of a teenager. Michael realised he must have been a very brave soldier when he fought in Iraq.

Nervous himself, Michael slipped his thoughts into Hodges's thoughts, sensing that Alex was there also, silently perceiving. Hodges was thinking about his day — checking in with Sergeant Macaulay, filling the car with petrol and other apparently trivial chores — in the hope that he could get back home in time to catch the Arsenal football game on the telly at seven o'clock. Michael smiled to himself, it was all very normal stuff. He pushed those surface thoughts aside and went in deeper.

It was dark inside Hodges's mind. The scars of post-traumatic stress and a broken relationship had left their mark. Beneath the cheery, optimistic exterior of his personality were pockets of depression and regions of pain hidden away in little clusters. Michael skirted around them, not wanting to reawaken any of the man's demons.

Michael rested inside Hodges's consciousness, getting a feel of his mind, almost as if constructing a map of his brain. Usually, if he was going in deep, Michael would aim for the section where memories were stored, causing neurons to fire and bring them to a place where he could read them. But this was different. He had to find somewhere to hide a set of instructions, somewhere where he wouldn't be detected, a place where those instructions would lay dormant until activated. Like walking into a person's room and planting a loaded gun in a forgotten drawer.

Hodges's forgotten drawer lay just behind his thoughts about the day. It was the perfect place to hide a little subroutine. Like planting a gun, he would have to do it secretly, putting back everything where he found it and wiping down his fingerprints on the way, so it appeared that nothing had been disturbed.

A moment's apprehension made him pause. Michael suddenly realised he was not prepared. It was only minutes since he and his friends had formulated the idea. He should have made more of an effort to plan what he was going to do, to work out every possibility in meticulous detail. But Hodges had been there, offering up his mind for experimentation and Michael decided to go for it. Perhaps it was a foolhardy decision.

In his hesitation, Michael's concentration faltered.

Hodges gasped.

Michael perceived his shock, and steadied his mind. He focussed his perception so it lay undetected in the subconscious area of Hodges's brain. "Are you all right?" he whispered to Hodges.

"Yes," said Hodges. "Just a twinge."

Michael decided to plant the instructions and get out.

Rather than constructing a new routine in Hodges's mind, he decided to attach his instructions to one that already existed: Hodges's plan to fill up the car with petrol. Michael's plan was simple, to add a couple of commands to his habit of driving to the petrol pump, checking the gauge was at zero before starting to fill, paying at the kiosk and trying to avoid the tempting chocolate bars on the counter. It was all so easy.

Michael pulled out his perception, steadily and gently so Hodges didn't feel a thing, wiping down his fingerprints as he left.

They faced each other on the tarmac of the car park, their minds separate again.

"Thank you," said Michael.

"What?" said Hodges. He looked around at his surroundings like a person who had just woken from sleepwalking.

"Michael!" he said, surprised to see him.

Michael perceived his confusion.

Hodges looked behind him and saw Alex standing there with Pauline sitting on the edge of the back seat of the car with a blanket on her lap and an orange in her hand. "I didn't give you a set of keys for the car so you could have a picnic with your friends," he said.

In his mind, it was like he had just arrived in the car park. And yet, he felt there was something out of place. The sun was higher in the sky than it should be and the air around him warmer.

Michael shivered at the thought that he might have wiped too much as he exited from Hodges's mind.

Pauline got up from her seat and threw Alex's orange like a ball over to him. Alex turned and snatched the orange out of the air with the instinct of cricket player. Pauline folded the blanket into a neat square and walked over to where Hodges stood. "Thank you, Mr Hodges," she said, handing it to him. "We've got to go, we've got roll call. Come on Alex."

Alex took a couple of steps to catch up with her. They began the walk back towards Galen House, but Michael stayed for a moment: watching Hodges, perceiving him.

"Are you all right?" Michael asked.

"Of course," said Hodges. "Is there a reason I shouldn't be?"

"No," said Michael. "No reason at all."

MICHAEL, Alex and Pauline arrived back at Galen House just as the perceivers who had been to roll call were filing out of the building. Dodging the bodies, like fish trying to swim upstream, they didn't notice Norm the Norm standing there until the last minute. He had his arms folded and a scowl so severe it looked like his facial muscles were on steroids.

"YOU THREE!" he barked.

They stopped in their tracks. *Oh terrific*, said Michael's thoughts.

Where are we going to say we've been? thought Alex, deliberately meaning for the others to perceive.

We could say we were helping Hodges with the car, thought Pauline.

That's not going to work, thought Michael. *Hodges doesn't need any help, at least not from the three of us.*

We went for a run and got lost, suggested Alex.

We're not even out of breath! thought Pauline.

"WHERE THE HELL HAVE YOU BEEN?" Norm bellowed so loud, some of the other perceivers turned to look, then thought better of it, turned back and hurried away.

"We were—" began Pauline.

"I don't want to hear it!" said Norm.

Michael and Pauline were relieved at not having to lie, but Alex thought, *If he doesn't care, then we're really going to get it.*

"SARKIS!"

Pauline jumped at her name being bellowed at her.

"Toilet cleaning duty for you today."

"But sir, I'm supposed to have drill this morning," said Pauline.

"ARE YOU QUESTIONING MY ORDERS, SARKIS?"

"N-no, sir," she stammered. "Sorry sir."

"BUCKLEY!"

Alex jumped at his name, even though he'd intended not to.

"Toilet cleaning for you tomorrow. SANDERSON! You can do the day after."

"Yes, sir," said Alex.

"Yes, sir," said Michael. He cursed himself for being so stupid. They should have come back for roll call and picked another time to go into Hodges's head. Another day wasn't going to make any difference, and now he was going to lose a day with his head stuck down a bog cleaning off somebody else's poo.

"SARKIS, BUCKLEY — DISMISSED!"

Alex and Pauline turned abruptly and headed to their quarters. Michael took a step to join them.

"NOT YOU, SANDERSON!"

Michael stopped mid-stride, his stomach knotting itself in apprehension and lack of breakfast. He perceived the concern of his friends as they walked away.

"You're with me," Norm ordered.

Norm took long strides towards the stairs which led to his office, with Michael following behind, not understanding why his misdemeanour should be any worse than theirs. He tried to perceive the sergeant, but there was an old song going round in his head, masking his thoughts: *Daisy, Daisy, give me your answer do…*

It was a simple technique to block perception, especially if a perceiver was inexperienced or not very strong. Michael was neither of those and could, if he wanted, make the effort to perceive deeper, but reading the mind of a superior officer was against regulations and he didn't want to risk adding to the trouble he was already in.

He followed Norm up the stairs to the administration floor: *I'm half crazy all for the love of you…*

And into his office … *It won't by a stylish marriage …* with its window overlooking the landscaped grounds, giving him a bird's-eye view of everything going on below. … *I can't afford a carriage …* It was a spacious office, carpeted with solid furniture cleaned to military precision, and a bookshelf down one side full of hardcover military history books. … *But you'll look sweet, upon a seat …* It was plush surroundings for a man of limited rank, but it supposedly made up for being put in charge of a bunch of teenagers, most of whom had no real interest in soldiering. *Of a bicycle—*

The singing suddenly stopped.

Norm the Norm thought, *I must be far enough away now.*

Far enough away, Michael assumed, from the other perceivers. So it was *them* he was trying to mask his thoughts from, not Michael.

"Where is your phone, Sanderson?" said Norm, closing the door behind them.

"It got destroyed in the fire, sir," said Michael. "I haven't got a new one yet."

Norm nodded. The emotion Michael perceived from him was … sympathy. So unexpected, it took him a moment to be sure. "I thought you young people would be rushing out to get whatever new and shiny gadget is in this month."

"I have to claim on the insurance," said Michael. "I can't face the hassle at the moment."

"I understand," said Norm the Norm, with a nod. Then — totally unexpectedly — he put a reassuring hand on Michael's shoulder. "I know it must be difficult for you at the moment … with your father and everything."

"Yes, sir," said Michael, bemused.

"Even so, you should perhaps get yourself a new phone."

"Yes, sir."

Sympathy did not come easy for the commanding officer, and yet it was there in his thoughts. Norm let his hand drop from Michael's shoulder and he walked round to the back of his desk.

Michael had been ordered up to the office before when he was in trouble. He knew the drill: Norm would sit down in his large leather chair and lean back while Michael stood to attention and listened to everything he had done wrong, followed by the punishment details he would have to complete. But this time, Norm did not sit. He picked up the receiver from the landline telephone on his desk and dialled a number. It was only four digits and, therefore, an internal extension. In the quiet of the office, it was possible to hear the ringing at the other end, and it being answered. "This is Sergeant Macaulay," he told the person down the line. "Can you get that call back for me please?"

A tinny voice replied through the receiver, "Yes, sir." Norm replaced the receiver.

He turned to Michael. "When it rings, it'll be for you. But this is the last time I act as your personal telephone service. Do you understand, Sanderson?"

"Yes, sir," said Michael. "Sorry, sir." Not really sure what he was apologising for.

Norm left the office and closed the door behind him.

Alone, and feeling a little exposed, not sure whether to look out the window, browse the bookshelves or just stand to attention, he wished he'd made more of an effort to perceive Norm to find out what the hell was going on.

He jumped as the phone rang. He composed himself as it rang once more, then answered. "Hello?"

"Michael?" It was a woman's voice.

"Yes."

"At last! I've been trying to ring you."

She sounded familiar, but because he couldn't perceive her, he wasn't quite sure who it was. "Sorry," he said. "My phone got damaged."

"No wonder it keeps going to voicemail."

There was something about the way she said 'voicemail' that clicked with his memory. "Doctor Page?"

"I wanted to tell you I've been doing a bit of digging into Doctor Saul Lucas," she said, not acknowledging his question, although it was definitely her.

It took a moment for Michael to remember. "Oh, the man who fudged the cure records."

"That's him," said Page. "He was substantially over-qualified to be working in a cure clinic, especially as all he was doing was overseeing injections. Normally that role is given to a nurse. But Lucas has a medical degree and a specialism in neuroscience. He worked in research for many years before he got a job with us."

"So what was he doing at a cure clinic?" said Michael.

"I've been thinking about that," said Page. "At first I assumed that, as a neuroscientist, he was interested in researching perception, but it must have been obvious even before he took the job that he's not going to find out anything by injecting a load of teenagers in the arm. So it has to be something to do with that Hetherington kid. As far as I can work out, Lucas quit the job as soon as he forged the records to say Hetherington had been cured."

"That doesn't explain why."

"As far as I can figure out, there are two possibilities," said Page. "He might have been at the clinic purely to save Hetherington from the cure for some reason — the boy might have been his nephew, the son of a friend, or someone paid him to do it. The other possibility is that he wanted a perceiver for his own research. Hetherington came along, Lucas somehow knew he had strong powers, realised he could work with the boy and so he forged the database and the kid officially became a norm."

"Why would he be researching perceivers?" said Michael.

"You'd have to perceive him to find that out," said Page. "Or maybe you could get your police friends to ask him."

"I suppose," said Michael, trying to think how the hell he was going to explain all this to Jones and Patterson. "Do you know where Doctor Lucas is now?"

"He went off the radar as far as the neurological research community is concerned. He hasn't published any papers or anything, but he does seem to be working out of a private lab at UCL. I can text you the details."

"I haven't got a phone," he reminded her.

"Well, maybe you can write it down. Do young people still know how to use a pen and paper?"

"Ha ha." Michael grabbed a piece of paper from Norm's desk. It was a uniform requisition form which was blank on the back. He turned it over and found a pen. "Okay, I'm ready."

Michael wrote, in unpractised spidery writing, the address of Lucas's lab at the Andrew Huxley Building at University College London on Euston Road.

"While I've got you on the phone, Michael, I know you don't like talking about it, but have you thought any more about seeing your father?"

Michael frowned. "I've been busy."

"He might not be a free man for much longer," she said. "I don't mean to pressure you, but …"

So that's why Norm the Norm had been hiding his thoughts from the other perceivers. He believed Page's call was about his father, something he knew Michael didn't want the others at Galen House to know about. It was the sort of consideration he never thought Norm the Norm would have.

"I'll think about it," said Michael.

"Good," said Page, and paused. "Well anyway, I hope that information on Lucas helps."

"Yeah, it might. Thanks."

"Goodbye then, Michael."

"Bye." He put the receiver back down on the phone base.

It was suddenly quiet in Norm's office. He read the piece of paper with the address of Lucas's lab one more time, then folded it up and put it away in his pocket.

THE boots of five soldiers stomped on the surface of the road, the simultaneous clap of rubber soles sounding out across the camp. Everyone who turned their head to look knew they were perceivers because of the grey uniforms they wore and because they were so young compared to regular soldiers. The uneven-numbered troops looked lopsided without Pauline taking up the sixth position at the rear. Not as if the drill sergeant seemed to care as he marched behind them, shouting, "LEFT! LEFT! LEFT!" to keep them in step.

Michael stopped just outside the entrance to Galen House and watched them pass. In front of him was Alex, changed into a civilian shirt and tie with his jacket hung over one arm. Waiting to be picked up. "Do you remember that?" he said.

"God, yes," said Michael. They were often made to go out and perform marching drills, even now after basic training was over, but he knew what Alex meant. He meant that first shock of arriving in the Perceivers Corps and being treated like army recruits.

"I don't get the point of it, I really don't," said Alex. "I mean, what does it matter if I'm out of step? I'm still going to get wherever it is we're going."

Michael chuckled.

"What?"

"Pauline said something similar."

The sound of marching boots became distant and the five perceivers with their shouting soldier chaperone disappeared around some trees, heading towards the parade ground.

"What did Norm the Norm want?" said Alex.

"I had a phone call." Michael let his discomfort about talking about it slip through his perception filters on purpose, suggesting that Alex shouldn't probe any further. "You in court today?" he said, changing the subject.

"Yeah, not as if my perception is going to be any use. The pathologist is giving evidence. The guy was beaten to death with a hammer, I don't think she's likely to lie about it."

"If I wanted to go to court," said Michael, "how easy is it to get in?"

"If you commit a crime and get caught, dead easy."

"No!" Michael nudged Alex in the ribs. "To watch. Like, you know, a member of the public?"

"You just walk into the public gallery. It's a principle of the legal system that people should be able to see justice being done."

"Even at the Old Bailey?"

A moment of understanding passed across Alex's mind. "You want to see the perceivers trial."

"What's wrong with that?" said Michael, suddenly feeling defensive.

"Nothing. I thought you weren't interested, that's all."

"I might have changed my mind. I haven't decided yet."

"It's likely to be packed and the press are all over that case," said Alex. "You're better off watching it on the television. Reporters are going to look at any teenagers who turn up and wonder if they're perceivers."

The sound of an approaching car engine caused Alex to look up. A black Audi A4 was driving towards them. For a moment, Michael thought it might be Hodges, but the number plate was different and the driver was a woman. "This is my ride," said Alex.

The car drew up to the kerb. Alex opened the back door and threw in his jacket. He was about to get in when Michael stopped him. He'd seen another black car enter the camp, and this one had the right number plate.

"Hodges," said Michael.

"Is he …?" said Alex. *Doing what you programmed him to do?*

"I think so," said Michael. "I'm not sure." He tried perceiving Hodges, but at a distance, in a moving car with other people around, it wasn't easy.

They both watched as Hodges approached and pulled up at the kerb in front of Alex's car. Hodges unclipped his seatbelt, reached over for something in the passenger seat and got out of the driver's door. In his hand was a large bunch of flowers, with blooms of red, yellow and purple arching out of their cellophane wrapper on fresh green stalks.

Alex's chauffeur wound down her window and shouted at Hodges. "Hey, you can't park there!"

He ignored her, shut the door behind him and headed towards the entrance of Galen House.

Alex turned to Michael. "This is it?"

"Yeah," he said, suddenly apprehensive.

Alex leant into the car. "I'll deal with this, I won't be a minute."

"We need to leave soon," said his chauffeur. "Or we'll get stuck in traffic."

Alex barely heard her as he and Michael followed Hodges inside the building.

It was just their luck that Norm the Norm was heading to the stairs that led to his office at the same time as Hodges was walking in the other direction. The sight of a man in a suit striding towards him with a bunch of flowers was too much for Norm to ignore.

"Mr Hodges?" said Norm. "What are you doing?"

"I'm looking for Pauline Sarkis," said Hodges.

"She's on toilet cleaning duty," said Norm, "but—"

"Thank you, Sergeant," said Hodges and walked straight off towards the living quarters, the flowers nodding their red, yellow and purple heads in unison with his movement. Michael tried to perceive him, even though he was retreating. He caught only one thought: *this way*.

He and Alex followed, perceiving Norm's curious glance as he watched them from the foot of the stairs.

"What's Hodges doing?" whispered Alex.

"What I asked him to, I hope," said Michael.

Into the corridor that led to the perceiver quarters, he walked past locked bedroom door after locked door. His mind said only one thing, *this way*, before he branched off into a corridor that led to the washrooms. At the end was a door with a sign indicating the room beyond was only meant for girls. Hodges continued regardless, pushing the door which swung open wide enough for him and the flowers to pass through untouched.

Michael went to follow, but Alex put out a hand to stop him. "That's the women's," he said.

"Not scared of women are you?" said Michael, pushing Alex's hand aside and stepping forward.

Damp hung in the room and, with it, the perfume of half a dozen shampoos and soaps. Extractor fans struggled to suck out the moisture caused by the morning showers and cleansing routines of the female perceivers. Michael hadn't been in there before and it struck him that it was very much like the men's washroom, except where Michael was used to seeing a line of urinals there was another row of sinks.

Ahead of them, Hodges walked down the line of toilet cubicles, slamming his hand against each one so it swung open to reveal no one inside. At the end, he moved onto the showers, looking inside each one until he confirmed they were all empty. He about-turned and walked back the way he had come, directly towards Michael and Alex.

"What's he doing?" Alex asked.

Michael's perception found nothing in Hodges's head other than a couple of phrases: *not in here … this way.*

Michael pulled Alex out of the way as Hodges headed straight for the door. He didn't even acknowledge they were there.

"His mind is … *blank*," said Alex.

"Like they all were," said Michael.

They followed Hodges back out into the corridor and to the men's washroom. Like before, he walked down the line, pushing open all the cubicle doors.

At the third one, he stopped.

Michael drew up behind him, with Alex at his back. They saw Hodges had found Pauline, kneeling beside the toilet bowl with her hair untidily tied back from her haggard face, yellow rubber gloves up to her elbows, a cloth in her hand and a bucket of greenish cleaning fluid next to her.

Hodges put his free hand behind his back like a waiter and bowed towards her, holding out the bunch of flowers. "For you, Miss."

Michael perceived her surprise and embarrassment as she took the flowers and tried to think of something to say.

With that, Hodges stood up straight and turned to walk out. Michael and Alex stumbled backwards out of the way as, without so much a glance in their direction, he continued out of the washroom.

Pauline, on her knees, peered around the cubicle door to watch him. "What was that about?" she said.

"That's what Michael programmed him to do," said Alex. "Right?"

Pauline blushed. She tried to hide her self-consciousness behind her filters, but she wasn't practiced enough to shield a sudden emotion.

"Yeah," said Michael.

"What happened to flashing his naked bottom at Norm the Norm?" she said.

"I thought this was less likely to get him fired." But even as he was talking to Pauline, he was worrying about Hodges. He'd perceived him as he passed and the blankness in his mind was still — worryingly — present. "Look, I'll see you later, okay?"

Michael rushed after Hodges.

"What do I do with these?" Pauline called after him.

He glanced back to see her holding up the bunch of flowers like the statue of liberty — a messy version of the statue of liberty who was in the middle of cleaning toilets. "Put them in water," he said.

Michael caught up with Hodges as he left the accommodation wing, striding as purposefully as the perceivers he'd seen marching towards the parade ground.

Norm was standing pretty much where they had left him, a hand resting on the rail of the stairs as he looked out onto the communal space of Galen House with a sense that he wasn't quite as in control as a commanding officer should be.

"Mr Hodges!" Norm called.

"Morning, Sergeant," said Hodges, as he approached like everything was perfectly normal.

"Mr Hodges, what are you doing?"

"I have to take Michael to his assignment," said Hodges. "Why, is there something else you want me to do?"

Michael smiled. He perceived Hodges's mind was back to normal, full of thoughts about the best route to go to avoid the traffic, whether it would be warm enough in the car to take off his jacket and why the sergeant was glowering at him with such an annoyed expression.

Norm the Norm appeared to have no retort and stood, gripping tightly to the handrail, as Hodges passed him.

He still had that annoyed expression as he watched Michael follow. "Sanderson?" he asked.

"Sorry, sir," said Michael. "I really wanted to give a girl a bunch of flowers."

EIGHTEEN

THE security guard at the Andrew Huxley Building at UCL rang ahead to inform Doctor Saul Lucas that he had a visit from the police. So it was a smiling and nervous Doctor Saul Lucas who answered his door to Michael and Sergeant Patterson.

With only a few dark strands in his otherwise white hair, he was an older man in his fifties with black-rimmed, square-lensed glasses that dominated his face. He looked every bit the scientist with a pristine white lab coat buttoned up so there was very little of his shirt and trousers visible underneath. "Come in, come in …"

He ushered Patterson and Michael inside to what was not really a laboratory or an office, but a strange mixture of the two. Down one side was a bench crammed with scientific equipment, some bits of which Michael recognised like the centrifuge, microscope and rack of pipettes, as well as some bits he didn't. Two stools, much like bar stools, were tucked under the bench at the near end, while at the far end a glass-fronted fridge quietly rumbled to keep cool its contents of neatly labelled test tubes. Next to it was a standard desk with computer, telephone and a mass of papers which didn't look so much piled up, as discarded on its surface. Above it, on the wall, was a corkboard literally covered with pieces of paper pinned on top of each other. To Michael's untrained eye, the spreadsheets of numbers and graphs meant nothing, although there were also a few colour pictures which he recognised as MRI brain scans.

"Welcome to my humble abode," said Doctor Lucas, sitting down behind his desk in the one and only chair in the room. He leant back as casually as if it had been a sofa.

He didn't, however, offer anyone else a seat. Michael perceived that Patterson didn't think that was very welcoming, but it was fine, as he felt more in control if he could stand. Michael, meanwhile, perched himself up on one of the stools.

"What can I do for the Metropolitan Police today?" said Lucas.

Patterson got out his phone and brought up an image of James Hetherington. It was a couple of years out of date because it had been pulled from school records, but it was a good likeness. "What can you tell me about this boy?"

Lucas leant forward, peering at Patterson's phone first with his glasses on, then pushing his glasses up onto his forehead to stare with naked eyes. The picture gave him a sting of recognition: *James Hetherington*, said his mind, but his body language said the opposite as he sat back in his chair and shook his head. "I'm sorry, I don't know him."

"His name is James Hetherington," said Patterson.

"Really?"

"He was a perceiver who you signed off after being cured."

"Was he?" said Lucas. His mind was racing, trying to work out what the police knew, what they wanted to know and how he could deflect their interest. "That was a long time ago, Sergeant Patterson, I can't possibly remember every child I saw."

"It was only a year ago."

"Really? It was a blip in my career, I've mostly forgotten about it."

"Why were you working at the cure clinic, Doctor Lucas? It seems a strange thing for a neuroscientist to be doing."

Lucas dodged the question with one of his own. "Have you ever worked in science, Sergeant Patterson?"

Patterson grimaced at his facetious question. "Funnily enough, I haven't."

Lucas smiled, calming himself with the belief he was steering the policeman away from the sort of questions he didn't want to answer. "Scientific research is all about chasing grants. Writing proposals to get the money to carry out the research that you want to carry out, constantly under pressure to publish papers to show your research is garnering results in order to keep getting the grants so you can keep working. Unfortunately, a year ago, I entered a dry patch. No one wanted to pay for neuroscience research and I needed the work. The cure clinics were hiring and so I got a job there, but it's not something I put on my CV. I'd be grateful if you didn't mention it to my colleagues."

"Of course," said Patterson. "It's just that this boy, James Hetherington, wasn't cured at all. He's still a perceiver. Do you know anything about that?"

Lucas shook his head again, but inside he was panicking. He needed to find out what the policeman knew, but without tipping his hand. And he needed to warn the boy, to call him as soon as the police were out of his office. Except, *what if they'd tapped his phone? What if they got a warrant to search his office?* He needed to get rid of them, and get rid of them soon. "I don't know anything about that, I'm afraid," said Lucas. "I just administered the injections, I didn't monitor if they were effective or not. Perhaps you should address your questions to the people who run the cure programme."

"Of course," said Patterson, playing the man at his own game, stringing him along by acting ignorant. "It's just that your name was on the form and I needed to start somewhere."

"I understand," said Lucas, getting up from his chair and walking over to Patterson as if to show him out. "As I say, I gave the injections and signed the form. I don't even remember this boy. Sorry you had a wasted journey."

Michael jumped off his stool. As they were talking and he was perceiving them, he was also looking at the images on the wall. Especially one particular brain scan with a large area lit up in red. "Isn't that the area where perception is active?" he said.

"What?" said Lucas.

"That area of the brain," said Michael, approaching the scan on the pin board. "Isn't that the bit that lights up in perceivers?"

Lucas, disgruntled at having his efforts to get the police contingent out of his lab interrupted, viewed the scan with a cursory look. "That's the primary somatic sensory cortex," he said. "I think that scan was taken when the subject was eating chocolate and listening to Mozart."

"I thought it only lit up like that in a perceiver," said Michael, knowing his own brain was lighting up at that very moment as he perceived Lucas was lying. He noticed that, on the bottom of the scan was printed a date which showed it was taken three months earlier and there was a subject code which said simply: 'E48'.

"I wouldn't know," said Lucas. "It's been a long time since I read about that area of research." *Who is this kid?*

"What *is* your area of research?" asked Michael.

Lucas turned to Patterson. "Sergeant, are these questions really necessary? I have a report to write and I'm close to my deadline."

Another lie. It meant Lucas really didn't want Michael poking around in his lab, which only gave him the incentive to poke around some more.

Now closer to the desk, Michael cast his eye over the scattered papers. There were more spreadsheets, pages of hand-written notes that he couldn't easily decipher and one cardboard file which he desperately wanted to look inside because it had the code E48 typed on the cover.

"I'm just interested," said Michael, turning to look at the bench of the lab, still not recognising any of the equipment beyond the centrifuge, microscope and pipettes.

"If you must know," said Lucas, his irritation starting to show in his voice. "I'm looking into neurological development in adolescents and its possible application in the treatment of dementia."

Michael crouched down in front of the fridge. Now that he could see directly through the glass door, he realised the test tubes inside were actually vials of liquid, some of it clear and some blood red.

"No, not in there!" Lucas rushed over as Michael touched the handle of the fridge. "The temperature is strictly controlled. It should only be opened if absolutely necessary."

There was an element of truth to what Lucas was saying, but Michael perceived he was also afraid of Michael finding out what the fridge contained. Each blood sample was labelled with a date and a code, many of which read E48. Lucas stepped in front of the fridge, blocking his view and forcing him to drop his grip on the handle. Just before he did so, Michael read the label on a vial of blood on the top shelf. The date was the day of the fire that nearly killed him and the label did not contain a code, but a name in quotation marks: 'Michael'.

Michael felt a chill run through him as he stepped back from the fridge and away from the scientist. Was that what the man was hiding? Samples of his own blood kept ready to be experimented on? He remembered the stab of the needle in the derelict office and the way Hetherington had stared at him with cold, hazel eyes.

"Now I must insist you leave," said Lucas. "I really have to write that report."

He really didn't, but Michael had perceived enough and joined Patterson at the door.

"Thank you for your time, Doctor Lucas," said Patterson and they left.

Out in the corridor, just far enough away so Lucas couldn't hear, Michael stopped. "He's lying," he said to Patterson.

"I figured," said the policeman.

"About a lot of things," said Michael.

PATTERSON and Michael joined Jones in his office and closed the door. Now that a perceiver was at the centre of their investigation, it was no longer appropriate to hold a briefing involving all of the officers working on the inquiry.

Jones didn't take a seat, but stood behind his desk, hands on his hips with the flaps of his jacket pushed back so the paunch of his stomach was visible hanging over the belt of his trousers. Michael perceived the man was worried, the investigation was slipping away from him, and the crazy secrets that surrounded the perceivers programme were hampering his ability to pull in all the resources he would usually employ.

Not Patterson. Patterson was excited. He stood on the other side of the desk, his eyes wide as he went through all the evidence in his head. Soon, he believed, they would have enough to make an arrest, if not several arrests.

Michael stood somewhere in the middle, both literally and figuratively. He was tired and wanted to sit down, but because the detectives were standing, he leant against the side wall of Jones's office, watching and perceiving them both in equal measure. He trusted the detectives to do their job, but he wasn't sure arresting people would be enough. If they caught Hetherington, they could charge him with something like conspiracy to murder, but they couldn't try him in open court without letting some very large and unpredictable cats out of the bag. They could hand him over to the cure programme and have him stripped of his perception, but all that would achieve would be to stop Hetherington doing it again. Michael wasn't sure that was enough. He also couldn't get the image out of his head of the vials of his blood in Lucas's fridge. He feared the whole thing was much larger than one boy pushing his will onto others.

"It's the Russians," Patterson announced.

"Russians?" said Jones.

"Tania's been working up some background on the case. It's sort of complicated, but—" Patterson looked around the office. "Have you got any paper?"

"Yeah," said Jones. He pulled out the tray of the printer on his desk and drew out a pristine white sheet.

"Perfect." Patterson laid it on the desk in front of him. Jones peered over his computer monitor to see.

Patterson reached for Jones's desk tidy and took the first pen his hand touched. It was a retractable biro. He clicked the top, revealing the tip, and wrote a large 'R' at the top left hand corner in faltering blue ink. He swore. He reached back to the desk tidy, fingered through the other pens and found one that was sleek, black and more to his liking. He pulled off the lid to reveal a fibre tip. He traced over the 'R', making a clear mark in black ink and continued with other letters until it read, 'Rublev'.

"We know Rublev was a Russian dissident, right?" He looked round the room to make sure the others were following. "Not exactly a popular guy with the current Russian administration. If anyone wanted him dead, it was them."

"Except we know he was killed — well, fatally poisoned — by a British journalist," said Jones.

"Elkins did the deed," said Patterson, "but like Michael said before, he might have been programmed to do it. I think the Russians were behind it."

"How do you work that out?" said Jones.

"I'm coming to that," said Patterson, letting it show that he was frustrated by the interruptions. "The bombing at the hotel we originally didn't think had a motive, just some mindless terrorism. But Tania looked closer into the conference that was taking place there, and it was a trade conference at which a prominent Russian delegate was present. This man, Pavlovsky—" he wrote 'Pavlovsky' under 'Rublev' on the piece of paper "—is also not very popular with the Russian administration. His companies are so successful he's using his money and influence to get his own way. So, from the Russian administration's point of view, how better to get rid of him than having him 'tragically' killed in a British terrorist atrocity?"

Patterson wrote 'Russia' in the middle of the paper, circled it, and drew arrows linking it to the names. "Michael thinks both of these assassinations and attempted assassinations were arranged by James Hetherington — that boy we saw meeting with Elkins on the CCTV."

"Yes," said Michael. "Hetherington is a perceiver. A strong one. I think he used his power to program Elkins and Bailecki to administer the poison and set off the bomb. Records show that he was cured of perception a year ago, but it seems those records were forged by Doctor Lucas."

"Who's Doctor Lucas?" said Jones.

Patterson was getting frustrated that his mind was racing faster than Jones could keep up. "We think he's what links the Hetherington boy with Russia." He wrote 'Hetherington' and 'Lucas' on the sheet of paper. "Lucas denied knowing Hetherington, but I showed the boy's picture to the security guard at the lab where he works and he confirmed he's one of Lucas's research subjects."

Jones looked at all the names written on the paper in front of him, and squinted as if that would help him understand better. "What's that got to do with Russia?"

"That's sort of speculation at the moment," said Patterson. "But Tania's been looking at the money trail and what she's found out so far looks interesting. Lucas has a lab at UCL, but it's actually rented by him privately by way of a grant he receives to carry out his work."

"Funded by Russia?" said Jones.

Patterson made an uncertain gesture with his hands. "We can't prove it — yet — the money comes from a corporation registered in the Philippines which we suspect is routing through money from the Russian government, possibly via several other countries."

Jones leant forward and plucked the pen from Patterson's hand. He drew an arrow from 'Russia' to 'Lucas', writing a pound symbol with a question mark above it.

Patterson grinned, seeing his boss was getting it. "The other interesting thing is that UCL entitles him to have sensitive parcels delivered by courier. Lucas is a neuroscientist who occasionally uses radioactive tracers when carrying out MRI brain scans. Obviously the ones they use in medicine don't kill people, but if you wanted a lethal dose of radiation delivered to you, what better way to disguise it than by having it shipped labelled as a medical-grade isotope?"

"So the Russians," said Jones, "could have arranged for a radioactive substance to be delivered to Lucas under the guise of hazardous medical supplies." He scrubbed over the arrow he had already drawn between Russia and Lucas and made it thicker. "Lucas gives the radiation to the perceiver boy." He drew an arrow from Lucas to Hetherington. "The boy gives it to Elkins and programs him to poison Rublev." Jones wrote the name Elkins in a space on the paper because they'd forgotten to do it earlier, and linked everyone up with arrows.

"That's about it in a nutshell. I suspect the same supply route and method was used to get explosives to Tyler and Bailecki," said Patterson. "Can I have my pen back, sir?"

"Sure," said Jones and handed over the black fibre tip.

Patterson added the names Tyler and Bailecki on what little space there was left and drew arrows from Russia to Lucas to Hetherington to Tyler and Bailecki, and finally to Pavlovsky. "Tyler was probably trying to blow up the hotel, but got arrested before he reached there. Bailecki obviously managed to blow himself up, but — if I'm right — missed his target."

"I wouldn't be surprised if some of that Russian money was paid to Hetherington," said Michael. "That's how he was able to give his gang all those shiny gadgets and new trainers to keep them loyal."

All three of them looked down at the piece of paper, a mess of names and arrows.

"That's a lot of supposition, but not a lot of evidence," said Jones. "I think you need to start bringing in a few people for questioning."

"Yes, sir," said Patterson. "Hetherington's gone AWOL, but I bet if we get Lucas in here, he should be able to lead us to the boy."

"Then you better get a move on," said Jones. "Before Lucas goes AWOL too."

NINETEEN

DOCTOR Saul Lucas did not wait around for the police to arrest him. By the time Sergeant Patterson and his team conducted dawn raids on Lucas's home and lab, he was gone. The officers were able to seize some of his computer and lab equipment, but the man himself had made a hasty escape. So it was a sweaty and frustrated Patterson who returned to the police station. He had no one to question and Michael was left with no one to perceive.

It left Michael at a bit of a loose end. As he sat around the police station, his mind went back to his telephone conversation with Doctor Page, and he began to think about his father.

SOME of the most despicable men and women ever to have lived in Britain had sat in the dock of Court One in the Old Bailey. The wood panelling that lined the four walls of the institution had absorbed the words of many murderers and rapists who had gone on trial in an attempt to persuade a jury of twelve of their peers that they were innocent of the crime of which they were accused. The men and women who prosecuted and defended the alleged criminals still wore the same costumes of black gowns and horsehair wigs that their forebears had worn down the centuries. It gave the court a sense of theatre: one where, at the end of the play, the curtain would come down in judgement on a person's life.

Michael watched from the front row of the public gallery, high up above the court like a theatre-goer who could only afford the cheap seats. On either side, pressed up so close on the bench that he could feel their body heat, were other members of the public. Three further packed rows sat behind him. Most of them were parents of perceivers, their anger so loud it crowded his perceptions. He blocked them all out and, at first, used only his eyes to observe the court.

That morning, Brian Ransom had been called to the witness stand. It was almost two years since Michael had seen him, but his father had aged far more than that. His hair, which once retained streaks of its original brown, was now almost entirely grey. His beard, although short and neatly trimmed, had become old and wiry. Even the way he stood was more slouched and stooped than Michael remembered him.

Ransom adjusted his jacket to make sure it sat squarely on his shoulders and prepared to be questioned.

The judge, a woman in gown and wig sitting alone at the head of the court on a raised bench above the other officials, spoke directly to him. "Can I remind you, Mr Ransom, that you are still under oath."

"Yes, Your Honour," said Ransom, his voice just strong enough to be picked up by the microphone on the stand in front of him, but still not easy to hear in the public gallery. Some of the shuffling of people sitting with Michael settled down as they strained to listen.

The judge addressed a barrister sitting below. "Mr Panich, you may continue your questioning."

"Thank you, Your Honour," said Panich, a man in his thirties or forties wearing a dark sombre suit beneath his gown. He stood and placed a folder of notes on a lectern in front of him. "You may remember in your testimony yesterday, Mr Ransom, that you admitted the so-called 'vitamin pills' that you distributed free to pregnant women were the cause of their children being changed at a genetic level in the womb. Is that correct, Mr Ransom?"

Ransom nodded. "It is, yes."

"Do you also accept that you lied to these women?"

"No, because the pills also contained vitamins," said Ransom.

Mr Panich smiled, as if it were funny. "But that is not the point, is it, Mr Ransom? The fact remains that you knew the mothers who took these pills would give birth to children who would, in time, go on to become perceivers."

"Yes," Ransom answered simply and directly.

"Then what do you say to the mother we heard testify, Mrs Croucher, whose daughter had to be cured of perception at the age of thirteen?"

"Giving perceivers a cure was not my idea," said Ransom.

"But it became necessary because you caused these children to be perceivers."

"No."

"I say it was, Mr Ransom. Your vitamin pills created a disease for which science had to find a cure. Do you not feel sorry for the people like Mrs Croucher's daughter who, we heard, was never the same after the cure?"

"It wasn't my intension to hurt anyone," said Ransom.

"You put a foetus-altering substance inside a pill and lied to pregnant women in order to make them take it — how could you possibly have expected that not to hurt anyone?"

"Perception should have been a gift," said Ransom, a little bit of passion now in his words. "We were living in a world of prejudice, of religious, racial and class intolerance. I believed, if only people could understand each other, *perceive* that we are all the same, then intolerance would be a thing of the past."

"So you admit you created the perceiver epidemic on purpose?"

"It's not an epidemic."

"You deliberately poisoned pregnant women. In the words of the charges against you, you 'administered a noxious substance with intent to cause bodily harm'. Is that not true, Mr Ransom?"

"No," he said, his voice clear and loud. "I created perception with intent to bring about a generation of enhanced people. To promote peace and understanding."

The underswell of disquiet around Michael erupted into a cry of, "Shame!" from behind him. Several others muttered approval at the woman's outburst.

The judge looked up at the public gallery with small, but fiercely disapproving eyes. She wasn't looking directly at Michael, but it felt like she was. He opened his perception just a little bit so he could reassure himself that her stare was directed to the woman behind. As he did so, his head was immediately filled with the tension. There were so many emotionally charged minds in the public gallery, and in the packed court below, that he could barely make out the judge among them.

In that moment, he felt a familiar presence at the edge of his perception. It was his father, instantly recognisable as the only other perceiver in the crowded courtroom. Ransom looked up at the public gallery and his gaze met that of his son.

Michael?

The word entered his head.

Yes, Michael replied with a single thought.

In that moment, he was able to filter out the jumble of other minds. They were still there, but if he concentrated hard he could reduce them to a background rumble. Pulling the perception of his father to the foreground, he perceived Ransom's nervousness. But there was also a fear, a fear that he would soon be sent to jail. He was happy to see Michael in the courtroom, but he also felt shame at being seen in such a situation.

While Michael perceived, the judge told members of the public that they must be quiet, or she would clear the public gallery.

I need to see you, Ransom thought.

How? thought Michael. There was no way down from the public gallery to the part of the building where the barristers, witnesses and defendants congregated; while meeting him at the entrance wasn't possible without being seen by the press and their cameras.

Warwick Lane, came Ransom's thoughts. *Where the taxis are.*

Michael had no idea where that was and he didn't get the opportunity to ask because court business was resuming.

"Please continue, Mr Panich," said the judge.

Michael felt Ransom retreat from his mind. Michael also withdrew his perception.

"Thank you, Your Honour," said Mr Panich and looked down at his notes on the lectern in front of him.

Ransom faced his questioner again: the man whose job it was to get him sent to jail.

THE security guard at the public entrance to the Old Bailey knew the way to Warwick Lane and gave Michael directions. It was literally just around the corner. Michael questioned whether it was too close to where the press were camping out to cover the perceivers trial, but apparently their cameras were only interested in capturing pictures of people going in and out of court, or if they decided to make a statement. The guard explained that, if someone decided against making a statement to the press, being chased down the road by a bunch of journalists and film crews wasn't going to change their minds.

Warwick Lane was a relatively quiet street off the main road. Not only devoid of the press and barristers, but also of much activity at all. While there was noise of central London close by, Warwick Lane itself was the conduit for only the occasional passing car.

There was a small layby outside one of the many grey block office buildings that lined the street with a couple of taxis parked up. Michael walked down to stand near them, wondering how long Ransom would be, and leant against the cold concrete of the building. He wished he had got around to sorting out his insurance and getting a new phone so he had something to distract himself while he waited.

It was as much as fifteen minutes before Ransom came round the corner. Michael saw him before he perceived him. He was actually smiling, an expression he had not worn on the news. Then, as Michael let the perceptions filter through, he felt his father's love. Stronger than he remembered it and enhanced by a loneliness drawn out by weeks of listening to people give witness against him.

"Michael!" Ransom said, as he got close enough. He held out his arms and Michael allowed himself to be hugged. He felt, under Ransom's suit, the bones of his rib cage press against him. He realised Ransom's clothes disguised how much weight he had lost during the trial. "It's good to see you."

Ransom released Michael and the pair of them stood back at a respectable distance from each other. Michael knew his father would perceive that his love was not reciprocated, but there was no point in blocking that from him. He already knew how Michael felt.

"Doctor Page said I should come," said Michael.

"Ah," said Ransom, smiling at the mention of her name. "That's the sort of thing Rachel would do."

"So, um …" Michael felt uncomfortable. Knowing that Ransom would perceive how uncomfortable he felt made it worse. He averted his eyes, looking at the ground where his feet kicked at an old cigarette butt someone had discarded. "How's it going?"

"My lawyers say I have a chance," said Ransom. "Although I perceive they're lying to me, so perhaps it's not going so good."

Michael nodded. "I've seen the news."

"Do you want to go for lunch or something?" said Ransom. "My lawyers usually get a taxi to whisk us off somewhere away from the press. I need to be back in court for two o'clock, though."

Michael wasn't hungry. His stomach didn't want food after being confronted by the hatred so many people had for his father. Again, as soon as he felt the emotion inside of him, he knew Ransom had perceived it. Instinctively, he increased his filters. He wanted to be open with his father, if this really was the last opportunity he would have to see him before he went to jail, but the reality was too painful.

"Maybe a coffee, then," said Ransom. "Let's at least get out of the street." He headed towards the first of the taxis in the queue.

"We're going to *drive* to a coffee shop?" said Michael in surprise.

"I know somewhere without lawyers or journalists. It's less than five minutes in a cab." He bowed down so his face was level with the open window of the first taxi in the row. "The Barbican?"

The driver, a skinny man with a day's worth of stubble, turned down the babble of the radio he was listening to and nodded.

"Mr Ransom?" came a call from behind. It was the driver from the second taxi who had got out of the driver's seat to beckon him over. He was a young man with slicked back hair and a black T-shirt with a rock music logo on the front, who looked more like a student than a cabbie.

Michael perceived Ransom's unease. He was about to perceive the young taxi driver, too, when his perception was overwhelmed by the anger blasting from the first driver.

"Oi!" said the skinny man, getting out of the driver's seat and glaring at the man behind. "I'm at the front of the queue."

"But I'm Mr Ransom's ride," said the young driver.

"He asked to ride with me!" The skinny man took one threatening step towards his rival.

Ransom took a step back, his hands up in surrender. "Look, it's fine. We can walk instead, it's not far."

"No, no, Mr Ransom!" called the young driver. "Mr Applegate booked me to pick you up."

Michael perceived from Ransom that Applegate was the name of his solicitor.

"If you have a booking," shouted the thin man, "why did you join the queue?"

"Let's go," Ransom whispered to Michael, clearly not wanting to get in the middle of taxi cab rivalry.

"Yeah," said Michael.

They were about to turn and walk away when someone else got out of the back of the second cab: another young man, but this one dressed completely differently. He was in blue jogging bottoms and a football shirt as if he had just come from the gym.

Michael perceived an uncertainty from Ransom that reflected his own.

I can't perceive them, came Ransom's thoughts. *But they're not perceivers, they're not blocking me.*

Michael tried to perceive them too, but there was nothing on the surface. So he went deeper, and that's when he realised why Ransom was having difficulty. The minds of the two men were blank. Devoid of thought like Tyler and Bailecki.

"We need to go," said Michael.

"What's going on?" said Ransom, perceiving his son's concern.

"Can you run?" said Michael.

"Why?"

"Just run!"

Michael broke into a sprint, turning his head to make sure his father was following him. Older, out of shape, dressed in a suit and confused, Ransom stumbled into a run. Behind him, the two young men from the second cab started after them. Michael — a stronger perceiver than his father — heard their minds cry, in unison, *CATCH HIM!*

They sprinted as best they could to the top of the road, but the one in the gym clothes was faster than them all and was soon at Ransom's heel.

"Dad!" Michael heard himself shout.

The gym man grabbed Ransom's jacket and yanked him back so hard that Ransom lost his balance. He fell to the ground, his hands slapping down on the pavement to save his face from bashing onto concrete. A blast of his father's fear, confusion and pain ripped through Michael's perception.

"No!" cried Michael as the young driver joined his conspirator standing above their fallen prey. Each grabbed one of Ransom's arms and pulled him to his feet.

Ransom struggled, trying to wrest his arms from their grip as they pulled him back towards his cab. Michael turned his head, looking for someone to help them, but there was no one. Even the other taxi driver had got in his cab and driven away.

Michael ran after his father and grabbed at the young one's elbow to pull him away. The man lashed out with his fist, striking Michael in the jaw and sending him, stumbling, backwards. He reached out for the wall of the nearest building as pain rang round his head. As he recovered, he tasted the saltiness of blood and realised he had bitten his tongue.

Ransom took his chance and shook the young one free from his arm. He kicked out, striking the shins of the gym man with one foot after another, struggling to break away. The blows did nothing to the gym man except cause him to retaliate, jabbing a fist hard into the side of Ransom's head.

Michael perceived Ransom's pain as the world blurred around him. He could have pulled out his perception, he should have put up his blocks, but he didn't want to leave his father. Another punch struck Ransom's temple and knocked his reality into a swirling mess of concussion.

Run, Michael, run! Ransom's mind screamed, using the remains of his consciousness.

But Michael couldn't leave him. The men, with their blank minds, were not interested in Michael, they were only interested in Ransom.

I'll get help, I promise, Michael thought. *I'll—*

But Ransom had passed out.

Michael watched, helpless, as the two mindless men dragged the unconscious body of his father back to the cab and bundled him into the back. The gym man got in with him and the young man got in the driver's seat.

The cab sped past Michael, to the top of the road. He ran after it, the ringing still in his head, as he tried to perceive the minds of his father's captors. They held only one thought: *turn left*.

The taxi turned left onto the main road, taking his father away to God knows where. At the last moment, Michael took note of its receding number plate. The only thing he could do.

TWENTY

MICHAEL sat in the same interrogation room he had been in several times before, but this time he was the one who sat across the table from Sergeant Patterson. Despite the painkillers he had taken, his jaw still ached from where he had been hit in the face, although the doctor who examined him at the hospital assured him nothing was broken. He was told he was lucky not to have been more badly hurt, although 'lucky' was not the word Michael would have used.

The police had been nice to him. They gave him a cup of their machine-dispensed coffee and allowed Patterson to take his statement, even though the inquiry was not officially anything to do with the anti-terrorist squad.

Michael clutched the cardboard coffee cup without drinking it, feeling its heat slowly dissipate as he went through the details of what had happened.

"How can you be sure Hetherington was behind the kidnap?" asked Patterson.

"I can't," said Michael. "But the minds of the men who took him had been programmed, I'm sure of it."

Patterson leant back in his seat. "I don't know how we could present any of this evidence in court," he said.

"I don't care about that," said Michael. "I want my father back." He sipped at his coffee, it was cold and tasted of plastic from the machine, but he drank it anyway.

"I had no idea Brian Ransom was your father," said Patterson.

"If your dad was on trial for being public enemy number one, would you go around telling people?"

"I suppose not."

"I don't think it's a coincidence that they took him from outside the trial," said Michael.

"They knew that's where he would be," said Patterson. "It's all over the news."

"I meant, they wanted him because of what he was on trial for."

Patterson responded only with a confused look.

"Lucas was researching into perceivers, right? Who do you think knows more about perception—?"

"—than the man who invented it," finished Patterson.

That wasn't exactly what his father had done, but it was close enough.

"Lucas is on the run," said Patterson. "You think he could still be working with the Hetherington kid to program people?"

"I saw into their minds," said Michael. "I'm sure."

There was a knock on the door and Jones entered. He looked a lot better than the last time Michael had seen him. He'd clearly been able to get a bit of sleep, he'd also had a shave that morning and done his tie up all the way to his shirt collar. "We found the cab," he said straight away.

Michael and Patterson turned to face him, waiting for more.

"It was abandoned at a taxi rank in Hounslow," Jones continued.

"Hounslow?" said Michael, trying to remember whereabouts in London Hounslow was.

"Other taxi drivers were annoyed because it was parked in the way and there wasn't a driver to move it," said Jones. "They complained to a passing copper, who matched it to the number plate you gave us, Michael, and that's when we were alerted."

"Any sign of Ransom?" said Patterson.

Jones shook his head. "CID are working on the theory the kidnappers switched cars at some point. They're checking CCTV, but it could take a while."

"What do we do now?" said Michael, thinking of bored police officers sitting in front of TV screens for hour after hour while the kidnappers did whatever they wanted with Ransom.

"*We* do nothing," said Jones. "This is a CID inquiry. Tony will forward your statement to them and they will take it from there."

Patterson let out an ironic chuckle. "When I figure out what I'm going to put in the statement. It's all about Michael's perceptions."

"Put in the statement what you would normally put in," said Jones. "Just the facts of what happened and physical descriptions of the men. Let's not mention anything about perceivers unless we have to."

"But what about my father?" said Michael, agitated. "While you waste time with CCTV and writing statements, Lucas could be doing anything to him."

"Lucas?" said Jones, glancing at Patterson for clarification.

"Michael thinks Doctor Lucas might be behind the kidnapping," he said.

"I very much doubt that," said Jones. "That was the other thing I came to tell you. We've had confirmation that Doctor Saul Lucas boarded a flight to Moscow yesterday."

"Russia?" said Michael.

"Yes," said Jones.

"We have to go after him!"

"We can't."

"But he kidnapped my dad!"

"We have no jurisdiction in Russia," said Jones. "Any dealings would have to be through diplomatic channels."

"Diplomatic channels?" said Michael. "But you're the police, you're supposed to catch criminals."

"Not when they're in another country," said Jones. "That's the job of Interpol and MI6."

"MI6? CID? CCTV?" Michael was furious. "Is no one out there finding my father? We need to *do* something, we need to go to Russia!"

Patterson leant forward across the interrogation table. "Look, Michael, I know you're upset, but you have to wait, okay? Lucas might have gone to Russia, but we don't know where the Hetherington boy is and, if you're right, he's the one we should be looking for. Let's trace the movements of the taxi and see if we can find out the identities of the two men you saw carry out the abduction. Meanwhile, we'll put an alert out at airports in case they're going abroad."

Michael perceived that Patterson was toying with the idea of reaching out a reassuring hand to touch him, but decided not to and went for a reassuring smile instead.

Michael sighed and willed himself to calm down. "This is going to be all over the news, isn't it?" he said.

"Already is," said Patterson. "At least if the kidnappers are planning to move Ransom out of the country, it will make it more difficult for them."

"I suppose," said Michael. He had gone from anger to despondency, all within the space of a couple of minutes.

"The best thing you can do," said Patterson, "is go home. We'll keep working on it and I'll call you in the morning with an update."

Michael, despite his doubts, agreed that it was the best course of action. It was probably the only course of action. So he thanked the two policemen and went out to find Hodges to take him back to Galen House.

It was only when he left the police station that he remembered Patterson would have difficulty calling him in the morning because he still didn't have a phone.

THE only bright thing in Michael's quarters was his phone, an expensive new phone with a bright, shiny screen that glowed in the palm of his hand. He had bought it on the way home from the police station with money he didn't really have. He told the man in the shop he was taking out a credit agreement while waiting for the insurance to come through on his old phone, but the truth was he never got round to making a claim and it had got to a point where he didn't really care. The new phone with its screen of high resolution multi-coloured pixels was the latest model, the best available and he wanted it.

Everything else in the room was dark: from the window where the curtains were drawn, to his mood.

Patterson had rung him on his bright, shiny, new phone that morning to tell him some depressing news. A boy matching James Hetherington's description had caught a plane to Moscow the previous day. So, it appeared, that at the same time that Michael was sipping at a cardboard cup of cold, plastic-tasting coffee, Hetherington had been enjoying an inflight meal courtesy of British Airways.

The two men who had kidnapped Ransom off the street had been arrested, having been found wandering around Hounslow in a bit of a daze. The one in the rock T-shirt had been discovered by a suspicious security guard as he scoured the floors of a multi-storey car park looking for his car which he had actually parked in a near-identical multi-storey twenty miles away in Bromley. The one in the gym clothes had been so lost and confused that he'd actually walked up to a policeman to ask for help.

Patterson had invited Michael down to the police station to perceive the pair while they were being interviewed, but Michael doubted he would get anything from their minds and turned down the offer. If they were anything like Elkins — and he was certain they were — then Hetherington would have made sure they had no memories of what had happened.

There was no news, however, about Ransom.

A knock on the door jolted Michael from his thoughts. His phone slipped from his lap and landed on the floor, corner first. He picked it up and examined the corner which had been saved from a massive dent by the carpet, but it did not bode well for the future of his very expensive gadget.

He perceived the person outside was Pauline.

Opening the door, he saw that she was dressed in regulation greys with her hair put neatly away in a bun, as had become her routine. Sympathy poured from her mind. Like all of them in the building, she had seen the news that Ransom had been kidnapped outside his own trial and seen Michael had come back to Galen House with a bloodied shirt. The others understood that Michael had tried to stop the kidnappers, but she was the only one who knew why. She felt sorry for him and her concern was uncomfortable for him to perceive.

"Norm the Norm asked me to remind you that you have toilet cleaning duty today," she said.

With all the crazy things going on in his life, trust Norm the Norm to be worried about the most trivial. "God!" Michael leant back against the doorframe. "I'd forgotten all about that."

"I thought he might let you off under the circumstances," said Pauline. "But apparently not."

"It's military bollocks," said Michael. "Discipline has to be maintained."

"Yeah, but…"

"The man's a soldier at heart. He fought in real wars where you keep fighting even though your friends are dying around you. I don't think he's going to let me off cleaning a few toilets."

"Alex cleaned them yesterday and I cleaned them the day before, so they're probably not that bad."

"You don't know some of the disgusting things men do in the toilets after they've been eating army catering," said Michael.

Pauline wrinkled her nose at that. "Having been in there the day before yesterday, I actually do."

He found a smile from somewhere inside of him which he hoped would let her know he appreciated the sentiment. "Tell Norm the Norm I'll be there soon."

"Okay," said Pauline. "Are you sure you're all right? I mean, there seems to be something going round in your head."

"You're a good perceiver, Pauline," said Michael. "I can see why they recruited you."

He closed the door on her and perceived her disquiet at being dismissed. But he couldn't worry about her now. He went back to contemplating his phone.

MICHAEL knelt down in front of the toilet and felt something wet soak into the knee of his trousers. He tried to tell himself it was water splashed onto the floor from the flushing mechanism, but as he looked down at what remained of the puddle beneath him, he saw a yellow stain around the edge where it had started to dry. Even though it was the men's toilets and there were plenty of urinals, someone had decided to take a pee in one of the cubicles and missed.

I can't stay here, Michael thought.

Not while Hetherington and Lucas were in Russia plotting to do God-knows-what with their knowledge of perceivers.

Not while his father was being held by people who were planning to do God-knows-what with him.

Not as if he knew what the hell he could do about it.

He dunked his cloth into the slightly soiled bucket of water next to him, squeezed it and wiped it over the toilet seat, thinking about Russia. All arrows led to that vast country. A country where the British police had no jurisdiction, where the British government had precious little influence and where Michael couldn't even speak the language. He needed a way in, someone on the inside who could help him, and he thought back to Victor Rublev.

Skazhi Andrei Orlov chto on bil prav, the Russian had thought as he was dying. It translated as 'tell Andrei Orlov he was right', according to an online translator. Michael probably should have done something about it at the time, but he was too busy persuading Patterson to investigate Rublev's murder and infiltrating Hetherington's gang, so he had almost forgotten about it. But now the thoughts were back in his mind.

Michael snapped off his right rubber glove, recoiling as some liquid flicked back onto his face. With his naked hand, he pulled his phone from his pocket and ran a search on the name 'Andrei Orlov'. Hundreds of results came up, but there were only a few that cross-referenced with Victor Rublev. Michael allowed his body to move from kneeling up to sitting down and leant his back against the side of the toilet cubicle. He realised he had just sat in the urine patch, but tried not to think about it soaking up into the seat of his trousers. With his buttocks damp, he read about the exploits of Rublev and Orlov when they were in their twenties and the many times they were arrested at anti-corruption protests.

Michael was going to search further when his phone rang with the unpleasant sound of the default ringtone.

"Hello?" said Michael, not knowing who it was because he hadn't got around to storing anyone's details in his contacts list.

"Hi, Michael, it's Tony Patterson again."

Michael felt both anticipation and dread. "Any news?"

"CID traced the car they think the kidnappers transferred Ransom into from the cab," he said.

"Where is it?"

"It was recorded getting on a ferry for France at Dover."

"Can you intercept it at the other end?"

"I'm sorry, Michael, it's too late," said Patterson. "The ferry reached Calais yesterday. The kidnappers obviously worked to get him out of the country as soon as possible. He was gone before we even had a chance to alert the ports."

"France? Why France?"

"CID's guess — and I agree with them — is that flying a kidnap victim against his will on a commercial airline was going to be near impossible, so they had to drive."

"Drive to Russia?"

"Seems likely. From mainland Europe, the journey is all over land. Interpol have been alerted, but the kidnappers have a head start and could have taken any number of routes to get there."

Patterson continued to talk about how they were going to do their best and how Interpol had good relations with other police forces on mainland Europe, but Michael heard none of it.

He knew then what he had to do. He had to go to Russia.

TWENTY-ONE

THE lights shining from the buildings could have come from any city in any developed nation as they streaked by on the roadside while the taxi drove through the streets at night. Only the traffic signs in an unfamiliar language reminded Michael that he was not at home anymore. That, and the perceptions from the taxi driver whose mind rambled away in Russian at breakneck speed. The bearded man, who wore a flat cap to cover his apparent baldness, couldn't speak English, but turned out to be a big football fan. He kept shouting out random football-related words in order to form some kind of connection with his passenger.

"Manchester United!" he said in a heavy Russian accent.

"Yes," replied Michael, nodding and hoping the man would take the hint that he wasn't in the mood to talk.

"Five-nil!" He laughed, as if it was a great joke. "Five-nil!"

"Yes," said Michael, trying to think of something that would pacify him and realising how little he knew about the English national game. "Old Trafford!" he said, remembering the name of Manchester United's football ground from somewhere.

"Yes, yes, Old Trafford," The taxi driver laughed. "Manchester United! Old Trafford!" He laughed some more and went back to concentrating on the road as they drove into a tunnel.

The black of night disappeared as the streaking lights of buildings were replaced by the glowing overhead bulbs that turned the tunnel's grey concrete into a dirty yellow. Its walls and roof enclosed him just as the taxi cab enclosed him, a bubble within a bubble, a tiny space of safety within a scary foreign city. He tried to relax back into the seat and let the soporific rumbling movement of the drive soothe the knots in his stomach, but it did not work. The constant reminder of how rash it was to jump on a plane to Moscow wouldn't leave him. He didn't know the city, he didn't know the language, he didn't know anybody there, he didn't even know for sure that the kidnappers had brought Ransom to Moscow. All he had was a ten-year-old address for Andrei Orlov pulled off the internet and information that Victor Rublev had been murdered.

Michael had spent more money he didn't have by checking into a tourist hotel in the city centre where he could be sure there was someone who spoke English. A man on the reception desk with impressive language skills had arranged for a taxi, and was able to tell the driver to take Michael to Orlov's address, by showing him the webpage on his phone with it written out in Cyrillic lettering.

They emerged from the tunnel and kept driving until the wide Moscow streets narrowed and the lights from the buildings became fewer and less bright. Like driving out of the centre of London to some of the poorer suburbs, the outskirts of Moscow had the feel of some-where yet to see the benefit of regeneration. In London there would be rows of terraced houses interspersed with the occasional tower block from the sixties, whereas in Moscow it was almost entirely square concrete apartment blocks from the Soviet era. All of them looked the same. It was a reminder of the communist ideal of everyone being equal, which meant they all had to live in unattractive, homogenous buildings at the side of old, dimly lit streets.

After only a few minutes into the outskirts of the city, the driver pulled up alongside the kerb. Keeping the engine running, he turned round to Michael and asked him something in Russian.

"Are we here?" said Michael. "How much?" He reached into his pocket where he had a bundle of rouble notes.

"No," said the driver in English. He mimed putting a telephone to his ear with his hand and slowly repeated a couple of Russian words which were close enough to English for Michael to understand. "*Telefon. Adres.*"

Michael pulled his phone from his pocket and reactivated the screen with Orlov's address on it. The driver read it, nodded and pointed to the block near where he had stopped. But he didn't look happy. "*Tochno?*"

"It's okay," said Michael, smiling to try to convey that this was where he wanted to be. He put his phone away and pulled out his Russian currency. He held out the notes to the driver and hoped the man was honest enough not to overcharge him.

The taxi driver chose a couple of notes and Michael got out of the cab, where it was a couple of degrees colder than it had been an hour ago in the centre of the city. He was under the impression that Russia was always freezing, but it was approaching summer in that part of northern Europe and it wasn't that cold. Just as well, as he was only wearing a jacket over his jeans and shirt. He pulled out his phone and switched to the screen with Orlov's address translated into English and tried to work out how to find the right apartment. As he did that, he noticed the driver hadn't left yet and was calling out to him in Russian.

Michael turned to see the man had wound down his window and was beckoning him over. Perceiving him, he realised the driver was concerned for his safety in the area where they had stopped.

Michael knew he should be concerned too, but was trying to ignore his own instinct.

The driver was still yammering away in Russian, so Michael walked back to the cab to try to reassure him. "It's okay," he said. "Really."

The driver caught hold of Michael's hand and pressed something into it. Michael looked down and saw it was a business card written in Russian. The driver jabbed at it with his finger, pointing to a telephone number printed in the bottom right hand corner in Western Arabic numerals. "*Telefon*," he said. "*Kagda ti gotov. Telefon.*"

"I'll call you when I'm finished, sure," said Michael, using a combination of perception and body language to understand what he was saying.

"Boris," said the driver, tapping his chest with his hand. "*Menya Zovut* Boris."

"Thank you, Boris," said Michael. "*Dosvidanya.*"

He laughed at hearing Michael's badly pronounced Russia.

"*Dosvidanya!*" he said.

He rolled up the window and drove off, leaving Michael alone in the remote area of Moscow that scared even the local man who had taken him there.

THE inside of the apartment building was as grey as its outer concrete shell, with barely functioning lights that brought gloom to the communal areas. On the second floor, an ageing corridor was merely a conduit to the doors that led into individual apartments. Doors that were thin enough for the noise of TVs and radios to bleed through to the outside.

Michael stopped at number 27, a black-painted door that was neither at the beginning of the corridor nor at the end, and listened to the chatter from the television. His perception told him there was a human consciousness inside, but he couldn't be certain it was Orlov or if Orlov was alone. If he widened his sensitivity, the interference from other people in the block drowned out what was coming from number 27.

The only thing to do was knock.

He waited, listening for noises of movement as he perceived that someone was alerted to his presence.

A man, with a complexion as grey as the walls, opened the door. In his late thirties or early forties, he still had much of his natural blonde hair which was overdue a cut and was tucked behind each ear to keep it back from his face. Dressed like someone's granddad, he wore a floppy cardigan over his shirt and trousers, which he'd tied around the waist with a knitted belt. Michael perceived that uncomfortable feeling of someone who was irritated to see him.

"Andrei Orlov?" said Michael in what he hoped was close to the correct Russian pronunciation.

The man's mind recognised his own name. "*Kto vi?*" he said.

"Do you speak English?" said Michael, realising what he had to say was going to be really difficult if he did not.

"What if I do?" he said in a strong Russian accent.

Michael let his relief show. "Victor Rublev sent me," he said.

Orlov bristled at the mention of the name. He hustled Michael inside. "*Pridi suda!*"

The door to Orlov's apartment led straight into his living room, a small space with only room for a television, an armchair and a single person's dining table near the curtained window. Like everywhere Michael had seen outside the city centre, it was dimly lit, with a single energy saving light bulb hanging from the ceiling in a yellow tasselled lampshade. The brightest area of the room was by the gas fire which had to be the best part of twenty years old and threw heat into the room with flickering blue fingers of flame. Above it, a mantelpiece was cluttered with photographs of children, at various ages from babies cradled in a woman's arms to portraits in school uniform. They seemed to be of three individuals, two boys and a girl, with the oldest boy being about fifteen. In the middle of the clustered gallery was a single portrait of the same woman who was cradling the babies, a woman about ten years younger than Orlov.

It was all very different to Rublev's opulent London home.

Orlov turned off the television and the background Russian chatter abruptly stopped. "How is Victor?" he said.

Michael swallowed. "I'm sorry to say that Victor died," he said.

Orlov nodded. There was no surprise in his mind, only confirmation of something he suspected. He sat down in his armchair and let the cushions take his weight, as the news soaked into his consciousness. "How did they kill him?"

A normal person might have assumed he had died from a heart attack or had been run over by a bus. Like Rublev himself, Orlov automatically assumed it was murder. "Radiation poisoning," said Michael. "Something was slipped into his tea, we think."

"A slow and painful death. I am not surprised." He sat and contemplated.

"He wanted me to tell you …" Michael tried to remember the words Rublev had used. "*Skazhi Andrei Orlov chto on bil prav.*"

"He only admits it when he's dying," said Orlov. "How much like Victor."

"I think it means, tell Andrei Orlov he was right. Right about what?"

"Don't throw your life away for a cause. Sometimes I think I should have listened to myself."

Michael tried to perceive what Orlov meant, but there was just a feeling of melancholy.

Orlov tried to push the feeling away. "You don't have telephones in London?" he said suddenly.

"Pardon?" said Michael.

"You could have told me this over the telephone, yet you travelled all the way to Moscow."

"I was with Rublev when he died. It didn't seem right to say something like that over the phone."

"I have a feeling this is not all you have come to say," said Orlov.

"No," said Michael.

"Then sit down, young man."

Michael looked around the room. The only other seat was the single dining chair. He pulled it out from the table and turned it around so it faced Orlov. Part of him wanted to come straight out and ask for his help, but he knew the man wouldn't be ready to give it. He had to gain the man's trust first.

"There were things I should have asked Victor Rublev before he died, but I didn't get the chance," said Michael. "His mind was confused at the end, but he had one clear thought of a young woman I think he might have known in Russia. He remembered her wearing a white summer dress painted with yellow flowers — do you know who she was?"

Orlov smiled. "Valeriya," he said. "We were young then."

"Was that when you were involved in protests against the Russian government? The internet says you and Victor Rublev were activists together."

"Valeriya didn't like it. She wanted to have a career, she didn't want to get in trouble with the authorities. She told Victor, either marry her or be a troublemaker, don't be both. He chose to make trouble. I think he regretted that."

Regretted it until the day he died, Michael thought. "There's been nothing on the internet about you for the last ten years. What happened? Did the movement go underground?"

"Is the internet all there is for you young people?"

Michael wasn't sure how to answer.

But it turned out to be a rhetorical question. "I was young when people wrote about me on the internet," said Orlov. "Then I got older." There was more to his story than that, Michael perceived it, but he would need to look deeper to find out what it was because Orlov was making an effort to keep those painful memories hidden.

"You didn't seem surprised when I said Rublev had died," said Michael.

"When Valeriya left him, he became more militant than I had ever been. Then his father died and he inherited all that money — his father did well with the fall of communism, you know. He used the money to leave Russia, turning his back on his country and all of his friends. He said he could have more influence in Britain, the land of free speech, but I think he was running away. To be honest, I haven't spoken to him in many years. It would not have done me any good if I had. Consorting with enemies of the state is frowned upon in my country."

There was regret in Orlov's mind. Michael couldn't be sure if he regretted losing touch with his friend, turning his back on the cause he championed in his youth, or getting involved in the whole thing in the first place.

"But you haven't come here to chat to a man more than twice your age about his memories," said Orlov.

Michael smiled at the man's intuition. "No."

"You could start with telling me your name."

"Oh," said Michael, realising he had forgotten to introduce himself properly. "I'm Michael Sanderson, I'm … it's complicated."

"But you want my help — yes?"

"Yes."

"I don't usually give my help to young English men who appear out of nowhere on my doorstep. But I believe you have a saying in Britain: if you don't ask, you don't get. So, ask."

Michael paused, thinking about where to start. "My father is … well, my father knows a lot about perceivers. Have you heard about perceivers?"

"We have the news in Russia," said Orlov. "In our own way."

"I think the Russian authorities kidnapped my father because of what he knows. I thought you might still be involved with the dissident movement, I thought you might be able to ask some questions."

"If Russian agents did what you say, then do you think they would have told anyone about it?" he said.

"No," said Michael. Now that he had said it out loud, it sounded ridiculous. "But I thought you might have some contacts, people you could ask. I don't know …" Michael felt embarrassed at asking what now sounded like a stupid question. "I didn't know anybody else in Russia. I can't even speak the language. I didn't know what else to do."

Orlov rose from his seat. "I am sorry to hear about your father, but I left all that behind me many years ago. I cannot help you."

Michael perceived he genuinely felt sorry for him, but his mind was made up and there was no persuading him. Looking round at the shabby living room designed for one person, he realised how stupid he had been to think that one man living on the outskirts of Moscow could help him with what amounted to international espionage.

Orlov showed him to the door.

At the last minute, Michael decided to make one last appeal. "If you think of anyone or anything that can help me, can you ring me?" He fished in his pocket for something to write his telephone number on, but all he had was the taxi driver's card. He turned the card over to reveal its blank side. "Do you have a pen?"

"Yes, I have a pen, but I don't need to write anything down."

"Just in case," said Michael.

Orlov sighed. "Stay there."

Michael stood poised with the taxi driver's card in his palm, ready to write down his number, while Orlov went back to his armchair and plunged his hand down the side of the seat cushion. After a little rummage around he pulled out, not a pen, but a mobile phone. One which would have been the latest model only a year ago. He came back to Michael, tapped a couple of things on the screen and handed it to him. "You can type your number in here."

Michael did as he was asked. "Thank you," he said, handing the phone back. "If they killed Rublev in the middle of London, I daren't think what they will do to my dad if they've brought him to Russia.

If you think of anything — anything at all that could help — please call me."

"I won't," said Orlov, putting the phone in his trouser pocket. He showed Michael to the door and — as they said goodbye, and Michael thanked him again — he perceived that Orlov was true to his word. He didn't want to get involved with anything that could put him on a collision course with the Russian authorities. He had accepted Michael's phone number to be polite, but he had no intention of calling Michael or ever speaking to him again.

TWENTY-TWO

THE hotel room in Moscow was very plush, and so it should be from the amount of money Michael had paid for it. It had an enormous double bed big enough for four of him, a pristine carpet, desk, chair, sofa and television. If it wasn't for the fire evacuation sign written in Russian, as well as in English, French, Spanish and German, it could have been any expensive hotel room in any city across the world.

It might as well have been somewhere else in the world for all the good it had done him. He had one lead — Andrei Orlov — and that had come to nothing.

He thought eating something would fuel his brain to come up with more ideas, but the room service he had ordered sat largely uneaten on the bed next to him. He'd munched on a couple of chips, but the potato had sat claggy in his mouth and it was difficult to swallow. Not that it was the fault of the chips, it was his own stupid fault for coming to a foreign country and expecting to investigate an international kidnapping as if he were James Bond.

He thought of calling Patterson back in London and asking if he could put him in touch with the British security services in Moscow. But he doubted even they could help.

He turned on the telly. Being a tourist hotel, it was fed with satellite channels, including a sports channel which the last person in the room must have been watching. It was showing a British football match. For a moment, he thought that serendipity had arranged for Manchester United to be playing at Old Trafford, but as he looked closer he saw that it was Chelsea versus Liverpool — and Chelsea were doing rather well, leading 2-1 approaching full time.

Yeah, he might as well have stayed in England.

His phone rang. He picked it up from the pillow where he had dropped it. The display had only a strange-looking phone number on it. A Russian number, he suspected.

"Hello?" he said, answering.

"It's Andrei Orlov," said the caller.

"Andrei Orlov?" Suddenly full of surprise and hope and bewilderment. "I didn't think you'd call me. I mean, thanks for calling."

"I lost my father five years ago," said Orlov, his tone matter-of-fact. "Cancer. I understand the pain. I called an old friend. Your father is Brian Ransom — yes?"

"Yes!" said Michael, desperately wanting to ask if Orlov knew where he was, but holding himself back.

"I can see why my government might think he was valuable to them. Perceivers scare them."

"You will help me?"

"No, not me," said Orlov. "But my friend might be interested. He says, can you meet him?"

"Yes!" said Michael, his heart pounding even faster now. "I can meet him. Where?"

"I can give you the address. Do you have a pen …?"

MICHAEL had called Boris, the football-loving taxi driver, using the number on his business card, but Boris had been reluctant to take him to the address Orlov had given him. The place was, as far as he could figure out from the man's wild gestures and loud exclamations in his native language, a Russian bar for hard-drinking Russians and not somewhere for foreign tourists. But the bar was his one possible hope of finding his father and that was where he insisted Boris take him.

As he walked in, Michael understood the taxi driver's concern. Even back in London, he would not have voluntarily gone into a dive like the one he had just entered. The light level was low, probably to disguise the state of the place as much as to give it atmosphere, and there were less than half a dozen people sitting huddled over tables down one side of the long, thin building. All of them, he perceived, were at different stages of inebriation. Only a barman — a tall thin man with a ridiculously big and bushy moustache like a circus strong-man — was totally sober. He eyed Michael curiously for a moment, then beckoned him over.

At first Michael wondered if this was the 'friend' Orlov had arranged for him to meet, but a cursory scan of the barman's thoughts revealed he was just a barman.

"English?" said the barman.

He wasn't sure if he was being asked if he was English or if he could speak English. Either way, the answer was the same. "Yes," said Michael.

"Up," said the barman, sticking out an index finger and pointing above his head. "Stair." He mimed his index and middle fingers walking up an imaginary set of stairs, and nodded towards the back of the room where a set of wooden stairs were half hidden by shadow.

"I'll sit on this table, and they can come down and find me," he told the barman, deciding the relative safety of downstairs where there were people was a better option. To indicate what he meant, he pointed at the table nearest the window and started to walk over.

"*Nyet!*" said the barman. "Up. Stair." He pointed above his head and did the walking motion with his fingers again.

There was no point arguing with him. Michael perceived the only English the man could speak was the few words he had already uttered. There was probably a reason Orlov's friend didn't want to meet in a brightly lit public place. So, against his better judgement, he went to the darkest corner of the bar and climbed the stairs.

Michael kept his perception wide open as he climbed the stairs, determined to be ready for whatever or whoever was up there waiting for him. Apart from the bubbling of inebriated Russian thoughts from the customers downstairs, he perceived nothing.

The wooden steps climbed into the dark to where there was a little landing before the stairs turned a forty-five degree angle for the final four steps to the floor above. Light shone from the entrance, like a beam from heaven. Michael walked up into the unknown.

The upper room of the pub might once have been a function room or a meeting room, but clearly hadn't been used for that purpose in years and had become little more than a store room. It was a vast space the size of the pub downstairs, illuminated by harsh strip lighting that revealed the true state of the scratched and peeling paintwork. It was filled with old tables and chairs piled on top of each other along with dumped cardboard boxes of miscellaneous stuff. One had an old electric heater sticking out of it and another was topped with a piece of scraggly Christmas tinsel. Judging by the grime that had accumulated on top of them, no one had touched them for a very long time.

Michael stood on the bare floorboards in the centre of the room and concentrated his perception. Still he sensed no one. He wondered if the meeting was real, or perhaps the person he was due to meet was late. He pulled his phone from his pocket and checked if he had any messages, but there were none. He thumbed through to recent calls and chose the number Orlov had used to call him. It rang. And rang. Until it clicked onto a recorded message in Russian. Michael disconnected.

Something rattled at the far end of the room. Beyond the furniture, half hidden by the legs of upside down tables, he saw there was a door with a sticker on it in green Cyrillic lettering. The door handle rattled again and opened, to reveal Andrei Orlov, standing at the top of a metal fire escape. Orlov stepped inside, negotiating a wiggly path between the junk, to face Michael in the centre of the room. He looked different than he had done the previous day in his apartment. It wasn't just that he had brushed his hair back neatly from his face, or that he had replaced his granddad cardigan with a smart, black showerproof coat. There was something else that Michael couldn't articulate.

"Thank you for coming," said Orlov in his impressive, but heavy accented English.

"Is your friend here?" asked Michael, still not perceiving anyone else close by.

"My friend is a little nervous. He wants to make sure you have brought no one with you and that you have no recording devices. You need to hand over your phone."

Michael looked down at the phone he was still holding. He didn't want to part with it — even though he had no one to call in a country where he knew no one — but he perceived no malice from Orlov, so handed it over.

As Orlov secreted the phone in his pocket, Michael realised he perceived very little from Orlov at all. No malice, no nervousness, no anticipation like he might expect. There was just a pleasant contented feeling, muffled like he was perceiving it through a veil.

He pushed deeper and the veil fell away.

He expected a rush of Orlov's emotions and thoughts, but his perception slammed up against a wall.

"You're blocking me." He spoke his realisation out loud, staring with disbelief at the Russian he knew wasn't a perceiver, but had somehow closed off access to his mind.

Michael pushed harder. The barrier was weak and cracked enough to let out one overwhelming feeling from Orlov's mind: remorse.

It was a trap. There was a perceiver somewhere close by, hiding their presence by shielding their mind while also masking Orlov's thoughts and feelings to lure Michael in. "You lied to me."

"No! Why would you think that?" said Orlov, but his mind was open now. Michael felt Orlov's guilt and his nervousness, and heard his thoughts tumbling in Russian, probably hoping the whole thing would be over soon. It meant whoever had been blocking him knew that he had been discovered.

The sound of heavy footsteps behind him made Michael jump. He turned to see two men enter from the stairs, led by the barman whose bushy moustache now appeared sinister rather than ridiculous in the bright strip lightning. He looked into their minds and saw the same blankness he had seen in the gang who had left him to burn.

Footsteps on metal climbed from the fire escape into the room. They belonged to another two men, their minds blank and their bodies blocking his exit.

Michael turned back to Orlov, the only other person in the room with a free mind. "What's going on?"

"*Prosti mne*," he said in Russian. Michael didn't understand the words, but he recognised the feelings behind them. He was sorry.

The men from the fire escape and the stairs closed in on him with slow steps like zombies.

"Why?" said Michael.

"My family," said Orlov as he thought of a woman and three children. The people from the photographs on his mantelpiece cascaded through his memories. He loved them and he missed them; forced to live, as he was, in a single person's apartment. In the mess of his emotions, Michael wasn't sure if Orlov had betrayed him to save his family, or betrayed him so he could be allowed to live with them again.

Orlov stepped aside and the men closed in.

Michael looked around, desperate for an escape route. All he saw was piled rubbish, solid walls and men coming towards him.

"Come out and face me!" Michael cried into the air. "I know you're there, perceiver." Whoever it was may have been able to keep their distance when sending in their programmed thugs, but they couldn't have blocked Orlov's mind without being close by, and Michael was relying on that. "Well? Where are you?"

Silence answered him, broken only by four sets of Russian boots clomping on the wooden floor. Close enough for Michael to see into their dead eyes. And past them to the daylight coming from the open fire escape door.

He made a break for it.

Dashing for the light, he took one step of freedom before a strong Russian hand gripped his arm and yanked him back; lifting him as he swung him round. Both arms were pulled behind his back as he wriggled in the grip of two strong hands and his feet kicked out against air.

"Help me! Help me, *please*! I'm up h—"

Cloth was pushed into his open mouth, stifling his scream. He tried to push it out with his tongue but more cloth was placed over the top and — even though he tossed his head to stop them — tied at the back so the gag was in tight. Inside, he was still screaming, but outside all that anyone heard was a muffled, "Mm mm *mmm*!"

The last thing he saw was the cold look from the moustached barman, before a black bag was placed over his head and tied securely with rope around his neck.

The world went dark. Sound was deadened. His own voice was silenced.

He struggled, but there was no breaking the grip of the four Russian programmed men as they dragged him away.

TWENTY-THREE

IN the daze of semi-consciousness, he felt the cold of the hard floor beneath him and the slimy damp of his own drool on his cheek. There was a musty smell in the air and the perception of someone familiar close by.

Michael's eyes squinted open to see the blurry white of ceramic floor tiles on which he lay and which had leached the heat out of him until he was as stiff as a corpse.

He moved, just a little, causing a rush of pain to run through his body. He heard himself groan.

"Michael?"

A man's voice. A recognisable voice. The familiar perception now identified; it filled his mind with love and concern.

"Dad?" he heard himself say.

Michael lifted his shoulders, and despite the pain from his aching body, pulled himself to a sitting position. A room no bigger than the one he lived in back at Galen House, enclosed him with white featureless walls. A narrow window high up behind him let in a crack of daylight and a closed door ahead of him suggested the rest of the building that lay beyond. Beside him, a grubby thin mattress from a child's single bed had been thrown on the floor and, in front of him, there was a plastic bucket that smelt of piss.

He leant his back against the wall and heard a chink of metal. Looking down, he saw a handcuff on his wrist was attached to a thick, unbreakable chain about a metre long that ran to a second cuff secured to a cast iron radiator.

A gentle hand touched his shoulder, the only warm thing in the whole room. It was Brian Ransom, still in the same suit he had worn in court, but his tie and shoelaces had been taken away. His beard had grown wild in the days since he had been kidnapped and his face had paled to match the grey of his hair. He was also chained to the radiator. He made no attempt to block his emotions, conflicted as they were with relief at seeing Michael and anger that he was there. Underneath was a fear, for himself and for his son.

"Michael, what are you doing here?"

"I came to find you," said Michael.

"I wish you hadn't."

Considering their current predicament, it was a wish Michael feared he was soon going to share. "Where are we?" he said.

"Moscow, I think," said Ransom.

That seemed right. He didn't know how long he'd been unconscious, but he didn't think it had been long enough to take him out of the city. He remembered being bundled into some kind of vehicle as he desperately tried to breathe through his nose inside the bag over his head until he passed out, possibly from some kind of drug. He felt pretty shitty, but he would have probably felt even worse if he'd been travelling for days.

"What do they want?" said Michael.

"The secret to perception," said Ransom.

"There's a secret?" said Michael.

"The boy who questioned me seems to think so."

"Boy?" It had to be James Hetherington. "An English boy about fourteen years old with hazel eyes — a perceiver?"

"You know him?"

"We've met," said Michael.

"I can't perceive him," said Ransom. "He's too strong."

"As strong as me," said Michael. "Stronger, maybe."

"What does he want with you?"

Michael shrugged. "I don't know. Perhaps he thinks I know something. Perhaps he just didn't like me coming to Moscow."

"I don't like it either," said his father.

Michael realised the ache in his bladder was getting stronger and it had nothing to do with the stiffness from lying unconscious on the floor. "I need a pee," he said.

Ransom pointed to the bucket.

"Really?" said Michael.

Ransom nodded.

Michael pulled himself to his feet. The chain attached to his wrist stretched out just long enough for him to stand over the bucket. Embarrassed, he turned his back on his father and emptied his bladder, watching the arc of yellow as it fell into the well of stale urine already there. When he had finished, he did up his fly. His body was relieved, but his mind was disgusted.

"Sit on the mattress with me," said Ransom. "It's not so cold here."

He did so and found it wasn't so much warm and soft, as less cold and hard than the floor. Opposite him was the door; ostensibly the only way out. His chain was not long enough for him to even reach the door handle, so he leant his back against the wall and cursed himself for being stupid enough to get himself caught.

Ransom put an arm round his shoulder. Michael initially shrunk back from him, but there was something comforting about the warmth from his body and from his mind and, after only a moment, he relaxed against his father's side. He dropped his barriers around his perception and allowed his own disorientation and fear to mingle with the concern and anxiety coming from his father.

MICHAEL lifted his head at the sound of the turning door handle.

James Hetherington stepped into the room with his mind totally closed behind his impenetrable blocks. Looking clean, fresh and well-rested on the outside, he brought with him the perfume of modern toiletries, accentuating the otherwise musty smell of stale human sweat that pervaded the room. He relaxed back against the doorframe, placing his hands casually in his trouser pockets, knowing he was safe at more than a chain's length from his captives.

What's he doing? Michael thought.

I don't know, I can't perceive him, Ransom replied.

Michael tried to see the rest of the building through the open door, but it was just a corridor with another white-painted wall on the opposite side. It was soon obscured by the barman with the bushy moustache as he turned from the corridor and into the room: his face and his mind both still blank, and a single instruction in Russian looping in his head. In his hand, he carried a padlock.

Walking straight past Hetherington as if he wasn't there, he approached Ransom, who flinched as the barman reached out to him. He didn't touch him, instead he took hold of the chain which secured Ransom to the radiator.

"What are you doing?" said Ransom, addressing his question to Hetherington.

"You'll see," said the boy. "Infuriating not to be able to perceive someone's intentions, isn't it?"

The barman pulled two parts of the chain together and secured them with the padlock, creating a loop. It effectively shortened the chain and restricted Ransom's movements.

"Michael is your son, isn't he?" said Hetherington.

Ransom said nothing.

"I perceive he is," said the boy.

Michael had his blocks up to stop his thoughts being perceived, but Ransom wasn't as strong as him and, worn down by days of incarceration, he put up little resistance.

"What of it?" said Ransom, his mind desperately wondering why his chain had been shortened.

Without warning, the barman grabbed Michael's elbow and dragged him by his arm across the floor. Michael scrambled to stop him, but his feet slipped on the tiles. At the halfway point, the chain pulled taut and yanked at his wrist, preventing the barman from pulling him any further.

"Michael!" called Ransom. He reached out a hand to help him, but the shortened chain stopped him from getting very far.

"It was very good of your son to join us in Russia," said Hetherington. "He can be my bargaining chip."

The barman reached into his back pocket and pulled out the handle of a penknife. With a flick, a blade extended and Michael felt its steel at his throat.

He gasped, the sharp movement enlarging his larynx and pressing his neck into the blade. He forced himself to take shallower breaths as he frantically searched with his perception to understand what was happening. All he sensed were the barman's looped Russian thoughts and his father's terror.

"What are you doing?" cried Ransom.

"You wouldn't tell me how you created a generation of perceivers," replied Hetherington. "Which made me realise you needed more persuasion."

"It was the vitamin pills," said Ransom, desperately. "Everybody knows that."

"But *how*?" said Hetherington. "What did you put in the pills that turned ordinary children into perceivers?"

"The scientists did it, I don't know how."

"Do you really want to play this game?" said Hetherington, his voice playful, like he was enjoying it. "Do you want to lie to me while you watch your son's throat being slit?"

Michael's body was yanked round so he faced his father square on and the blade was pressed closer to his neck. His shallow breaths became faster as he felt the steel break skin and a drip of warm blood flow to his collar.

"You're a perceiver, you know I'm not lying!" pleaded Ransom. "I owned a pharmaceutical company, I paid people to do the science, I didn't do it myself. I can't tell you what was put in those vitamin pills, because I don't know!"

"Then show me."

"Anything. Just don't kill my son."

Hetherington left his position by the door and walked over to where Ransom was kneeling by the radiator. Ransom opened his arms wide. "Perceive me," he said.

Even though Michael's body was under the barman's control, his mind was free. It allowed him to sense his father's mind — which he tried to do subtly so no one would feel it — as Hetherington probed with his perception.

Tentatively at first, then deeper. Ransom released any remaining blocks and left himself open. Hetherington searched through all the random rubbish of the man's mind, down into his memories and back to a time when he was supervising the vitamin pill project. He pulled out images of scientific reports with reams of text and pages of coloured graphs.

Michael sensed Hetherington's impatience. The boy grabbed Ransom's head — both hands clutching at his temples — and pulled him close. Hetherington locked his eyes with him and leant in closer until their foreheads almost touched. Ransom did not resist as Hetherington violated deeper and deeper into the centre of his mind. Too deep for Michael to follow. So deep that it hurt.

Ransom cried out and clenched his head — his larger adult hands over the top of the smaller child hands of his jailer — pain piercing his mind. He wanted to wrench the boy's hands away, but the fear of what would happen to Michael if he did, stopped him. His moaning became a wailing. Hetherington still pushed.

"Stop!" cried Michael. "He doesn't know anything else!"

Hetherington was locked inside Ransom's mind. He probably didn't even hear. He certainly didn't care.

Ransom swayed, his head only held upright by Hetherington's hands, as the boy's perception burned through his consciousness.

Michael — helpless in the barman's grasp — feared it might kill him. He didn't know if a perceiver could strangle another person's mind to death and he didn't want to find out. Looking around the cell for something — anything — he could use, he saw only the mattress, the bucket and the radiator. Even if they could help, he couldn't reach them. His arms flapped uselessly at his side as more blood dripped from his neck.

Ransom let out a final weak scream.

"Dad!" Michael yelled.

The bucket flew at Hetherington with the force of a football being kicked into goal. Urine spilled out in a stream of yellow which splashed over his body.

The shock caused him to let go of Ransom and the connection with his mind was suddenly severed. Ransom collapsed onto the mattress.

Hetherington turned to the barman, his shirt dripping with piss. "What the hell are you doing?" His anger so loud, it echoed off the walls and floor.

The barman seemed confused, he lessened his grip on Michael.

"Well?" Hetherington demanded.

"*Ya ne znaynu*," answered the barman.

Hetherington let out a cry of frustration. He kicked the bucket at his feet and it went spinning across the room, spilling the last showery drips of urine as it did so, before it collided against the opposite wall and crashed to the ground. Still furious, Hetherington kicked Ransom who lay barely conscious and groaning on the mattress.

"Come on!" Hetherington ordered the barman. He stomped towards the door, walking with his legs wide like he had just pissed himself.

The barman let go of Michael. The knife was suddenly no longer at his throat. Michael fell forward onto his hands and knees.

Behind him, the door closed and he was left in the room with his father, wondering what the hell had just happened.

TWENTY-FOUR

So much urine had been spilt in the room that Michael could taste it. There was a puddle of it drying in front of him and the mattress next to him was soaked with it. Every time he breathed he couldn't help but take in its rancid particles which had evaporated into the air. No one from their little prison had bothered to come in and clean it up, they hadn't even moved the bucket back in case the prisoners had to use it again. They had just left them to sit in their own filth.

The only acknowledgement that they were living human beings came with the delivery of plastic mugs of water and an anaemic-looking cheese sandwich which the zombie barman had brought them. Michael knew he needed the food and hydration, but every time he thought about eating or drinking it, he tasted his own piss in his mouth.

Ransom's head rested on Michael's lap. He had fallen unconscious after Hetherington had left the room, and was going in and out of a dream state. At first, Michael slipped his perception into his father's dreams, trying to find out if Hetherington had done any damage, but he only glimpsed his father's nightmares. Normal, he hoped, for their current situation.

He kept thinking about the bucket. Hetherington had clearly blamed the barman for throwing it over him, or for allowing Michael to kick it at him. But the more Michael re-ran the events in his head, the more he was convinced that no one had touched it. Like the wires back at the derelict office, the only thing that had touched the bucket was his mind.

Ransom stirred and moaned.

"Are you okay?" said Michael.

"Headache," he mumbled.

Michael was relieved. Ransom had both understood his question and answered it coherently: a good sign.

Ransom pulled himself to a sitting position, clutching his head with one hand, as full consciousness brought full-on pain. Michael had been perceiving him to try to ascertain if he was all right, but pulled out when he realised the headache was too much to share.

"What happened?" said Ransom.

"He almost killed you," said Michael.

"You can't kill people with perception."

"Are you sure?"

Ransom wasn't up for a discussion, he just clutched his head and moaned.

"Here," said Michael, handing over a plastic mug of water. "This might help."

Ransom took it and gulped. "Thanks." He passed it back, half-emptied, dropped his hands to his lap and leant the back of his skull against the wall.

"Did you give him what he wanted?" asked Michael.

"I gave him what there was. I have a bioscience degree, so I understand the research, but I couldn't replicate it. Not without the genius of the people who worked for me."

"So he didn't find what he was looking for?"

"His frustration was all over my mind. He kept pushing and pushing, looking for something that wasn't there, then there was a sudden terrible smell and he pulled out."

"Someone threw the toilet bucket over him," said Michael.

"Really?" Ransom laughed, it was so ridiculous. "Ow!" He clutched his head.

Michael indicated the puddle in front of them and the upturned bucket against the far wall.

"Who did that?" said Ransom.

"I think…" Michael trailed off, not knowing how to phrase it. "Do you think perceivers are capable of telekinesis?"

"Telekinesis?"

"Moving objects with your mind," said Michael.

"I know what the word means, I wasn't sure I heard you properly."

"I think… I think I might have thrown the bucket with my perception."

"Not possible," said Ransom.

"Are you sure?" Michael had now seen it happen twice with his own eyes and he wasn't about to dismiss the idea. "I was only able to do it when I was highly stressed, but if I can find a way to do it on demand, I could use it to get out of here."

Ransom raised his arm with the metal cuff locked to his wrist. "Can your mind unlock this? I can't even do it with my hands. Unless we can get out of these chains, we're not going anywhere."

Michael sensed something at the edge of his perception. "Do you perceive that?" he said.

"What?" said Ransom.

It was a person, Michael was sure of it. Distant, but there. A presence he had felt before. With thoughts he couldn't quite distinguish, but which *felt* English. It wasn't Hetherington — the boy wouldn't be as stupid as to walk about with his mind open like that, even at a distance from his perceiving prisoners — but it *was* someone he had perceived before.

The more he concentrated, the closer the presence became. By the time the door handle turned, Michael had recognised the mind as belonging to Doctor Lucas.

Doctor Lucas's nose wrinkled at the smell as he stepped inside their cell and closed the door behind him. He appeared more stressed than the first time Michael had seen him and looked less of a scientist without his white coat.

Recognition flashed across through Lucas's mind as he saw Michael. "I thought it was strange the Metropolitan Police had such a young person on the force. But James tells me you are a perceiver, so it makes sense."

"Who are you?" said Ransom, revealing this was the first time he had encountered Doctor Lucas.

"Your son knows," said Lucas. "Perhaps you could ask him."

Scientist researching perception, Michael thought. He hoped it was enough to answer Ransom's curiosity, because he needed to search Lucas's head for information which could be useful.

"I came here to continue my research, but I told them I needed more data," Lucas continued. "If they could acquire Brian Ransom's research, I said, it could advance my own work by years. I expected them to hack a computer and steal some documents, I didn't expect them to bring you here. I'm sorry."

And he really was sorry. He was embarrassed that his request had led to a violent kidnapping, and disgusted at seeing someone he admired chained up like a farm animal. So much so that he could barely look at him and kept staring at the crack of sky that could be seen through the tiny window above them.

"Release us," said Ransom.

"I'm not in charge of that." Lucas shook his head. "But I could offer you a way out."

He left a deliberately dramatic pause for his words to sink in.

"I'm listening," said Ransom.

"Work with me," said Lucas.

"The man who got me kidnapped? Are you serious?"

"Deadly," said Lucas. "James thought he could pull the knowledge from your head, but just because he can read your thoughts, it doesn't mean he can understand them. *I* can understand them, Mr Ransom. I've been studying perception for a long time, it would be a privilege to work with a pioneer of the field."

"Pioneer," said Ransom, with irony. "That's not what they call me in the media."

"Because they don't understand. You had a vision of a world where people could understand each other at a deeper level, because they could share their thoughts and feelings openly. I can offer you the chance to continue your research. Don't you want to see your work spread? I can offer you that. And I can offer you some of the best facilities available to the Russian government."

His voice was full of optimism and promise, but his head was full of doubt. The building he was in, out in the industrial wastes of Moscow, was an empty shell with little equipment and fewer staff. His Russian handlers said his sudden escape from Britain had caught them by surprise and it would take time to arrange a work environment for him. Part of him believed that the cogs of Russian bureaucracy turned slowly, but another part wondered if the people who had recruited him back in England really had the full backing of an administration that could provide him with all the resources he had been promised.

"I was wrong," said Ransom. "I thought perception would bring peace, but instead it brought violence. Don't you remember the rioting on the streets of London two years ago? People *died* because of me."

"Ignorant people killed each other because they didn't understand, Mr Ransom. What would have happened if you had been able to explain to them? What would have happened if women understood that taking a pill would see their children grow up to have special powers? Wouldn't they have embraced that chance? I'm offering you the possibility to start again, to learn from the mistakes of the past. You and I, we could work together to improve your gene therapy. In years to come, it will be seen as a gift to the world."

"And if I refuse?" said Ransom.

"Maybe they will let you go home, I don't know," said Lucas. "That's if you really want to go back to Britain to spend the rest of your life in jail."

Noise of footsteps in the corridor made Lucas jump. Worried, he stood up straight as the door was thrown open and Hetherington came in with his face full of anger.

"What the hell are you doing in here?" he shouted, throwing his blocks around the man's mind so Michael's perception was suddenly shut out.

"I just came to see," said Lucas, looking intimidated by the boy forty years younger and six inches shorter than him.

"I told you not to! They can perceive everything in your head, don't you understand? *Everything!*"

"Don't worry, I'm going now," said Lucas as he tried to hold onto his dignity. "The place is filthy, by the way. You should get someone in here to clean up before the scientist I need dies of dysentery."

Lucas side stepped Hetherington and headed for the door. "Think about my offer, Mr Ransom," he called back. "It's the best you're going to get."

THE barman looked ill when he walked into the cell. There was a paleness about his skin and a growth of stubble on his chin which had started to blend into the line of his moustache. The blankness remained in his head, but the Russian words looping inside it seemed different. Not just different because they were different words, but different as they repeated, like there was glitches in the recording. Michael wondered how much Hetherington had exerted control over him. When he thought about the control Hetherington had over the kids in the gang back in London, he remembered them being of independent minds most of the time. It was only when he had a deadly job for them to do did he take over completely. The barman looked like he hadn't been his own man since the moment he had directed Michael upstairs to meet his kidnappers. It was a long time to be separated from his own thoughts and his own willpower.

Michael flinched as he saw the barman was coming for him. He realised his reaction was making him as timid as his father. The barman grabbed his elbow, like before, and dragged him away from the radiator. A flash of memory of the penknife at his throat panicked him and Michael kicked out harder and more desperate than the last time.

"Michael!" shouted Ransom. He reached out for his son, but the shorter chain tugged him back. Michael felt the fleeting touch of his father's hand on his foot before he was dragged away.

At the full stretch of the chain, the barman stopped; still holding tight to Michael's struggling body.

"If you kill him, you'll have to kill me!" Ransom shouted. "I'll never work for you."

The barman was oblivious to his pleas. He only had his instructions, instructions in another language that Michael couldn't understand.

The barman reached into his back pocket and pulled out — not his knife — but a set of keys. Relief spread through Michael's muscles as he watched the cuff around his wrist being unlocked. Freed from the chain, the barman dragged him all the way to the door.

"What are you doing?" cried Ransom. "Where are you taking him?"

"It's okay, Dad. Don't worry, I'll be fine," said Michael. It was a lie, he didn't know what was going to be done to him, and he knew his father would perceive the lie. But he felt the need to say the words anyway.

In the corridor, he saw a glimpse of light from a door that might lead to the outside, before a cloth was rammed over his face so it blocked his eyes, mouth and nose. He gasped and breathed in a chemical smell like rotting fruit. In that moment, he realised the cloth must be infused with a drug. He struggled, his hands bounced uselessly off the arms of the man holding him, as he tried not to take another breath. Until he could resist it no longer and his hold on consciousness slipped away.

TWENTY-FIVE

RANSOM'S hand rocked Michael's shoulder and gently shook him awake.

His eyes opened to see that he was back in the cell with his head lying in his father's lap. His whole body ached, especially his head, which remained groggy from the drug.

"Are you okay? Did they hurt you?" said Ransom.

"They drugged me. I don't know. Was I gone long?"

"A few hours."

Michael tried to remember those hours, but they were lost in the blackness of sleep.

"Sorry to wake you, Michael, but something's going on."

"What?" Michael pulled himself up to a sitting position and closed his eyes for a moment to let his vertigo settle. He felt the handcuff locked tight again around his wrist and heard the clink of the chain as he moved. Looking at the room, he saw the cell was the same: mattress, radiator and the toilet bucket moved back to where they could reach it. The only difference was the distant noise of people shouting.

"Do you hear that?" said Ransom. "I can't perceive them, but I thought maybe you could."

Michael concentrated on the sound. They were men's voices — at least two of them, possibly three — shouting in Russian. A younger voice occasionally interjected in English, recognisably that of James Hetherington. Michael focussed his foggy mind on them all. Hetherington had his blocks up — there was no breaking through that wall — but the Russians were norms and therefore easier to crack. He confirmed there were three of them, all angry about something, but the distance meant his perception could only reach their surface thoughts, which were all in their native language.

"They're angry," said Michael.

"I can hear that," said Ransom. "About what?"

Michael tried to push his perception further, but he was already at his limit. "They're too far away. And they're thinking in Russian."

"They're probably arguing about what to do with us."

"You don't know that," said Michael.

"What use are we to them now? The boy pulled everything from my head, there's nothing left for him to take."

"Then accept Lucas's job offer."

"Work for the Russians?" said Ransom.

"Better than dying for them."

Ransom touched Michael's arm and gestured for him to be quiet. They both listened. The shouting had stopped.

Michael perceived the Russian men. He could still sense their presence, but it was getting fainter. "They're leaving," he said.

"We have to get out of here," said Ransom.

"Yeah." The single word was not enough to express how much he agreed.

Michael stood and climbed up on the radiator; its ancient cast iron frame robust enough to hold his weight. He hoped to be able to see out of the window, but even on tiptoe, he only managed to get face to face with more blank wall.

Ransom got to his feet, knowing — perhaps *perceiving* — what Michael was up to. "Stand on my shoulders."

Michael stepped from the radiator to his father's shoulders. He rested his hand on the wall for support until he stood as tall as the ceiling and easily high enough to look out of the window. What he saw was depressingly deserted. Beyond the wall of the cell was a flat, neglected car park with specs of green where weeds were growing through the cracks. There was a car at the far end which might have been parked, but by the rusty state of it had probably been abandoned. On the other side of a wire fence, waist-high grass swayed in the Moscow breeze.

Michael clambered down again.

"Well?" said Ransom.

"Lucas's mind was right, looks like we're in the middle of nowhere. He seemed to think this was in an old industrial area, but if there are any other buildings, then they have to be on the other side. No one's going to hear us if we shout for help."

"What else did you see in Lucas's mind?"

"Nothing very useful. There are a few members of staff who work here, but they're told to keep well away from this room in case we perceive them. It's a forty-five minute journey from wherever Lucas's accommodation is, so we're not far from civilisation, but unless we can get out of this room …"

"Then we have to get out of this room," said Ransom.

"Yeah."

Michael gathered up the chain that secured him to the radiator and pulled hard. The cuff at the end clanged against the cast iron and proved the lock was secure. It was probably easier to gnaw his own arm off than to break through the metal.

He sat back down on the floor and his foot inadvertently kicked the paper plate which had once contained the now-eaten sandwich. It made him think of the barman and his zombied brain.

"There's one weak link in the chain," said Michael; excited as a plan formed in his mind. "The man Hetherington controls, the one who unchained me to take me away."

"I tried to perceive him, but there's nothing there."

"The control over him is strong, but I think it might be weakening. I'm not sure if I can break through on my own, but with the two of us we might be able to do it."

"Then what?" said Ransom. "Persuade him to help us?"

"He's Russian, he won't be able to understand us. But we might be able to take control of his mind and re-program him."

"Perceivers can't do that."

"Natural borns like you, maybe not," said Michael. "But second generation kids like me can. I'll show you."

MANY hours passed before the door handle turned. The gentle click as the latch released from the doorframe alerted Michael and Ransom. They sat up straight.

Ready? came Ransom's thought.

Michael nodded silently.

The barman nudged the door open with his toe as he carried in two plastic mugs of water balanced on top of each other and an anaemic sandwich on a paper plate.

Michael searched all of his senses for signs of Hetherington. The boy kept his mind firmly shut, so there was no detecting him with perception and, instead, he had to watch and listen. The only sound was the barman's boots on the tiled floor. The only view through the open door was the opposite corridor wall. There was no smell in the air which indicated the perfume from Hetherington's modern toiletries. He was as certain as he could be that Hetherington was nowhere close.

The barman stopped just before the point where Michael's chain could reach. His mind was as blank as before, with one singular instruction circling in Russian: *karmi ix*. He squatted down and placed the mugs of water in front of him — pushing them over the invisible line so they could be collected by the prisoners.

Now!

At the signal from Michael's thoughts, he and Ransom plunged their perception into the barman's mind.

It was like punching air. They stumbled into blankness, they floundered for something to grab hold of and clutched at nothing.

The barman must have been able to feel them because he stopped mid-movement. The sandwich plate was only halfway to being placed on the floor.

Karmi ix, said his strangled thoughts.

The instruction, planted by Hetherington, was a point of weakness and Michael seized upon it. As he took hold, it buzzed like a bee trapped in a jar and he struggled to contain it. Ransom's presence was suddenly at his side, bolstering his strength until the instruction was tamed. Michael used his perception to trace the thought from where it had emerged. He burrowed deeper and deeper into the barman's mind, he pushed at the blankness and forced his way through Hetherington's mental controls until—

The barman's mind snapped. Like a balloon popped by a pin, his inner self exploded out from the barriers. Pain and confusion bottled up from days under Hetherington's control spiralled to the surface in an overwhelming rush. He screamed and fell over backwards, sending the sandwich flying over his shoulder in individual slices of bread and ham.

Michael realised the barman had fallen beyond the reach of the chain, which was a problem if they needed to physically restrain him.

The distraction disrupted Michael's hold on the man's mind.

Concentrate, Ransom's thoughts told him.

Michael refocused his energy, which caused the barman to cry out as he touched the tender part where Hetherington had meddled. The man's brain had been scarred where it had been repeatedly over-written with Hetherington's instructions. If Michael was to reprogram him, he would have to press his thoughts into that painful scar.

Us or him, came Ransom's thoughts.

Michael pushed away his reticence and conjured up images of the barman reaching for his keys, releasing their handcuffs and escorting them out of the building to freedom. He laid the images on top of the scarred part of his mind, over and over, until they began to stick. Until—

Blackness fell across Michael's perception. He was thrown out of the barman's head, with such energy that he was physically knocked backwards and his head slammed against the radiator.

At first, he thought the barman had passed out. But then he saw Hetherington walk through the open doorway and he knew the boy had blocked him.

The barman rolled on the floor moaning to himself.

Red-faced with anger, Hetherington glared at Michael and Ransom. "I don't believe I argued for you to be kept alive. But they're right, you're a liability!"

Hetherington kicked at the pathetic body of the barman curled up on the ground. "Nikolay!" The barman, who now had a name, spasmed as the boy's shoe hit his spine. Then he stopped groaning, unfurled himself and stood up.

Hetherington must have re-taken control.

So easily.

Realising he was outmatched, Michael felt the sinking feeling of defeat in his stomach. He stood and clasped a length of his chain between his two hands and got ready to wrap it round the neck of anyone who came near him. He would strangle them to death if he had to. Ransom also stood and took up position by his side.

"I've had enough of this," said Hetherington. "Sod Lucas, sod the lot of them!" He nodded to the barman who began walking towards them.

Michael braced himself for whatever was going to come. He might be about to die chained to a radiator, but he was going to go down fighting.

The barman reached into his back pocket, pulled out the handle of his penknife and flicked out the blade.

Ransom stepped forward and put his body between Michael and the knife. "If you want to kill my son, you have to go through me."

"Dad, stop!"

"I'm the only one who can tell you how to make more perceivers," Ransom appealed to Hetherington. "Those scientific reports you saw in my head, I understand them. Doctor Lucas knows it. If the Russians want their own perceivers, I'm the best chance you've got. You kill *me* and what are they going to do to *you*?"

It was frustratingly impossible to tell if Ransom's words moved Hetherington at all. His mind was closed behind his outward smile that watched from the safety of the far wall.

The barman's blade got closer.

Michael leapt from the wall — his head bent forward like a human battering ram — and charged at the barman. Still in Hetherington's control and unable to react like a thinking person, the barman took the full force of Michael's attack. He dropped the knife and its blade pinged to the floor as it tumbled across the tiles.

The barman stumbled backwards.

Michael ran forward full pelt and charged again. But the barman had stumbled over the invisible line and Michael's chain pulled him up short; the handcuff cutting into his wrist. His unchained hand swiped at air as the barman stood safely out of reach.

Hetherington continued to watch with an unwavering smile.

Infuriated, Michael realised he had been attacking the puppet when his real enemy was the puppet master. He swung round with all his anger and uselessly screamed his frustration like a chained dog barking at an intruder. Hetherington was out of reach. They were all out of reach. The puppet master, his puppet and the knife.

The knife.

On the floor where it had been knocked from the barman's hand.

Michael focussed on the knife. It twitched. Almost unable to believe it, he watched its metal blade tinkling on the tile in the control of his mind. Taking a breath — quick before Hetherington noticed — he concentrated his rage, frustration and fear in a blast of raw emotion.

The knife lifted from the floor and flew like a spear across the room. It struck Hetherington's chest with a thud.

Hetherington cried out and clasped his breast where the blade had imbedded itself between the bones of his rib cage. The boy's blocks faltered and Michael perceived his shock and pain for a moment before he regained control. Blood wept through his shirt onto his fingers as they clustered around the wound. He staggered on his feet, but he did not go down. His eyes stared wide and crazed.

Hetherington launched his perception at Michael's mind. He rammed it hard against his blocks. Michael fought to keep him out as he remembered how such an onslaught had nearly killed his father. But Hetherington's anger had made him strong and Michael struggled to hold on.

"Michael!" Ransom called out from somewhere behind him. But his father could be of no help.

A sudden noise cracked the air.

The mental onslaught ceased.

Hetherington's body jerked forward: hit from behind by something invisible.

Another shot rang out. Hetherington spasmed again. With the third one, he collapsed. Sinking to his knees, he held onto life for one last moment before he stopped breathing and fell face down onto the floor. On his back were three red circles made by the bullets that had killed him.

The barman, still standing, wavered without the control of his puppet master. Blood spurted from his chest: once, twice, three times, as he was shot in quick succession. He collapsed back against the wall and slid down it, leaving behind bright red smears on the white paintwork.

The sounds of gunfire echoing in his head, Michael looked to the doorway, expecting to see his Russian execution squad.

But what he saw was so incredible he wasn't sure it was true.

Hodges, a semi-automatic pistol clasped in his fingers, stood in front of him.

TWENTY-SIX

MICHAEL perceived the warm, familiar mind of his driver and almost wept at the gloriousness of it. He dropped every barrier, every filter in his head and drank in the sweet presence of Hodges. Even then, he had to use his eyes to confirm it. Hodges looked less groomed than usual, there was stubble on his chin from where he hadn't shaved that morning and his jeans, jumper and flak jacket made him look more like a civilian than the suit he usually wore, but it was him. It really was him.

The only fear left in the room came from his father. Michael turned to see Ransom crouching by the radiator, reeling from the gunfire.

"It's okay, Dad," said Michael. "This is Mr Hodges. He's a former British soldier. He's my friend."

Ransom relaxed, even though Michael could sense that, inside, he was still shaking.

The sense of other familiar minds filled Michael's perception. Immediately he knew who they were.

Pauline came in from the corridor and stopped short as she reached the doorway. "My God!" she breathed.

Alex came up behind her. He said nothing, but Michael perceived he was just as sickened at what he saw.

That's when Michael looked around the room and realised what a shit hole they had walked into. Hetherington's dead body lay face down in a pool of his own blood, the barman's lifeless body was slumped against the blood-splattered wall, and Ransom sat in filthy, crumpled clothes. Michael realised he must look equally pathetic.

"Are you all right?" said Alex.

Michael touched his own torso and assessed himself. No bullet holes, no knife wounds, he was physically in one piece. "Yeah. Yeah, I think so. How did you find us?"

"This one was worried when you ran off," said Hodges, pointing to Pauline. "She got me to talk to your policeman friend. He traced the payments you made to the airline and the hotel. The hotel was able to tell us which taxi driver you used and he directed us to—"

"Can we talk about this later?" said Ransom, pulling himself to his feet. "We need to get out of here."

"Don't worry," said Hodges. "I've got the hire car outside, it's less than an hour's drive to the British embassy."

"What about …?" Ransom pulled at his chain and the other end rattled against the radiator.

"Keys!" said Michael. "Check the barman's pockets."

Alex stepped past Pauline and knelt at the body of the unfortunate barman slumped on the floor with his dead eyes still open. Alex slipped his hands into the barman's front pockets, but found nothing. He reached round the man's back to get into his rear pockets. The barman fell sideways and his skull struck the floor with a hollow thump. Alex gasped and pulled his hands away. But the dead man had only moved through the force of gravity and, after catching his breath, Alex continued his search.

He found no keys on the barman. He checked Hetherington too, but stood up from the body with his hands empty.

"They must be in the building somewhere," said Michael.

"We haven't got time to check," said Hodges. "The few people who were here ran off when they saw the gun, but they must have alerted someone by now and I don't fancy my chances in a shoot-out with armed Russian police."

"But backup's on its way?" said Ransom.

"Unfortunately not," said Hodges. "This isn't exactly an 'official' operation."

Alex went up to the radiator and pulled at the chains where they were locked by a handcuff. "Could you shoot them off?" he asked Hodges.

"Even if I could be that accurate, there's no guarantee a bullet could cut through the chain. That's if it doesn't ricochet and kill one of us first."

A sense of panic was manifesting in the room. All the perceivers could feel it, while Hodges was trying to keep himself calm so he could think.

"We can't leave them!" said Pauline.

"We need bolt cutters or something," said Hodges. "Stay here."

Michael only had a chance to perceive that he was going out to the car before Hodges was gone.

"He can't have bolt cutters in the car, surely," said Pauline.

"Knowing Hodges, I wouldn't put it past him," said Michael.

Quiet descended as they waited for Hodges to return. Michael realised he was shaking from the after-effects of an adrenaline surge. He decided to sit on the floor before his legs collapsed from under him.

"Are you okay?" said Pauline.

"I'm just pleased to see you," he said. "Really, really pleased to see both of you."

"Are these your perceiver friends?" asked Ransom.

"Yes," said Michael. "Pauline and Alex."

"Natural born?" said Ransom.

"I think your pills created them," said Michael.

The three of them didn't have time to think about what that meant because Hodges came back carrying a tyre iron.

He held the metal lever aloft like a sword of victory as the others wondered what he was going to do with it. "We should be able to break the cuffs off the radiator with this," he explained. "If that doesn't work, I'm going to prise the entire radiator off the wall and take the whole bloody lot, with you two attached to it, back to the British embassy."

TWENTY-SEVEN

MICHAEL had waited for an hour in the London drizzle outside the Old Bailey to get a place on the front bench of the public gallery. Many of the people pressed in close on the benches around him had also braved the British weather to make sure they witnessed Brian Ransom being sent down for his crimes, and so the courtroom was full of the smell of damp clothes and hair.

The public were kept safely behind the brass railing atop the balustrade at the back of the court, but the anger and vindictiveness of their minds spilled out everywhere. Their hatred for his father pressed in on Michael's mind so forcefully that it hurt. He could have shut them out, but he wanted to feel every moment.

Pauline's fingers intertwined with his. Her hand felt warm and comforting as she sat by his side. Michael knew his own hand felt clammy with sweat, but he perceived she didn't care.

"All rise," said a court official from down below.

A collection of barristers in black robes and horsehair wigs stood in unison, like an army regiment brought to attention. Around him, Michael perceived the uncertainty of people in the public gallery wondering if they were supposed to stand up too. A man next to him in the front row did, followed by a woman behind him, and then the rest of them who got to their feet in ones and twos.

Standing made it easier to see Ransom in the dock. He looked respectable in his new suit, neatly washed and brushed hair, and trimmed beard. None of which stopped the nervousness leaking from his mind.

At the front of the court, an oak wood door set into the oak panelling of the wall opened and the judge entered. It was the same woman Michael had seen before, in wig and gown, looking diminutive in contrast to the amount of power she wielded.

She sat down.

The barristers sat as one.

The people crammed into the public gallery realised they should do the same and sat down in ones and twos.

"Remain standing, Mr Ransom," said the judge.

Michael perched on the edge of the bench and leant forward. He ignored the sign on the wall that told members of the public gallery not to lean over the rail.

The judge lifted her gaze from a folder of papers on the desk in front of her and looked directly at Ransom. "The prosecution alleges thousands of women and children were your victims, but in sentencing you I can only take account of the twenty cases placed before this court and for which the jury found you guilty," she said. "The charge of Administering a Noxious Substance with Intent to Cause Bodily Harm comes with a maximum sentence of five years' imprisonment. Given the severity of your crime, Mr Ransom, I have no hesitation in sentencing you to five years for each and every count, to be served consecutively. Giving you a total jail term of one hundred years."

The shock, Michael perceived, struck Ransom as hard as a punch. It knocked him dizzy and he stumbled sideways. The security guard next to him caught his arm.

An excited and vengeful thrill poured from the minds in the public gallery. "I hope you rot!" yelled one woman.

Michael gripped Pauline's hand tighter as he forced himself to keep perceiving. He was frightened that if he blocked out other people's feelings, he would have to face his own.

"Under British law, I cannot pass such a sentence," continued the judge, raising her voice above the disquiet which had also broken out among the stunned barristers in front of her. "However, due to the unprecedented nature of your crimes, Brian Christopher Ransom, I have no hesitation in commuting it to a full life term, meaning you will spend the rest of your days in prison without the prospect of parole. Take him away."

The security guard, already holding onto Ransom's arm, led him to exit the dock.

Michael grabbed the rail and leant out as far as he could. *Dad!* screamed his mind.

His father looked up from below as the security guard placed the metal jaws of a handcuff around his wrist. *Don't worry*, said Ransom's thoughts. *It's better than being a prisoner in Russia.*

I'll visit you!

Don't. You need to live your life and forget about me.

"No!" The word screamed from his lungs as he leant further out over the rail. Pauline grabbed his T-shirt to pull him back and stop him falling, but he didn't relent until his father was led from the court and so far away that his mind could no longer reach him.

MICHAEL gripped tight to Pauline's hand all the way out of the court. They didn't say anything, they didn't have to, as they perceived each other's thoughts and feelings with every step.

Emerging into the street, they saw the sun had broken through the morning cloud and started to dry the damp remnants of drizzle from the pavement. Anyone else might have felt the day was brightening up, but the sun brought no warmth to Michael.

Just outside the public entrance to the Old Bailey, leaning against the pole of a parking restriction sign, was Sergeant Patterson. He wore the same grey crumpled suit he had worn that first day in the interrogation room.

Michael self-consciously untangled his hand from Pauline's fingers.

Patterson held up an arm to catch their already-caught attention and the three of them met in the middle of the pavement. "Hello," he said.

"I didn't expect you to be here," said Michael.

"I tried to call you," said Patterson. "But I couldn't get through to your phone."

"I lost it in Russia."

"How many phones have you lost now?"

"Just the two."

"Who's this?" said Pauline.

Michael knew she knew who it was, as she could perceive it from both of them, but norms liked to hear themselves be introduced using actual words. So Michael obliged. "This is Sergeant Anthony Patterson," he said.

"Tony," corrected Patterson, holding out his hand for her to shake.

Pauline accepted. She blushed a little as they shook quickly and she reclaimed her hand to her side. Patterson, it seemed, was a bit of a charmer on the quiet.

"Look, Michael, I'm sorry about your father ..." Patterson said.

"Don't be," said Michael. "He committed the crime he was convicted of, there's nothing anyone could have done."

"Anyway," said Patterson. He filled the uncomfortable moment with a nervous cough. "I came to tell you that I have completed the report into your involvement with the Metropolitan Police."

"Did I get a gold star?" said Michael. It was his attempt to make a joke to break the tension.

Patterson smiled out of politeness. "My recommendation to the Chief Constable is that we continue to experiment with …" He was going to say *perceivers*, but thought better of it out in public. "… people like yourself within the investigative branches of the service in the hope that your skills may be utilised to greater affect in the future."

"That's a lot of long words, Sergeant Patterson," said Michael.

"Yeah, well, Inspector Jones may have written that bit," he said with a grin.

The sound of a car horn caused all three of them to look round. A black Audi A4 had pulled up at the kerb next to them. Hodges waved from the driver's seat.

"This is our ride," said Michael.

"Do you want a lift?" offered Pauline.

"No, no," said Patterson. "It's a short walk to the tube."

Hodges wound down his window. "Hurry up, I'm on a double yellow!"

Pauline hurried over and got into the back of the car, but Michael wasn't quite ready to leave. "Say hello to Inspector Jones for me, won't you?"

"Sure," said Patterson. "And I look forward to working with you again."

"Really?" said Michael, even though he perceived the policeman was being perfectly honest.

"Really," said Patterson. "Just try not to get involved with international espionage next time."

"It's a deal."

Hodges sounded the car horn again.

Michael didn't know what else to say and so he left Sergeant Patterson and got into the back of the car with Pauline.

He'd barely closed the door before Hodges was pulling away and attempting to reach a set of traffic lights before they changed to red. Michael watched Patterson turn in the direction of the nearest tube station and walk away until a bus drew up behind them and blocked his view.

TWENTY-EIGHT

PAULINE sat next to Michael on the sofa in his room. There wasn't space for Alex, so he sat cross-legged on the floor for what felt like a party to celebrate their safe return from Russia. Although, as they were still inside the military base where they lived, it was a party without balloons, without alcohol and before 'lights out'. They drank fizzy sugary stuff from cans and listened to music streamed through the television speakers from Alex's phone and laughed about things that no one else would find funny.

"I found out today I got a job," said Pauline.

"Congratulations!" said Michael. He raised his can of Coke in salute and took a sip. "Doing what?"

"Stacking shelves?" said Alex.

Pauline kicked his knee with her toe. "An assignment," she clarified. "I'm going to be working with the police, like Michael."

"After this last week, I hope not like Michael," said Alex.

It was Michael who kicked Alex's knee this time.

"Tell me again why I'm the one who has to sit on the floor?" said Alex.

"Because it's my sofa," said Michael.

"I'll be assigned to CID," Pauline interrupted before the boys got into a pointless argument. "So, looking into the minds of murderers, that sort of thing."

"Well, I'm pleased," said Alex. He raised his can of some sort of fizzy orange stuff and sipped. "They're keeping me in the court system for a while longer, so it looks like perceivers really are being deployed out there in the world."

"Yes," said Michael. Not that he really believed it. He'd been ordered to write a report on his experiences so far working with the police force, but he had a feeling his suggestions would be ignored. He may have won over Patterson, but he doubted many norms were ready to accept perceivers working alongside them just yet. Especially when they were all still so young compared to the people they were working with.

Michael finished off the last of his Coke and allowed his body to gather all of its bubbles inside of him and let them out in one, large, resonating burp.

"Euw!" said Pauline. She pushed him away from her playfully. "*Not* attractive."

"Sorry," said Michael, but he wasn't really thinking about her anymore. He was thinking about the empty Coke can. He put it down on the floor in front of him.

Alex went to pick it up.

"Don't," said Michael.

"I was only going to put it in the bin," he said.

"I want to try something."

He could tell the others perceived there was something going on in his head, but they did not see enough to understand what.

Michael stared at the Coke can. He stared at it until he thought he knew every inch of it, from the dent in the side where Alex had squeezed it with his thumb, to the angle of the ring pull at the top. Once he had assessed it with his eyes, he covered it with his perception, as if holding it in his mind. He concentrated. He wanted the can to go into the rubbish bin. He wanted it badly, to the exclusion of everything. There was no sofa, no Pauline and Alex, no room, only the can and the bin. As he focussed all of his willpower, the can wobbled on the carpet.

"My God," Pauline whispered.

"Are *you* doing that?" said Alex.

He barely heard them. Michael visualised the can lifting into the air and — in front of him — the can levitated. Only a few centimetres, but it was suspended above the carpet by nothing other than his thoughts. He gasped as he saw it and his concentration faltered. The can dropped to the floor and tipped over. A brown remnant of Coke dripped from the can onto the carpet.

Michael sat back into his seat, amazed at what he saw, but knowing that he had done it: he had moved the can with the power of his mind.

"Was that a trick?" said Alex, looking from the can to Michael and back to the can again. "No trick," said Michael.

Because they were perceivers, they knew he wasn't lying.

"How...?" said Pauline.

He shrugged. "I'm not really sure. When I thought I was going to die, it just happened. The first time I thought I was hallucinating or something, but after the second time I found I could do it if I really concentrated."

"Wow," said Alex. "Could you teach me to do it?"

"I don't know," said Michael. "We could try."

"Even with your super powers, you wouldn't have got out of Russia without our help," said Pauline.

"You're not going to let me forget that, are you?" said Michael, playfully.

"Nope," said Pauline. She disguised her grin behind her drinks can as she sipped.

Even though he didn't say it, he made sure she perceived how grateful he was. He knew, if she hadn't persuaded Hodges to fly them out to Moscow, he wouldn't have survived.

"Any idea what they did to you in Russia?" Alex asked Michael.

"Not in those missing hours," he replied.

Pauline turned to him. "Missing hours?"

"Didn't he tell you?" said Alex. "He was drugged and taken somewhere for several hours."

"No, he didn't tell me," said Pauline. She made her displeasure felt. "Taken where?"

"That's the thing," said Michael. "I was unconscious, I don't know. I can only imagine Hetherington wanted to perceive my mind while I wasn't awake to block him."

"Can you do that?" said Pauline. "Perceive someone while they're asleep? Apart from seeing into their dreams, I mean?"

Michael shrugged. "I don't know. I wouldn't put it past the Hetherington kid."

"Maybe they carried out some sort of secret experiment," said Alex.

"Like what?" said Michael.

"I don't know. They could have taken some of your genetic material to forward their research."

"They already had my blood," said Michael. "What more would they want?"

But Michael couldn't rule it out. Just as he couldn't rule out that Hetherington pulled from his mind out all sorts of classified information in those missing hours: details about the British perceiver programme, where they were based, who was in charge. He could have passed that information to anyone in the Russian administration and who knows how they would use it to their advantage.

Unless the kid hadn't got around to telling anybody and the information died at the same time as he was killed with Hodges's bullets.

The only person who survived for sure was Lucas. Hodges didn't remember seeing him in the complex and Michael hadn't perceived his presence as they ran away. Lucas had already fled England with a wealth of knowledge about perceivers and that made him dangerous. If the Russians ever got around to giving him all the resources they promised, there was no telling what he would be able to do.

The music streaming through the television speakers suddenly skipped tracks and blasted loud rock music into the room.

Broken out of his thoughts, Michael saw that Alex had his phone in his hand and had chosen something more lively to play. "This is supposed to be a celebration, right?"

"I suppose," said Michael.

"Then cheer up!" Alex drank the last of his fizzy sugary orange and put the empty can on the floor in front of him. "Teach me how to do that levitation thing."

"What, now?" said Michael.

"Why not now?" said Alex.

"Go on," said Pauline. "When he fails to do it, I can spend all week making fun of him."

Michael smiled. "Okay."

Alex grinned and sat up straight and put his fingers to his temples in the pose of someone who was ready to concentrate. "Tell me what to do."

~ END ~

When businessmen go mad, Michael investigates the shocking link to perceivers, as his relationship with Pauline grows, in:

Mind Evolution: Perceivers #3

The Perceivers series:

Mind Secrets
Mind Control
Mind Evolution
Mind Power